Poison

Joely Skye

A Samhain Publishing, Ltd. publication.

Samhain Publishing, Ltd.
577 Mulberry Street, Suite 1520
Macon, GA 31201
www.samhainpublishing.com

Poison
Copyright © 2009 by Joely Skye
Print ISBN: 978-1-60504-152-0
Digital ISBN: 1-59998-531-4

Editing by Sasha Knight
Cover by Anne Cain

First Samhain Publishing, Ltd. electronic publication: May 2008
First Samhain Publishing, Ltd. print publication: March 2009

Dedication

To C.

Prologue

"What is my name again?" Arel asked.

Lem cast Arel a look of disapproval. "Geln."

"God, it sounds like I've been castrated." Arel gazed at himself in the mirror. The long leather boots were soft and comfortable, as were the baggy pants that ended at the knees, but he disliked the high-necked jacket and the padded gloves. No doubt he didn't fully appreciate the importance of giving people the impression he had long fingers.

Arel sighed. How had he managed to land this assignment? He'd kept his head down in training, charmed his instructors, been a good student. Too good, he supposed. Now they thought he could infiltrate an alien society—or they could afford to throw him away if he failed.

What an appalling idea.

Don't show you're tense. The mirror is two-way. He forced himself to relax, though that act of will left him with the uncomfortable impression that he didn't belong to the mirrored green-eyed waif lost in layers of clothing. Thin but muscular, Arel felt too old to appear waiflike. His gaze rested on his face for a moment, in order to convince himself he was there, just undercover. His lips curved as if the entire prep amused him. Or perhaps he simply looked weary.

"Geln, try to muster up a bit more enthusiasm." Lem was

9

an ass. Arel didn't want to enter a feudal society and Lem knew it, but saying no to one's first assignment was unwise, if not impossible. "Do you think you're prepared?" A bit late for that question to be asked.

"Don't worry. I'm ready." Arel turned his green eyes on Lem. Were they lit with enthusiasm? Perhaps not, but the new emerald irises were stunning. Considered beautiful and lucky in the city of Riman, the green didn't quite match his dark complexion. He felt a pang of nostalgia for his liquid browns.

But the big greens worked. Lem relaxed and began to make soothing noises about Geln's talent and how the Alliance wouldn't have chosen Geln if he wasn't fully capable.

Arel tried to feel flattered. He was to accomplish two things—acquire information about the political situation on Rimania and pave the way for greater contact with the Alliance. Unfortunately, he was also a secondary operative. Someone else was in charge of where he should go and what he should do. Someone he would be forced to blindly trust.

"It's a typical first assignment," Lem added cheerfully.

Arel nodded in a manly, decisive way. After all, he was ambitious, arrogant, and poor enough to take this highly paid assignment in a violent culture on the cusp of change. He didn't have deep personal ties to hold him back. His ability to connect to and inspire confidence in different types of people would serve him well.

"Geln?"

Arel's head flipped up. Lost in thought, he'd been staring at his boots.

"Great!" Lem grinned. "You're responding to your name."

Great. Geln displayed a most winning smile through the mirror. He wanted them to remember his enthusiasm for this assignment.

10

Chapter One

Sunlight streamed in through the full wall of window. Tobias Smator squinted into overwhelming brightness while his mother lectured him, her voice clipped with purpose.

"You're now third in line for the lordship. Have you considered what you might do with your new position?"

"No." He rubbed his aching forehead. Even the tablecloth was too bright.

"Tobias. Look at me when I speak to you."

He shouldn't have agreed to lunch with his mother. He had thought she might be upset about her brother-in-law's recent death, but the event had only fueled her ambition for her son.

She eyed him. "Don't tell me you haven't examined the consequences of your uncle's passing."

"No." He did not intend to tell her he was sad.

She clicked her tongue in disapproval.

Annoyed, Tobias blurted out, "If I kill Serge and Ruel, the lordship will be mine. Is that what you mean by consequences?" Okay, immature, but he didn't care. "No? Good, since I don't want to commit murder."

Her long fingernails clattered against the tabletop in rhythmic irritation. "Must you sound like you're ten years old? Besides"—she looked over as if sizing him up—"you're quite incapable of any such action."

Tobias laughed too loudly at her odd response. "Don't get excited because there's one less warm body between the lordship and I. It won't even last. Serge's wife is pregnant."

"It might be a girl."

"It might. Leave me alone, Mother."

"You're not like your father."

Tobias pushed back his chair. "God, I hope not. Father's ambition got him killed. I have no desire to be lord and Serge knows it."

She rolled her eyes. "Yes, your goal in life is to amount to nothing."

He blinked, trying not to reveal how much her attack surprised him. "Not entirely. Someone killed Uncle Perrin. I intend to find out who."

"Don't start *that* again. Lord Eberly, *the Minister of State*"— his mother did like to stress that oh-so-important title of her latest conquest—"has himself concluded that Perrin died of a heart attack."

"He was fit," Tobias muttered. His mother was either flirting or having an affair with Perrin's old nemesis, so she chose not to see a conflict of interest in Eberly heading the too-brief investigation into Perrin's death. "Times are changing, Mother. If Rimania wants to have the benefits of becoming an affiliate of the Alliance, namely its gifts of technology, the ruling class must behave. Killing each other indiscriminately is rather frowned upon."

"Of course I don't think you should kill your cousins," she declared wearily. "But you can use some political savvy to gain power. You're closer to the lordship now and people will notice. If you let them."

He was not closer to the lordship. He was the son of Tomas, the second brother, the one who was not supposed to become lord. Serge and Ruel, the two sons of the first brother, were directly in line for the prize. Both were willing and eager to inherit the post. Tobias was not.

"You will attend the funeral tomorrow night," she said.

"I was planning to." He stood.

"For goodness' sake, Tobias, I'm talking to you. Sit down." She pointed to his chair.

His face heated.

"You are twenty-three years old. Is it possible to start acting your age? All you do is hang out at those stupid pubs and have affairs with the stupid women Ruel passes on to you. The intelligent women all leave him."

Unable to stomach this conversation, he turned and walked away. She chased after him, her tone less strident, even a hint of apology in her voice. "You're young. But not so young you can't appreciate intelligence in your partners." She placed a hand on his arm and he had to stop. "I know I like intelligent men."

Tobias stared down at his mother in consternation.

"It's been a while since I've heard rumors about you," she said delicately, tilting her head up. "Anything you'd like to share with me?"

God, no. What was with her today? He wanted to escape. He stared out the windows that no longer made him squint. The sky, as was its wont, had clouded over. Weather changed quickly in the city.

"You don't need to run away, Tobias," she persisted. "I am your mother. Even if you're not the only young man in my life."

Wonderful. She wanted to discuss her latest sycophant

13

with him. Something must have shown on his face because she removed her hand and a sneer marred her features.

"Prude. You're like your father in some ways." His mother had always made it clear that she thought his father a wastrel who'd managed to get killed while trying to wrest the lordship from his older, cleverer brother. Tomas Smator had left his infant to be raised by a woman whose main desire in life, despite her occasional political sallies, was to be fancied by young men or older men if they were powerful. Preferably both.

Tobias despised his mother. Technically, as his father's heir, he could kick her off his estate.

She smoothed her expression, as if aware she'd gone too far. "Come, come, it's not so bad. Go to Georg's for a new outfit and charge it to me." Her mouth fixed itself into a stiff smile.

Not trusting himself to speak, Tobias bowed and walked out of the house, then veered off the stone path onto the lawn. It was early spring and the heels of his boots cut into the new grass, spattering the good leather, leaving half-circles of mud in his wake. He didn't see where he was going. A blur of green surrounded him.

He ran a hand through his hair until the gesture irritated him and then he swung long arms in rhythm to his stride, a motion that reassured him. It took a while for the ball of anger in his chest to dissipate, for his heartbeat to subside to one consistent with a brisk walk.

Why had she ambushed him like that? Bringing up his social life when she had never before shown interest? Was it a new game? His private life had always been off limits.

He could threaten to remove her from the house, he thought a little desperately. But it wouldn't assuage the anger he felt about his uncle's death, his *murder*. Everyone else accepted the heart-attack story, but Perrin had been in excellent health. And two weeks ago, Perrin warned Tobias that politics could be dangerous. It made Tobias sick to think someone had killed a good man. There were so few of them. The back of his throat tasted of acid.

He wasn't looking forward to the funeral. Serge, with his heightened status, would be smug, not mournful. Not that his cousin was bright enough to arrange such a deceptive death as his father's. In fact, neither of Perrin's sons were strong men.

With his uncle gone, the political movement to withdraw Rimania from negotiations with the Alliance had lost its leader. Tobias hadn't necessarily agreed with Perrin's politics, but he had loved his uncle.

In mid-stride Tobias changed direction and headed across the estate. He ignored the light rain that began to fall, though he should have grabbed a hat before he left the house. No matter. The tailor wouldn't judge his matted hair and his mud-spattered boots.

ℰ

"Shall I add another half-inch to the fingers, sir?"

Tobias sighed. "No, thank you. My hands are large enough as it is."

"Yes, sir," said the tailor doubtfully while Tobias ignored the old man's muted disapproval. Padded tips were awkward and stupid, and his hands were already long and big, though not elegant. Much like the rest of him.

The bell over the door rang and Tobias turned to see Ruel walk in. Tobias looked a mess and Ruel would notice. On the other hand, Ruel might distract Tobias from his morbid thoughts.

"Hey, Tobias, preparing for the funeral?"

Well, maybe not. "Yes."

"Mommy sent you here, eh?" Ruel clapped Tobias on the shoulder.

Tobias frowned.

"Oh come on, Tobe." Tobias hated being called Tobe. "Try not to look like such a bedraggled pup. You're positively forlorn here."

Tobias found Ruel's determined manner of not being affected by his father's death wearying. It made him angry. Both sons had, like their mother, the depth of a tablecloth. They'd laughed off Tobias's suggestion that Perrin had been murdered.

Finger by finger, Tobias tugged off his new gloves. "I liked your father," he said quietly.

Ruel tousled Tobias's hair. "Such a sentimentalist. A mess of a sentimentalist," he added, theatrically shaking his now-wet hand. "What have you been doing? Wading through the family ponds? I suppose I should be so fortunate as to have family ponds to wade through but I've been denied the extravagance. They belong to my brother."

The tailor waited patiently for the two young men to finish their inane conversation. Tobias slapped the two gloves together and held them out. "Can you wrap these, please?" he asked the old man. "I'll pick up the suit tomorrow."

"Yes, sir."

"Tobias, wait for me and we'll head over to Fargo's."

"No." Since Tobias never said "no", Ruel looked taken aback. Tobias shrugged.

"Are you in one of your funks?" Ruel demanded and Tobias didn't react. Ruel smiled, charmingly. "I have a certain Ann-Marie on my back, Tobias. I know you find her green eyes beguiling."

Remembering his mother's words, Tobias felt his stomach churn.

Puzzled, Ruel let his charming smile fade. "Well, a sour face wasn't quite the reaction I expected. I thought you liked her. We usually have similar tastes. Doesn't Ann-Marie attract you?"

"No." Tobias wiped his face. He was beginning to sweat.

"But what will I do with her?" Ruel appeared genuinely stumped.

"I have to go."

This time, Ruel shrugged. "Met your mother's new boyfriend yet?"

Tobias took the barb full on, as Ruel planned. "Fuck, no." It was really time to leave. "Bye, Ruel." Tobias stalked out of the shop.

§⌒

Through the sealed glass case, Tobias examined his uncle's face one last time. Death and cosmetics couldn't quite erase the humor and kindness of the man. Nor could they tell Tobias who had killed him. Not everyone had loved Lord Perrin Smator, but he, perhaps out of guilt, had watched over Tobias, even protecting him from Serge from time to time.

Tobias didn't want to think about Serge. He looked at the people milling about, forming clusters and breaking apart. This funeral was a thinly disguised excuse for a party and no one seemed to care much about Perrin.

Miffed by yesterday's rebuff, Ruel ignored Tobias, so he stood by himself while Ann-Marie stuck to a disgruntled Ruel like glue. About one-quarter of the women Ruel ended up

17

dumping took Tobias's soft landing. After all, Tobias had an estate and if he lacked charm, well, at least he was tall. Women seemed to like that.

His affairs never lasted long. He didn't want them to. Tobias ground his teeth, annoyed at the direction of his thoughts.

Serge walked up, drink in one hand, the other extended, expecting Tobias's. They shook. Once Tobias had grown to his cousin's size, Serge had stopped trying to squeeze his hand to its breaking point during their formal greetings. They were alike, people said, which didn't please Tobias. Serge looked stupid, dull and mean.

"Tomorrow you can milord me," Serge said. "Wouldn't do to start protocol before Father is interred." He jerked his head towards Perrin's body with a wry grin that quickly disappeared.

Tobias nodded stiffly, hoping Serge would wander off. Instead his cousin stood there, drinking, as if they had something to say to each other. Perhaps Tobias should ask after Serge's wife. "And Lira? How is she—?"

"Fine, fine." Serge swept his hand between them, as if to clear out the question. Lira and Serge's marriage had not been a love match, but she would soon bear him an heir. "When are you thinking of settling down, Tobias? You can't take Ruel's castoffs forever, you know."

Tobias tried not to step back in alarm. He didn't quite understand what was going on. No one had ever felt the need to discuss his sex life before yesterday. Were his mother and Serge talking?

"Marriage needn't be restrictive," Serge added silkily.

Tobias thinned his lips, trying not to grimace.

"You know"—Serge did little to conceal his impatience—"in order to serve in any political capacity you will have to marry."

He leaned forward and Tobias could smell smoke on his breath. "Your mother has asked me to initiate this conversation, but you must contribute beyond this stunned expression of yours."

"I'll tell her you did your best."

Serge stared in disbelief. "Don't be an ass, Tobias. I'm going to need advisors. Family members I can trust."

Tobias tried not to gape. He didn't trust Serge an inch and had thought the feeling mutual.

"If you ever find your tongue, let me know." Serge turned on his heel and walked away while Tobias let out a long, shaky breath.

It was going to be a long evening. Tobias tried to ignore the odd rising panic. People were discussing a part of his life he considered deeply private. A line of pain throbbed across his temple, so he reached for another drink. Sometimes he found it hard to believe he had been born into Riman society. He belonged elsewhere.

A place that allowed him to be himself, that allowed him to *breathe*. He sometimes imagined himself living on an entirely different planet, although those fantasies were vague on specifics. Like how he would possibly get there. No one had actually left Rimania for hundreds of years.

Half an hour and a couple of drained glasses later, a servant approached a numb Tobias with yet another drink. He didn't recognize the man. New, or perhaps he'd been hired to work the funeral. Tobias lifted the glass off the tray.

"Your brother requests your presence in the courtyard."

Huh?

The servant bowed politely and withdrew.

Tobias didn't have a brother, but he wasn't going to yell that at the retreating servant's back. He gulped down his drink, placed the glass on a side table, and tried to walk in a straight line through the hall. At the moment, in his stupor, he was grateful that he knew this house and estate well. He'd spent too much of his youth here while his mother scampered off here and there.

The fresh air hit him with some relief. His head cleared a little. Enough to appreciate the light of the first moon on the patio. The way it fell across the tiles...

Tobias frowned. Why was he here? Something to do with Serge probably. Fuck, he hated Serge. His boyhood torment, though whenever he felt the need to unburden his old secret terrors, he became aware of how stupidly melodramatic and unexceptional the bullying had been.

Now Serge wanted him as an advisor. That made no sense. Serge despised him.

Tobias's head felt wavy. Not his usual reaction to alcohol...

This was the courtyard. Where was the supposed brother? He walked farther, glancing behind one bush, then another, feeling rather sick and rather sad.

He couldn't become weepy in a strange place. But, no, this was familiar. His childhood terror...

Yes, yes, he'd just been through that.

Despite his difficulty focusing, Tobias straightened in alarm. In the moonlight, he saw someone's feet, pointed up, and the rest of the body lay in shadow. Tobias very slowly—time seemed wrong now—moved closer. With some trepidation, his gaze followed the legs up to the torso, to find the hilt of a jeweled knife. Its blade embedded in a man's very bloody chest.

Shit. Finding it impossible to believe what he saw, Tobias blinked as sweat ran into his eyes. *That's Serge.* Tobias's heart pounded harder than his aching head.

He could hardly move, despite his desire to vomit.

"Tobias?" His mother's voice floated out to him.

With supreme effort, Tobias turned to look at her.

She appeared in his line of vision, attached to the arm of a tall, slender green-eyed boy. Or man. It was difficult to see clearly. The waves now extended to Tobias's sight.

His mother spoke and her distorted words echoed. "What is the matter with you?"

Then she seemed to notice something behind him.

"Tobias?" Her voice rose on his name, high and out of control, reverberating. Or maybe it was Tobias who shook.

She leaned on the boy-man. Her mouth continued to move but Tobias could no longer hear. He dragged his gaze over to her companion whose face blurred and all Tobias could see were his exceptional, weirdly green eyes. Leaning forward, Tobias lost his balance. The cement tiles rushed up to his face and obliterated consciousness.

Chapter Two

Tobias's insides cramped and the side of his face felt smashed in. Why was he in such pain? Even groaning hurt. He lay prone till someone turned him over, face up. He wished they'd leave him alone, he couldn't even open his eyes to glare at whoever hovered over him. A hand explored his mouth. Unpleasant, that. A finger pushed against his tongue. Against his will a quick, sharp taste blossomed.

"Swallow" was hissed in his ear. Tobias obeyed, hoping the voice would go away.

The next thing Tobias knew, he came awake with a vengeance and was on his knees, vomiting, his stomach being turned inside out while that same voice repeated "you're okay" like a mantra.

Tobias wanted to believe, but the spasms *hurt*. And they didn't stop. He had trouble catching his breath. But the man stayed with him and a strange hand rested on his back, his only source of comfort.

"Good, good," came that encouraging voice, almost an accent there, but not quite.

"Good" was not the word that came to Tobias's mind. "Hell" was more like it, he thought just before he collapsed.

$\wp$

Tobias woke at home. His entire body ached and a sense of nightmare gripped him. Bad dream, he decided while he tried to open his eyes. And failed. Hmmm. The lethargy confused him. Hangover? Possibly, though a bizarre one.

At least he was in his bed. That was familiar. What had he been drinking? He'd actually attempted to cut back on the alcohol lately, fearful that he'd give himself away when he was under the influence.

At his second attempt to open his eyes, he succeeded, and promptly shut them again. The morning's light was too bright. He hadn't a clue why he should feel so awful and this lapse of memory made him uneasy. As did his throbbing cheek. Had he walked into something?

He rested, trying to recall the night before and managed to remember Perrin's funeral had been held. The fresh realization cut deep. Uncle Perrin was dead, and he'd drunk too much— that was no way to respect the dead. With some self-loathing, Tobias struggled to sit up. The effort made him tremble. This time he forced his eyes to stay open.

To his alarm, a stranger was stationed at the corner of his room—a thickset, middle-aged man in uniform. Tobias blinked in astonishment.

"Good morning, sir." The policeman stepped forward. "I'm Officer Lahane."

"Hello," said Tobias cautiously and winced. The side of his face was tender and numb, as if it had been injured then treated. He was appalled by a sudden rush of memory.

Serge had been murdered. Knifed. Tobias had seen him. As had his mother and the man with the green eyes.

The police would be questioning Tobias, no escaping that. In fact, Lahane *was* the police. With a sinking feeling, Tobias saw he was being either guarded or detained.

His horror deepened when he realized only Ruel stood between himself and the lordship.

"*Fuck.*"

Lahane didn't approve of the outburst. "Sir?"

Tobias strove to keep the panic out of his voice. "Why are you here?"

"To protect you, sir."

"From whom?"

"We don't know that yet." The slightly sinister tone was also portentous. "We'll need to question you."

"Question?" repeated Tobias weakly, trying to hide his absolute dread.

"About last night."

"Someone tried to poison me."

"Possibly." Lahane's tone cast doubt on Tobias's statement.

Dr. Tran's arrival didn't improve the situation. Through the open door, Tobias could hear his mother's frantic voice demanding to know what would happen to her son in a way that suggested he'd already been found guilty of murder.

The doctor escaped Tobias's mother as Lahane shut the door on her. Dr. Tran was here to check him over: pupil size, reflexes, temperature, blood pressure, etc. The doctor's movements were abrupt and nervous, though he tried to hide it behind a bracing you're-in-top-shape kind of manner. By the time he left, Tobias felt doomed.

Next stop, apparently, was the police station. It was paramount that Tobias not talk to anyone, not even his mother, before being questioned. Something about contamination.

All Tobias knew was he did not want to go to the city's station again. He breathed deeply against the panic and reminded himself that he was no longer a vulnerable thirteen-year-old boy.

℘

"Your mother said you spoke of killing Serge and Ruel." The man—Tobias's questioner—delivered this statement in a neutral way, as if they were discussing the weather.

"It was a stupid joke," Tobias said lamely. "I loathe the idea of being a lord, as my mother knows. Did she mention *that*?" Okay, the last question sounded too anxious, too angry. Right now, Tobias felt most inclined to kill his mother for even mentioning their discussion, but decided it was best to keep quiet about those murderous thoughts.

He peered at the questioner. The man's smooth, round face gave nothing away, and most of his lanky body was hidden behind a massive desk. Not that Tobias felt particularly adept at reading body language. God knows he'd made his mistakes in the past.

"Your mother's statement forces us to question you. Formally."

Formal. *Crap.* Though he had expected no less, given where he now sat, still Tobias's heart sank.

"Do you understand what that entails?" The man hit a number of keys, probably flipping through the documents on his screen. "Yes, you do. You were similarly questioned when you were thirteen years old and your aunt's diamonds went missing." His eyebrows rose just a fraction before he met Tobias's gaze. "Rather an unusual situation."

Tobias shrugged. Sixteen-year-old Serge had framed him, but he wasn't going to say that now.

"I'm very surprised that Lord Perrin Smator allowed what was essentially a family affair to reach such a high level."

"He was away," Tobias said shortly.

"Ah, well." The man set down his monitor and used his palm to wipe nonexistent dust off the desk's polished wood. "Now we have a more serious matter on our hands. We want to identify Lord Serge Smator's murderer." A strategic pause. "I assume you'll cooperate."

"Of course." Tobias had no choice.

"You understand that the physical restraints are for your own safety?"

"Yes." His situation was demeaning, but he tried not to sound surly. He was currently engulfed by metal while the other man sat at a desk, and moved around when he was so inclined. The questioner had no intention of ever introducing himself. His role allowed anonymity—a privilege in the upper ranks of the police force—while Tobias could be grilled about his personal life and his private thoughts. The idea had him breaking out in a light sweat.

"Sir, please place your arms in their restraints."

Spoken as if Tobias was balking. He obeyed.

His hands were wet when he lifted his arms and placed them in the shelf-like slots, allowing them to be trapped. A force field immobilized Tobias's arms and chest. He could press against the field but it winded him.

"Try to relax, Mr. Smator."

Tobias snorted.

"It's important that you don't move."

A metal globe descended from above to surround his head,

and all Tobias could see was silver. *Don't panic, don't panic.*

The metal echoed with the questioner's voice. "Are you comfortable, Mr. Smator?"

Was that a trick question? "I suppose," he ventured.

"I understand you underwent this procedure ten years ago, but nevertheless I will remind you that using functional MRI during formal questioning is harmless and painless. It allows us to detect whether or not you are lying. I encourage you to tell the truth and the entire truth, so we don't have to explore other methods of interrogation." The old-fashioned kind—torture.

Tobias could be grateful for his high status right now. After his experience at thirteen, he'd become somewhat obsessed by all forms of interrogation, including the crude drugs and beatings that were administered to the lower classes and the recalcitrant elite who had no one to protect them.

"I will tell the truth," promised Tobias. He didn't like pain.

"Good. Let us begin." Mr. Anonymous paused for dramatic effect. "Did you kill Serge Smator?"

"No."

"Did you know that Serge Smator would be killed?"

"No."

"Were you involved, in any way, in the murder of Serge Smator?"

"No."

"Why did you talk to your mother about killing your cousins?"

"I didn't. It was a stupid throwaway line, said to annoy her." He should have known better. "I have no political ambition and she resents it. I sincerely wish Serge were still alive." All true. Tobias hoped the questioner could "see" that live in Tobias's brain.

"Did you meet anyone new at the funeral last night?"

"No," he said more slowly.

"But...?"

"But I did see two people I had never before laid eyes on."

"Who were they?"

"A servant who gave me a drink laced with poison, and my mother's new admirer."

"Ah." This syllable uttered with some satisfaction. "I know the identity of the latter. Geln Marac."

"Who?"

"A worker."

Tobias frowned. The green-eyed one? He'd been dressed in high fashion, nothing a worker could afford.

"He has somehow ingratiated himself with some of the elite," the man explained. "Including your mother. Don't worry, we'll be doing something about his deception. Under the circumstances, it is quite suspicious."

Tobias recalled how Geln Marac had—he thought, his memories weren't the best—helped him last night, and couldn't make sense of what this new friend of his mother's was doing. Knifing Serge and comforting Tobias? That hand on the back didn't make sense. "What will you do with Marac?"

"He's not someone you need concern yourself with, Mr. Smator. Let's get back on track. Who gave you emolio?"

"Emolio?" The word was new to Tobias.

"You overdosed on emolio last night. It is an offworld drug and illegal."

"Offworld?"

"No need to repeat everything I say, Mr. Smator."

Tobias gritted his teeth. "Someone poisoned me."

"This is Lord Smator's murder investigation, not yours." The man's dry tone implied that Tobias was an attention-getter who wanted to steal his dead cousin's thunder. "Now, who gave you the emolio?"

"The servant I didn't recognize. I told you."

"Why were you in the courtyard?"

"Someone wanted to talk to me. That same servant directed me there." There was a long pause and Tobias could feel sweat bead on his forehead. This metal globe was making him hot.

"Do you believe your mother could be involved in the murder of Serge Smator?"

"No." His mother was many things, but not a murderess.

Another long pause and Tobias began to fear that his anxiety was going to take control of him, though he'd kept it on a tight leash till now.

Then the metal globe rose, his arms were released, and Tobias was free of the threat of invasive questioning. He hadn't given himself away, hadn't come close. Something of triumph rose in him, despite the awful situation.

The questioner delivered his verdict with a small smile. Perhaps Tobias's obvious fears amused him. "It appears you are not involved in the murder of your cousin, Serge Smator."

౭ఎ

Five hours later, after many tedious but *in*formal questions by Officer Lahane, Tobias returned home to watch his mother fly down the stairs and throw herself on his shoulder, sobbing theatrically. He put an arm around her, though he couldn't remember the last time they'd hugged and he felt too weary for this kind of display.

"I thought you were going to be imprisoned, or *worse*." She pulled back to look at him, as if he'd just come home from a three-month vacation and she was proud of his adventures. She lifted a hand towards his face. "Your cheek is healing nicely."

"I guess." It still hurt to talk and he'd been forced to talk all day.

"Did they treat you well?"

"It was fine."

"Fine? When I've been frantic, not knowing what they'd do to you." A long shaky sigh was wrung from her. Then she brightened a little. "Fortunately, I've had Geln to keep me company. He's been a wonderful distraction."

Tobias stiffened. "Geln Marac is here?"

"Yes." His mother turned her head and looked up. Tobias followed her gaze and saw the green-eyed boy leaning on the balustrade observing this tender family scene. He was too young for her, and a worker. She'd hate that. "I needed the emotional support."

Support? Tobias frowned while Geln grinned as if sincerely glad to see him. He raised one hand and, in a parody of a wave, waggled his fingers.

"I'm pleased to meet you standing, Tobias." The voice was rich, though not deep, and full of humor.

Geln's attempt to charm annoyed Tobias. One enthralled Smator was surely more than enough. He didn't respond to Geln's greeting, though he kept his gaze on that pretty face as he spoke. "Geln's a worker, Mother."

"Worker?" she repeated, tone implying Tobias had made a bad joke.

Geln went very still. With that one word, *worker*, his friendly smile vanished, his expression dimmed, and Tobias felt regretful, like he'd just lost something.

"The police are very interested in him," Tobias continued, ostensibly talking to his mother. But he didn't wish the police on anyone, especially a worker, and Geln deserved the warning. Tobias disliked his mother's sycophants, but had some loyalty for the man who had helped him vomit up poison. It was why he'd said as little as possible about Geln to the police.

"Geln?" His mother spun around to look up at the young beauty. She spoke too quickly. "What's Tobias talking about? You can't be a worker." Her polished smile was slipping.

"No, I can't," he drawled. "But life can get complicated. Excuse me a moment." He disappeared from view.

She turned back to Tobias. "Worker? Are you sure?"

Tobias felt bad. "That's what the police said. Look, Mother, I'm exhausted." Tobias reached for the bell-pull and rang for his man.

They waited in awkward silence, his mother looking away from him, lost in thought.

"The police say he's a worker?" she asked yet again, this time in a quiet, small voice, right before Sandorl entered the foyer.

"Yes," Tobias sighed. Perhaps he had just ended a promising relationship, but he hadn't wanted that man with his mother anyway.

Tobias handed Sandorl his overcoat and trudged up to his room.

Chapter Three

Geln slammed his fist against the brick wall, abrading the skin. "Shit. Major fuck up. Major, *major* fuck up. Shit shit *shit*."

Kleemach didn't respond right away. Then it sounded amused. "Sound-damping comes in handy at times, doesn't it?"

"I am fucked. I am screwed. I am—"

"Stop that." Kleemach's voice changed, likely a subroutine kicking in. "Breathe slowly and get yourself under control. Now."

"Major is such a stupid word." Geln whimpered.

"Calm down, Geln. We'll handle this."

"Right. Yeah."

"You're not alone."

In theory, no. Geln had Kleemach's extensive support. But physically and emotionally Geln was alone, marooned on a feudal planet with an AI floating far above him. It took all of Geln's will not to scream *bullshit*. He wrapped his arms around himself and dug fingers into his skin—the dank washroom was cold.

"Okay," said Kleemach, all business. "Let's go over this. How much do they know?"

"They believe I'm a worker. They're going to bloody well interrogate me. Not only do their drugs and violence scare the shit out of me, but I'll reveal what I know about the cadre. The cadre can be pathetic and violent, but I don't want to betray them."

"You have more potent secrets."

Kleemach didn't give a shit about the homegrown cadre, a rather motley group of men with unrealistic aspirations that involved overthrowing the government. What the AI didn't want Rimanians to discover was Alliance espionage. Well, neither did Geln, given that he was a spy. "Yes, Kleemach. Hell knows what the Rimanians will do once they realize I'm an Alliance operative. Hell knows what the *Alliance* will do."

"The Alliance is on your side. Don't be needlessly paranoid, Geln."

Geln snorted. "From now on I'll save my paranoia for situations that warrant it."

Kleemach didn't answer. Its pauses, rare and unsettling, indicated it was searching for an appropriate response. "We'll have to convince them you're elite," it said in a clipped I'm-on-top-of-this-mess tone. "Why do they think you're a worker?"

"Fuck if I know, Klee. But the police told Tobias Smator I am." His voice was rising again.

"Calm down, man." Perhaps Klee thought "man" was a term of affection? Though how its affection was supposed to help him now, Geln couldn't fathom. "We're going to change your birthright from worker to elite. Though it will take some finagling."

"I don't have time." The strangled words came out between clenched teeth, but that was better than high-pitched panic.

"Yes, you do." Klee's voice sounded dismissive, as if it was already working hard on Geln's case.

It would find a solution, Geln tried to reassure himself. Klee was good at this shit, it had been specifically created to oversee Geln's operations. The Alliance wouldn't abandon Geln. He was gathering all kinds of useful information, having been accepted as a member of the cadre *and* as an admirer of the Minister of State's mistress, just as Peo, his primary operative, had ordered.

Geln's trembling, now caused by a sweat-induced chill, started up again. He'd been leaning against the brick of the heat-sucking manor trying not to faint. He detached himself from the wall.

"We've got time," Klee continued. "The police aren't terribly efficient here. They've already sent someone to collect you at your lodgings, so don't go home."

Geln rolled his eyes. As if he would even consider such a stupid move.

"But get out of this house. Even the police will twig to the fact that you could be here."

He would leave as soon as his legs could carry him out. It occurred to Geln that he'd better wash his face, get his act together and stop reacting like a total amateur.

"Geln, you're important, but not that important. The Rimanians haven't mobilized the entire police force in order to locate you in the next two hours. If you're careful, they won't find you this evening. Go to a bar you don't frequent, say Fargo's, and keep a low profile."

Fuck. Klee was winging it, projecting a persona that was programmed to reassure skittish operatives.

Klee's voice continued on inexorably, smooth and confident. "Contact me once you're at Fargo's. In the meantime, I'm setting you up as an elite. That way you'll get the MRI inquiry and you can lie through your teeth with a little help from our chemical friend, stosh. No Rimanian drugs. No beatings. You'll get clear. Okay?"

"Yes," Geln agreed, sounding stronger than he felt. He supposed stosh-induced amnesia was preferable to Rimanian drugs, but he wasn't keen on a temporary brain-wipe. Even if the memories came back. Mostly.

It would be something of a relief not to think about everything for a while.

"You'll be fine, Geln."

"Yeah? Is that what Peo thinks?"

"Your *primary operative*"—for some reason Klee disliked Geln's nickname for this woman—"trusts my judgment."

Klee's pat answer.

"Right." Though Geln hadn't thought it possible, he felt even more desperate than usual to meet his PO. But it wasn't allowed and, this way, the police would not be able to extract a useful name from him, no matter what drug they fed him.

Well, he had his own secrets. He hadn't told Klee he'd saved Tobias's life last night. Why the hell had he done that anyway? Klee, meaning the Alliance, would disapprove. Geln wasn't to interfere in Rimanian politics, whatever form they took.

But the whites of Tobias's eyes had yellowed, a symptom of emolio poisoning which smacked distinctly of offworld politics. Geln had had seconds to choose his course of action and saving a life had been the easy moral choice of the moment, even if a little thought tagged Peo as the likely source of the drug. He hoped she wasn't the poisoner. Fuck. No wonder he was so panicked.

But Geln just didn't have time to dwell on the emergency pill he'd given away last night. He had to concentrate on the crisis at hand. "I'll need my cover, Klee, and I'll need to believe it."

"I'll get you one. Stay out of the police's way until we talk again."

"I'll try." Geln closed down the connection, schooled his face and calmly left the washroom. Upon retrieving his overcoat, he walked out the front door. He was badly chilled and the stupid elite garb didn't keep him warm. He preferred the plainer, warmer worker clothing he'd worn when he'd stayed his first four months with the cadre—before Peo had decided they were a lost cause and there were better places on Rimania for Geln to infiltrate. But now, after only two months as an elite, he was on the run.

No one saw him leave. The police could waste time looking for him in Dressia's manor. He hurried down the large stone stairs, taking the wide, shallow steps by twos. It seemed the longer the staircase, the greater the glory, or something like that. He finally slipped into shadow.

He cut around the back of the estate and walked through the fields. Hiding out here was not a safe option. Bandits from the countryside liked to sneak into the city from time to time, so each estate's security had its own methods of deterrence. Some involved physical maiming.

Geln reached the boundary of the estate and cut back up to the main road. He didn't want to get lassoed by one of their odd technical atrocities. Intelligent barbed wire was apparently popular on the black market. He shuddered. Such a trap would deliver him directly to the police, if it didn't kill him first.

⟡

Fargo's had the kind of plush, dark interior that Geln found

Poison

oppressive. The velvet doors, with their rich reds and blues, matched the chairs that were, thankfully, comfortable. He sank down into a corner, trying not to look furtive. How successfully he projected calm, he couldn't gauge. He was supposed to be a good actor, having spent four bloody years at it. Somehow acting in plays and acting in real life in a foreign culture were quite different—the feedback in real time usually needed interpretation, unless it was obvious one had failed badly.

The waiter brought Geln beer and a fried rice snack. Usually he liked such fare, but his appetite was shot. For appearance's sake, he nibbled.

Putting his elbow on the table, he rested his head on his hand so people wouldn't notice he was talking to his watch. It could sound-damp, but it couldn't hide his moving lips.

"Hey, Geln." Klee sounded inordinately friendly so Geln figured his AI was worried about his mental state. Lovely. "I'm inserting your history into the data banks as we speak."

"Do you know why the police decided I was a worker?"

"It's the default status."

Geln frowned.

"You're from the northern district of Rogan, a land of few people. All the elite are identified and, basically, you're not one of them. Or, you weren't. As of today, you are their bastard child, secretly raised by the Maracs, an unremarkable worker family who died out five years ago."

"Oh come on, this sounds ridiculous." The police would never buy it.

"Doesn't matter how it sounds," Klee said testily, as if Geln were tactlessly insulting its creation. "It's in their data banks and their data banks are incorruptible."

"God," declared Geln hopelessly.

37

"Your mother hid her pregnancy and handed you over to this unknown family to keep you secret. Your father, also elite of course, died before they could marry. Hence the scandal and the cover-up. But you're pureblood elite all the same and that's what we need."

"Who put this information in the data banks, then?"

"It's a mystery, but someone who wanted to protect your future, possibly your maternal grandmother. It wasn't to be revealed until your twenty-first birthday, which is, ta-daa, in two hours." Klee sounded triumphant.

"It sounds corny," Geln protested.

"It certainly does not."

"I'm thirty-one."

"Don't be stupid. You look twenty-one and that's what counts."

Geln groaned.

"It's perfect." The AI almost sounded conceited. "You can still identify with your cadre of workers because of your upbringing. With them you can reject the social hierarchy. You'll have access to two classes of Rimanians for the rest of your stay!"

Geln shook his head in disbelief. Klee was ridiculously optimistic about his assignment. "Forget the cadre right now. I'm too rattled to even think about them." Besides, the local leader, Arjes, gave him the creeps. Another thing Geln didn't want to share with Klee. "I've got to get my story straight and convince the police. Suppose my mother doesn't remember being pregnant?"

"Both she and *her* mother are dead, Geln. Until today, you've been a worker who wanted to believe he was elite because, as a boy, you were told such a story. When the police check your file before they interrogate you, they will find the 'truth'."

"What if they don't check my file?"

"Tell them you're elite and insist that they do."

"There's no reason for them to listen to me, Klee." Geln was trying not to whine, but fear was getting the best of him. "Can't Peo help me?"

"No. She must keep her cover."

"Fuck her cover," Geln muttered, though without much heat.

"Geln, I'll be monitoring the whole thing, okay? If necessary, I'll force them to notice that you're elite. But it will be more elegant if you can convince them to look on their own."

Elegance, yeah, that was key. Not, say, staying in one piece.

Geln gulped a deep breath and reached for optimism. After all, Klee could and did monitor a zillion things, even if it didn't understand all the information it accessed. Presumably if the AI's major goal was to get Geln identified as elite, it could do it.

"Okay." Geln wearily chewed on his now-cold snack. Klee was actually good at what it did, he reminded himself. "So, what do *I* do?"

"You wait. They're combing the bars. They'll come to you. And while you wait, I'll give you the details of your life so you'll have a story to tell them tomorrow."

Chapter Four

"I'm afraid you must pay a visit to your cousin Ruel," his mother informed Tobias during their late breakfast. She had waited to dine with him.

"Today?" His body still ached from the poison and his face had not yet healed. "Given Ruel's disinterest in both family and politics—"

"Ruel's brother has just been murdered. You were a prime suspect. Not only that, someone may have tried to kill you." She picked up her utensils and delicately cut off a piece of sausage. "I think it politic, if nothing else, to show your face, express your regrets, and make it clear that you haven't a clue what is going on, perhaps even voice some concern about your own personal safety."

"I proved my innocence yesterday."

"There are limits to every technique of inquiry, Tobias. While I personally have no doubt of your innocence, others will remember your antipathy towards Serge."

Tobias winced, pressing a palm against his forehead.

"Don't resent my advice," his mother continued on inexorably, and Tobias realized he would go to Ruel's simply to escape her lectures. "Don't you see that you want to place yourself on the same side as Ruel?"

Here, his mother was mistaken. Ruel didn't have a side and if he did, Tobias wouldn't like it. His cousin could be fun, but he was also amoral. "I have a headache, Mother."

She called for the maid to fetch an analgesic.

They waited five minutes for the painkiller to work. He really wasn't hungry, especially for sausage and eggs, so he pushed away from the table.

"I realize you don't feel well." She looked up. "Do you want me to accompany you when you pay your respects?"

"No," he declared flatly, and she managed to look a little hurt. But he could not deliver the required platitudes while his mother hovered over him. Besides, who knew what Ruel would be doing.

Preparing to go took longer than usual, and despite the analgesic, Tobias's head continued to throb dully, as did his face. On his way over to Ruel's apartments, the carriage seemed to hit every bump.

Still, he made it to Ruel's and Tobias was announced, then led into the rented rooms. He was now Ruel's heir, an appalling thought. Rumor had it that Ruel and a girl from the Pyadrez family—Tobias couldn't remember her name—would soon become engaged. He felt sorry for the girl, but also hoped she would start reproducing as quickly as possible.

It was now early afternoon and Ruel, somewhat drunk, stumbled as he approached.

"Greetings, Tobias." He shook hands rather unenthusiastically as one corner of his mouth dug into his cheek with a disgruntled expression of resignation. Evidently, Ruel didn't want a condolence visit and Tobias soon saw why. Ruel had company.

Behind him stood Ann-Marie. As usual her clothing was a little too gaudy, her makeup too strong, her eyes too green. No wonder Ruel didn't want him here. Tobias was interrupting a tryst, never mind that Ruel had recently tried to dump Ann-Marie, never mind that his father and brother were dead. Although, perhaps that was part of the explanation. Ruel looked haggard.

Ann-Marie tilted her head and raised her eyebrows, challenging Tobias to be shocked by her presence.

Instead, Tobias took her gloved hand and kissed it. "Hello, Ann-Marie." He sounded a little stiff. He probably looked awkward too.

"And to what do I owe the honor of this visit?" Ruel asked.

Somehow, at home, his mother's arguments had made sense, with their talk of murder and succession. But they crumbled in the face of his listless cousin.

"I wanted to offer my condolences." Tobias tried to sound sincere, not diffident.

"Thank you." Ruel did not sound sincere, only bored, and for a tense moment, Tobias thought he would have to turn around and leave right away. Then Ruel gestured down the hall and they trooped into the drawing room. Tobias sat.

"Well." Ruel still stood, listing slightly to the right. "They've cleared you, haven't they, with their little magnetic examination?"

Tobias nodded.

"I'm not surprised. Even if you and Serge hated each other." Ruel gave a loopy smile. "You must have been alarmed to be at the mercy of the truthteller. Again."

Tobias shrugged. He didn't want to talk about himself.

"Who knows what they could have asked you or what you might have been forced to say about yourself. A postadolescent interrogation must be different from the one in your youth."

It wasn't an interrogation, shithead. But no, Tobias didn't say the words. He had to stay calm. Even if Ruel enjoyed a taunt when he was in the right mood, he knew *nothing* about Tobias's inner life.

"You see, darling." Ruel captured a stray hair of Ann-Marie's between his index finger and thumb. "Tobias here is a little repressed."

Despite all that had gone on this past week, Tobias once again felt a sick panic when he realized that Ruel wanted to toy with him. Tobias schooled his face to keep his expression bland and met Ann-Marie's gaze, expecting that coy smile of hers she often used on Ruel, and occasionally on himself.

But Ruel's dig had not impressed Ann-Marie. She'd stiffened, moving away from Ruel's hand, and her stony displeasure caused Ruel to straighten.

Ruel coughed. "My mind is wandering. Bit of a shock, this whole thing. Not sure what will happen next. Suppose I ought to marry."

Marry? Well, sure, but an odd topic to raise with Ann-Marie in the room. This visit was surreal and it was the last time Tobias was taking his mother's advice. She had no idea what Ruel was really like.

"Bit of a problem, that," Ruel added, then momentarily covered his face.

"You don't want the lordship?" Tobias asked finally, since Ann-Marie just stood there and Ruel continued to shake his shoulders silently, perhaps laughing.

"Not like this, I bloody well don't." He dropped onto the couch, sinking into its pillows, and closed his eyes. "I don't mind the idea of the lordship. Can't do a worse job than Serge would have done and the perks are fun. But I might not get it anyway. Lira's due in a month or two, isn't she?"

Somehow, Tobias had forgotten the expected baby.

"Until the child is of age, you'll have the lordship in practice." Ann-Marie's voice was smooth and controlled.

As he nodded, Ruel's half-lidded eyes rested on her. He turned to face Tobias. "I don't wish to marry the Pyadrez girl, you see. I want to stay with Ann-Marie."

"Oh?" Tobias had been asked to take Ann-Marie off Ruel's hands two days ago. He didn't understand this drastic change of heart.

"You may disapprove"—Ruel slurred that word—"but it is not your decision."

Tobias opened his hands. He had no desire to argue the point. His head began to pound again and he just wanted to bow out of this conversation. "When will Serge's funeral take place?"

Ruel waved vaguely. "The police will take their time examining him postmortem." He passed a hand across his eyes. "I didn't like my brother but I miss him. His death completely fucks up my life. As the younger brother, I had the freedom to do as I wish. Now I'll lose that freedom without inheriting the lordship. I'll be regent, as it were." He shuddered. "The police have the bastard who knifed Serge. I hope they hang him for murder. I could wring his neck myself."

Tobias straightened, alert. "The police have who, exactly?"

"The bastard."

"Yes. *Who*?" Tobias persisted.

Ruel shrugged. "Some worker."

No, thought Tobias in dismay. A picture of the green-eyed boy came to mind, as well as the unreal memory of that sharp taste in his mouth, just before he vomited the emolio. He hadn't wanted Geln caught. "What's his name?"

"I don't know." Ruel appeared to find the question ridiculous, as if he wouldn't pay attention to such details. "Ann-Marie, do you remember his name?"

"I do." She shot Tobias a small, ironic smile. "It's Geln Marac."

℘

Hours after the police apprehended him, Geln finally convinced them to check his data file. It was midday. He thought. He'd begun to lose track of time.

He still feared they wouldn't actually pull up his file before they hauled him off for an injection. Klee had said it would monitor his situation, but its ability to insinuate itself was limited. Klee couldn't prevent someone from injecting a toxic drug into Geln's arm, for example.

In an attempt to control his trembling, Geln walked around and around his little cell. It was a bare cement room with a hole in the corner, quite lovely. He might have appreciated it more if his ribs and face hurt less.

His charm hadn't done much for him last night. They'd assaulted him and sneered when he'd claimed to be a Pyadrez.

Time passed, and passed again. He spent most of it sitting on the floor, holding his aching chest. It hurt when he breathed. Dehydration threatened, but no one came. He didn't think he had internal bleeding, but the longer he was held in this room, the more he worried about it. The discomfort of broken ribs kept him from sleeping.

This would be an awful way to die. Dehydration. Internal bleeding.

"Klee, where are you?" he asked, though the question made

no sense. They'd taken his watch and Klee couldn't hear him.

More time passed and he began to lose it. He no longer wanted to cry—at first he thought his strength of character had returned, but now he wasn't sure. Holding on to ideas became difficult. He feared the police would return and he'd let slip that he was from the Alliance, or that he was a member of the northern cadre for redistribution.

Wrong story, he admonished himself, trying to hang on to his cover. He was Geln Marac, bastard child, nephew of Hernan Pyadrez who lived in the city. He hoped his uncle would be able to rescue him, and soon.

Only much later did he come to know that the arresting officers had panicked when his file came up. Panicked to such an extent that they'd left him alone for longer than they meant to while trying to figure out how to handle a bad situation. For the police had assaulted a member of the elite.

By the time the doctor arrived, Geln was unconscious.

ℰↃ

Geln woke to find himself lying on a very comfortable bed. At first he thought he was back home, perhaps recovering from a night out, and the sense of relief was so overpowering he wanted to weep. That was when the nightmare began seeping back in, for the room smelled sterile and foreign. Dismay shuddered through him. This was no home of his.

Without actually moving, he blinked awake, trying to determine where he was. A man stood guard. Geln closed his eyes quickly, feigning more sleep while his dulled brain assessed the situation. He couldn't remember how he'd got here. Last he remembered, he'd been left to die in a cell.

It occurred to him that he'd been drugged, though he wasn't sure. Gingerly, he took a deep breath. His ribs no longer hurt. In fact, he'd been changed into clean clothes, which was quite presumptuous on their part. He surreptitiously touched his face. It was clean and his bruised lips were tender but no longer swollen.

He stopped pretending sleep and sat up, bracing himself for some kind of pain, and found none. No doubt he'd been dosed with healing agents.

"I hope you slept well, sir," said the officer. "Sir" was an awfully good sign. Yesterday, or whenever he'd last been awake, it had been "asshole" and the like. Geln let himself hope that he was being treated as an elite. "Your personal belongings are beside your bed, sir."

With a leap of joy, Geln realized the officer meant that his one link to Klee was beside his bed. Wanting to snatch up the watch, Geln forced himself to reach over and close his fingers around that watch without appearing to snatch it up. He attached it to his wrist. The separation from Klee had been traumatic.

For good measure, he glanced at the time and frowned. "I seem to have slept for two days."

"We didn't want to disturb you."

They'd drugged him. He felt like something of a puppet, but whose, he didn't know. Never mind. He just needed to get out of here, talk to Klee, and make sure his Pyadrez story still held.

"I'll let my superior know you are awake, sir. Possibly you are hungry."

"Possibly." He swung his feet off the bed and placed them on the plush carpet.

"No, no, sir. We will bring breakfast to you."

That sounded ominous, and Geln waited nervously, but the food they brought him was wonderful. Starving, he dug into the rice dish, the eggs, a fruit salad and rolls. He also enjoyed the steamed milk. Between mouthfuls, he asked, "Are you going to release me?"

"Of course, sir! We are just waiting for your uncle to arrive."

Geln decided not to question this good piece of news. Would he actually get out of here without using stosh? He stumbled over to what was evidently the washroom, closed the door, and took a seat on the edge of the tub. Then he activated his watch, calling up Klee and sound-damping so bugs could not pick up their conversation.

"Klee?"

"Geln! Are you okay? You should be."

"I am," he said, a bit alarmed by the massive relief he felt at talking to Klee. He was too emotionally dependent on the AI. Well, he would worry about *that* later.

"So they're treating you well, right?"

"I'm eating good food. I slept in a comfortable bed. But I seem to be a prisoner and I've been heavily drugged."

"They wanted to get rid of your injuries before your uncle saw you."

"Right."

"I'm glad you're okay, Geln," the AI declared warmly and Geln rolled his eyes. He *knew* the AI didn't have emotions, but it sure did play to him and Geln couldn't help but react.

"How's Tobias, by the way?"

"Tobias?" Klee repeated the name as if it hadn't a clue who the man was. Geln just waited until Klee decided it should answer the question. "Tobias Smator is fine. Why do you ask?"

"Because both he and I were there that fun-filled night his

cousin Serge was knifed to death." Silence. Klee had nothing more to say. But Geln did. "Not to change the subject entirely, but I have to know. Is Peo involved in these attacks on the Smators?"

"No," it said immediately and with total conviction.

Geln suppressed a snort. He didn't know why he asked Klee these kinds of questions, since it lied through its virtual teeth when ordered to.

"Why?" Klee asked.

Careful. "I'd like to talk to Peo."

"Geln, it's a very human desire, especially after captivity, for an operative to want to confide in another human. It's not possible, I'm afraid. But I'm here for you."

"You're here." Geln could agree with that much. But the operation, not Geln, was Klee's first priority and Geln would do well to remember—and stop asking questions about Tobias.

Besides, maybe Geln was wrong. Maybe he'd mistaken Tobias's symptoms the night of Perrin Smator's funeral and the kid hadn't been given emolio. How reassuring that would be. Otherwise, the possibility of a poisonous primary operative was disturbingly real. Being in charge of the op, Peo knew of Geln while he didn't know of her. Not only that, but worse, Klee was subordinate to Peo's AI.

"Geln, are you okay?"

"A little tired," he admitted, exhaustion hitting him hard. "I'm going back to bed where I can't talk to you because of my guard."

Under the watchful eyes of said guard, Geln crawled beneath the sheets and, before his uncle arrived, actually slept again. The knock on the door brought Geln full awake. He sat up while the officer opened the door and welcomed the stranger.

A middle-aged man with a long face stood on the threshold. He stared at Geln who gazed back thinking, *This is my cover's uncle?* Moustache, slight paunch, rather drab, nondescript. Kindly expression though.

The man broke eye contact and nodded in dismissal at the officer, who promptly left. The door shut and Geln and his "uncle" were alone.

As he stood, Geln tried to hide his nervousness. Not knowing what to expect, he was going to play follow the leader.

His uncle smiled, his face brightening significantly. "Hello, nephew." It hadn't occurred to Geln that Hernan Pyadrez would be pleased to see him. He'd assumed a newfound nephew would be a burden to shoulder.

"Hello, Uncle." They shook hands and clapped each other on the shoulder. Hernan was slightly shorter than Geln so at least height-wise he wouldn't seem strangely out of place in his new family.

Hernan lifted up his palms in bemused disbelief. "I can't believe I have a new relative."

Neither can I. Geln smiled back.

Hernan's smile dimmed. "And I can't believe they arrested you. How have they treated you?" Hernan searched Geln's face.

"Well," began Geln, not certain how or if he should describe the beating. Was it advantageous to let Hernan know they'd hurt and healed him?

Hernan looked away, as if he guessed what had happened. "How long have you been here?"

"Three days in total, I believe."

Hernan rubbed his moustache, disturbed. So his uncle wasn't stupid. "Did they rough you up badly?"

Geln shrugged. He didn't know how to rate beatings, and

what really mattered was getting out of here.

Quiet-faced, Hernan placed an index finger across his mouth and chin, thinking. He dropped his hand and spoke. "We're going to lodge a complaint. The Pyadrez family still has some political clout here."

Geln nodded cautiously.

As if to encourage him, Hernan chucked Geln on the shoulder. "I loved my sister very much. She was beautiful." He paused, again searching Geln's face. "You don't look at all like your mother."

Geln tried not to flinch. Klee hadn't taken appearances into his calculations. If the disjunction was too great, the cover could still fail.

"But you have your mother's lovely eyes," Hernan added kindly and for the first time Geln was grateful for his greens. "Green is a sign of the elite, you know."

"Ah yes." God knows Geln knew *that*, given he'd fought to keep his brown eyes before leaving on this assignment.

"And you will have so much more. I regret that you've been separated from us, Geln. Your mother felt... I understand that..." Here Hernan stopped, overwhelmed by the socially treacherous ground upon which he now trod.

Geln kept his features carefully bland. Social rules for bastards were no doubt complicated.

"Your mother loved you very much," Hernan concluded, reaching for something safe.

Geln sighed inwardly. He wouldn't enjoy deceiving this man. After an awkward silence, Geln asked, "Do you think we can leave soon?"

Hernan breathed in quickly, making a noise of regret. "They won't let you go until they've questioned you. I can't talk them out of it, despite their recent deplorable behavior."

Shit. Geln would have to take the stosh after all, when he was still reeling from the healing agents' overdose.

"The MRI machine will not hurt you," Hernan assured him.

The MRI machine would indicate that he lied. Geln fingered the pills that lay under the skin of his inner arm.

Hernan fidgeted with his ring, his knuckle. He looked up and blurted, "Did you do it, son?"

It took Geln a moment to realize Hernan was asking if he'd killed Serge Smator. Taken aback, Geln shook his head vigorously. "No. No I did not."

"I'm glad to hear it."

Shortly afterwards, they came for Geln. Before they took him, he retreated to the washroom. There he carefully parted the artificial soft flesh of his right arm and felt for the circular pill of stosh that lay against his real skin. Stosh was supposed to focus the mind, leaving little room for doubt, no matter how outrageous the lies. Sometimes the focus was so extreme, people forgot their past. Geln supposed he could take comfort in forgetting. He just hoped it wouldn't be permanent.

He placed the pill on his tongue and swallowed. If he didn't recover from this dose at least he had a newfound uncle to protect him.

Chapter Five

Three weeks ago, Tobias was questioned by the police. Since that time, little had changed in his routine, and yet he felt different, restless.

Because Tobias had a goal—to investigate his uncle's death and find his murderer. He intended to use his mother's increasingly close relationship with the Minister of State to his advantage. That in turn required he talk politics with his mother. As he did now, at breakfast. She was, as usual, giving him advice, not all of it bad.

"So what you need to do, Tobias, is explain to Ruel that increased trade will lead to increased wealth. That's a simple enough message for even the most simple-minded of cousins, and Ruel does like money."

"It's not easy to talk politics with Ruel. He's not interested."

"He will be soon. Once he marries."

Tobias thought of Ann-Marie. It was as if Ruel's lordship had reinvigorated a dying relationship. The two had become inseparable. "I'm not sure he *will* marry, Mother."

"Oh?" With a slight smile, she pushed an envelope across the table.

He picked it up, fished a card out of the gilded paper and stared at the marriage announcement in astonishment. "I find this hard to believe."

She was pleased by his reaction. "I think it's good news. It's time Ruel became responsible."

"Marriage makes one responsible?"

"It can." She eyed him speculatively and he resisted the urge to flinch. He didn't think he could stomach marriage himself.

"One can be responsible without marrying," he maintained.

"Not Ruel. He needs a woman to take charge."

"I guess." Tobias decided to shift the topic of conversation towards something of greater interest to him. "Any news on Serge's murder investigation?" For the moment, Tobias was working on the theory that the person behind Perrin's death had also killed Serge.

"Not since they ruled out Geln Marac." His mother shook her head and her distress seemed genuine. "That poor boy. You would have liked him, Tobias."

"Well, he's not dead, Mother."

She ignored his statement. "He was very charming."

Tobias sighed. Ever since he'd heard Geln had been apprehended by the police and come away from the station a vegetable, Tobias had felt guilty as hell, as if he was responsible for Geln's interrogation. He wasn't, he knew that, but he clearly remembered Geln's reaction to the news that the police thought him a worker, how Geln had straightened and stilled, trying to give nothing away and yet, to Tobias, telegraphing his fear in that suspended moment.

"Well, perhaps we'll meet Geln, or what's left of him, at the official engagement party." His mother didn't feel guilty, she never did, but she was angry about the green-eyed boy's fate.

"Will the Minister of State attend?" Tobias asked casually.

"Why?"

"I'd like you to introduce us."

"I will introduce you, of course, but not then. He's out of town for the week."

Tobias glanced down at the invitation again, still incredulous. The party was only two days from now. "My, Ruel and his bride are moving quickly. What's the rush?"

She placed her chin in her hand and let her gaze rest on him. "I believe, my dear, that Ruel has decided he wants heirs after all."

℘

Tobias held out his arm and Ann-Marie laid her small, elegant hand on him. She squeezed the muscle in approval and his heart sank. She was going to flirt with him. She might even like him.

He shouldn't try to placate an erratic Ruel by halfheartedly wooing his cousin's latest fling gone sour. For Ann-Marie was the worst kind, a young, sexually active widow who wanted to marry again, and this was the worst event, Ruel's engagement party.

Tobias didn't want to embark on another affair. Ruel's previous cast-off had run its course quickly. She'd been naive and inexperienced, Tobias had acted boring and circumspect, and the relationship, such as it was, fizzled within a couple of weeks. Ann-Marie might be more persistent, demanding. Unless she still had her sights set on Ruel.

She lifted her face towards Tobias, big green eyes cool with laughter, and spoke with calculated charm. "Are you looking forward to this chance to view the reclusive Ruel?"

Tobias couldn't help but smile. "Ruel? Reclusive?"

"Well, I haven't seen much of him these last few days, though perhaps reclusive is too strong a word." She widened her eyes, to include him in the joke.

Tobias shrugged noncommittally, embarrassed by his own dilemma, one which he'd created by obliging Ruel and asking her to the party. Rather desperately he looked around the ballroom as if the decorations interested him. The little floating jewel holograms made the air above them glitter like stardust. Less ethereally, the windows were painted in Smator and Pyadrez colors. The bright orange of the latter clashed with the smoky blue of his own family.

"I bore you," said Ann-Marie.

"Not at all," he protested. "I was just looking at the family colors."

"Fascinating," she murmured, "how so often none of the colors match. You'd think they'd take it as a sign that families shouldn't intermarry. Goodness knows, I should have."

Tobias didn't know what to make of her statement and her arch expression. She'd emerged fabulously wealthy after her short marriage to an old man. "Well then, who would one marry, if not a member of another family?"

"Workers, of course." She laughed gaily.

The joke irritated him. "Why is that funny?"

She pulled up short and tilted her head, surprised by his reaction. "It's not, of course. Excuse me." She disengaged her hand from his arm, and with some relief, Tobias watched her disappear into the crowd.

He glanced up at the stardust again, then around the room, trying to find someone he could chat with. He saw his mother and thought, *no*, until he realized she was talking to

Geln.

He hadn't thought Geln capable of attending a social event—rumors had made Geln out to be virtually incapacitated—and Tobias found himself inordinately pleased the man was here. An odd warmth spread through him, heating his face. He didn't move as he waited for his blush to fade. A strange woman was attached to Geln's arm, and Tobias surmised that she was a Pyadrez.

As if aware he was being watched, Geln looked away from the women and caught Tobias's gaze across the crowd. They locked eyes, and Geln's brow furrowed before he turned away. Tobias's curiosity exceeded his caution and he walked over to join the threesome.

On his way, Tobias tried to suppress the fantasy-Geln he'd created for himself over the past couple of weeks. He hadn't met Geln again but had nevertheless thought long and hard about the man, about his relationship with his mother, his ordeal with the police and, most intensely, Geln's actions after Tobias had been poisoned. Tobias had become convinced Geln had saved his life. Yet he suspected that conviction. It was so obviously cast in a romantic glare and Tobias didn't do well there.

"Tobias, darling." His mother called him over. "This is Evina Pyadrez and her cousin Geln."

Tobias bent and kissed Evina's hand. "Charmed," he murmured.

He turned to Geln and they shook hands. Geln's palm was dry, his shake steady, while Tobias felt ridiculously nervous.

"How are you?" Tobias asked, a little too loudly.

Geln looked puzzled, perhaps by Tobias's awkwardness, but he smiled politely. "I'm fine, thank you."

Tobias had the impression that Geln didn't recognize him. Before Evina could move away with Geln, Tobias put in, "A lovely engagement, no?" He clasped his hands behind his back and grinned, as if settling in for a long conversation.

"Quite." Evina's tone suggested the opposite.

"We're so glad to have our two families united," said his mother, all light tone and no meaning.

Evina smiled thinly. "Come, Geln—"

"Tobias," interrupted his mother. "You *must* ask Evina to dance."

"Ah." Tobias felt caught and tried to hide his reaction while Evina shifted away, her body language giving every indication that she had no desire to dance with him.

"I cannot leave my new cousin on his own," Evina explained.

"Don't worry, I'll take care of Geln." His mother linked her arm through Geln's protectively.

Evina protested further, his mother again insisted, and Geln stood bemused. Tobias moved away and beckoned to Geln, who disengaged from the women and approached him.

"Do you know who I am?" Tobias asked in a low voice and Geln stiffened, not quite a flinch, as if Tobias was threatening him. "Don't worry about it," added Tobias quickly, wanting to reassure.

Geln relaxed a fraction, still wary. "*Should* I know you?" His green eyes, too bright, pinned Tobias. There was a slight line across his brow.

"Well, maybe not," Tobias admitted, wondering what Geln made of his high color. "We had little to do with each other. But we met under...unusual circumstances."

"Oh?"

"I just..." Tobias stopped. This was not the time.

"What?" Geln asked, suddenly interested. There was an

openness about him, a lack of guile, that made him vulnerable, appealing. "You've made me curious, though I don't remember much." He offered Tobias a crooked smile.

"Why did you save my life?" Tobias couldn't help but ask.

The smile slipped and Geln looked at him with some alarm. "What the fuck are you talking about?"

Tobias should have kept his mouth shut. He'd known there was memory loss, but he'd hoped Geln had remembered something about that evening.

"Cousin," demanded Evina.

Geln lifted one finger, asking her to wait. "Maybe we could talk some time."

"Yes. I'll call at your house tomorrow." He bowed, Geln bowed, and they parted. Tobias put his slightly shaking hands in his pockets. *What* was he doing?

"Bitch," said his mother and Tobias dragged his mind away from Geln whose face was all sharp planes and dusky beauty. "Who does Evina think she is, treating Geln like a child? I don't know how he puts up with it."

Tobias lifted one shoulder in a shrug. "How is Evina related to the bride?"

"Cousins. I certainly hope Ruel's bride has a little more charm than *that*. I have yet to meet her. Do you see her?"

"No."

His mother craned her elegant neck, searching, and her gaze settled on Ruel who stood with a young girl on his arm. "Ah. Come, my dear, let's congratulate the charming, newly engaged couple."

Tobias wanted to think about his conversation with Geln, but congratulations were in order.

As was his wont, Ruel was drunk again but he functioned,

even if his bride-to-be kept darting looks of unease at her betrothed. Jina Pyadrez wasn't particularly pretty, but her smile was friendly and her expression sweet.

His mother coaxed an introduction out of Ruel, then chatted to the girl who seemed a little overcome by the intensity of his mother's curiosity.

"Well, Ruel." Tobias reached for a glass of wine from a passing waiter. "Congratulations."

"Ha."

With the crowd's noise, Tobias supposed Ruel's fiancée couldn't hear them, but his cousin's reaction made Tobias uncomfortable. He gulped more wine.

"Where's Ann-Marie?" asked Ruel.

"She left me. Not that we need discuss her now." Tobias lifted his wineglass. "Congratulations, again." He tried to move off.

"Don't be a twit, Tobias." Ruel reached out and grabbed his arm to prevent him from leaving. "Stop congratulating me as if you think I don't want this engagement. You're wrong."

"What?"

"You're wrong." Ruel raised his eyebrows significantly.

Tobias sighed. A drunk Ruel was emphatic and nonsensical. Tobias feared some kind of scene if Ruel's fiancée overheard their conversation.

"This engagement is *exactly* what Ann-Marie and I want."

"Good." The less he argued with Ruel, the sooner he could leave.

"I haven't given up Ann-Marie. Not at all."

Poor Jina.

"So don't worry, Ann-Marie isn't interested in you."

"I am relieved," Tobias said with some distaste. He looked down at Ruel's hand until he removed it from Tobias's arm. "Good night." Having shown his face, Tobias escaped the rest of the evening.

Chapter Six

"Geln," came that voice. "Please respond." Pause.

"Geln," it repeated. "Respond, please." Pause.

"Are you there? Geln?" Ah, thought Geln. *It* was changing its tone, which usually began as tentative, shifted to demanding or impatient, and ended in yelling. He swore the voice came out of his watch, a nondescript piece of jewelry made of dull metal and an old-fashioned face. Quite amazing that such a small object could hold a voice, and yet, he wasn't quite amazed.

He knew he used to know exactly what this was about. But until he did again—he was fairly optimistic that he would, he was getting less clueless by the day—he didn't respond to the disembodied voice. He couldn't disregard the feeling that the source of these words was a little dangerous and not to be trusted.

"Well, my boy," said an ever-solicitous Uncle Hernan. "How is that newspaper?"

Hernan. Kind, well-meaning Hernan meant, *How are you?* But his uncle didn't like to ask that question directly.

"Interesting," pronounced Geln as he laid aside the newspaper and resisted the urge to wipe the ink off his hands. He wasn't used to reading material that left ink on his skin. He didn't think. Nor did the post-dinner relax-in-the-den time seem familiar. Hernan liked to smoke a pipe and Geln tried not to betray how unpleasant and foreign he found the smell. "The Alliance doesn't seem to be popular, does it?" Geln offered, to show he understood something of what he'd read.

"No, it isn't," Hernan agreed eagerly. Last week Geln hadn't been able to make head or tails of the articles in the newspaper, so his uncle saw this comment as great progress.

"Rimanians, us, that is." Geln paused and gave a weak smile. He still wasn't sure about his own identity. It seemed fluid. "We prefer to be on our own, I gather?"

"It's more complicated than that, my boy. Much more complicated." Hernan shook his pipe at Geln. "You see, the Alliance cannot be trusted. They are powerful and secretive and only out for themselves. They seek to undermine the autonomy of our people."

The summary sounded a little simplistic to Geln. The article he'd just read suggested that the Alliance was putting pressure on Rimanians to enact some societal reform. For example, they didn't think people should die of hunger which seemed, as far as Geln could tell, a good idea. But he wasn't prepared to get into that type of conversation with his uncle.

"I see," said Geln.

Hernan nodded sagely before clamping the pipe in his mouth and returning to his book.

After thirty seconds of silence, the watch started talking again. Behind the newspaper, Geln rolled his eyes. The first time the watch had talked to him, a servant had been dusting the china. Geln had yelped and leapt to his feet while the servant attributed Geln's odd behavior to his police detention.

Since that first shock, he'd learned that only he could hear the watch. At first he'd wondered if he had a voice in his head telling him what to do. But after a time, he'd rejected that theory. There was memory, near to surfacing, that would explain more. He just wasn't ready yet.

"It's Kleemach, Geln," announced the now-weary and familiar voice. "The watch face is functional. It will sound-damp your voice, if that's your concern. I heard Hernan talking to you. Surely, surely, you're not this lost. It's been three weeks." Interesting how the watch never said more than that. Geln hadn't, obviously, asked it questions, but he had thought it might start telling him who he was and what he was doing. "*Geln.* I know you're there."

Geln sighed. A part of him wanted to remain lost, to not remember all the complications circling round his stay with the police and the murder of Serge Smator. Another part of him was desperate to know everything. Like why that young man Tobias seemed to think Geln had saved his life. It was flattering, in an alarming way. Was he the type of person who saved people's lives?

"Geln, you are there," it restated. It was nothing if not repetitive.

"I am," mouthed Geln behind his newspaper.

"I heard that!"

Geln straightened in alarm, crinkling his newspaper loudly.

"I heard that!" It, Kleemach, repeated. "You don't remember, perhaps, but I can pick up subvocalization. No need to, with the sound-damping, but I'll take anything at the moment. Thank the stars. Geln, why haven't you been talking to me?"

Geln snapped his teeth together and made himself think before he subvocalized again. He didn't trust Kleemach. Yet to resist for too long held its own danger. This thing was powerful, that much Geln knew.

"I'm not sure," offered Geln. A safe response.

"Do you know who I am?"

"No."

"Not at all?"

"No. But I think I will soon."

"Good, good." It sounded relieved. "It's just taking longer than expected. What I want—"

"Mr. Marac, sir?" Disoriented, Geln took a moment to realize a servant stood at the threshold of the room, addressing him. He slowly lowered the newspaper.

"Yes." To mask his discomfort, he smiled pleasantly. Servants made him uneasy, but no one seemed to find his unease strange. All his reactions were explained by whatever had happened at the police station. Geln shivered. He really did not want to remember *that*.

"Someone has called for you, sir."

"Good, good," said Hernan, ever the optimist. Geln, however, was confident that not all visitors were good. "Bring him in."

"Sir. The visitor is a woman. She insists that she should see Mr. Marac...alone."

"*Alone?*" echoed Hernan. "Who is she with?"

"No one, sir."

Hernan appeared to be astounded by this fact, and Geln could only assume there had been some break in protocol. Geln rather wished it weren't a woman but instead the amiable, if insubstantial, Tobias who regarded Geln as his savior. What an attractive image—Geln, the guy who saves lives, especially the lives of young bashful brown-eyed men.

Hernan stood and straightened his short jacket. "I am going to see this woman myself and find out why she is calling. I don't want some disreputable person from your past forcing themselves upon you."

"Well," said Geln, not sure how to respond. His curiosity piqued, he actually wanted to see this mysterious woman. "Why don't I come with you?"

Hernan became very stern. "You're in over your head, boy."

Geln was in over his head for reasons Hernan didn't understand. He was dead certain he'd been playing a very dangerous game and that it would be a while before he recognized all the players again. Best to try to stay informed.

"You'll be with me," Geln told Hernan who frowned, but did not argue further when Geln followed him out of the room.

"Shit, don't go," *it* announced, startling Geln who came to a stop. He lagged behind Hernan, not sure what to do about his lively watch.

"What's wrong?" Geln subvocalized.

"Refuse to see this woman. Let your uncle dismiss her."

"Dismiss?"

"Yes," it hissed.

"Uncle?" called Geln. Hernan turned, surprised Geln stood so far behind him. "Perhaps you're right and you should see this woman without me."

Hernan nodded. "I'll look after it, son."

Geln retreated from the hall, then raced to his room to take off his watch. He'd had enough of Kleemach startling him with unexpected speeches. Besides, it eavesdropped on everything he did and said, which struck him as quite invasive though presumably at some point in the past he'd been used to it. He ran back down to Jina—such a young thing to be engaged to that jerk, Ruel—and begged a favor of her.

Because Evina was poor company, Jina had been reading alone. Geln supposed that her loneliness helped explain why she was thrilled about her upcoming marriage to a drunkard. She liked any kind of attention. So once Geln explained about the mystery woman's visit, Jina was excited by an unusual event and Geln's interest. She wanted to see the lady who had dared call without an escort.

"It is something a paid woman might do," she stated rather breathlessly. Her cheeks pinked at the statement and she darted a glance at Geln, as if expecting him to scold her.

"Indeed." He hurried her out of the reading room and upstairs where they could get a decent view of the visitor. Jina directed him to her sitting room and pulled aside the drapes so they could both look out.

The strange woman was still there, but not for long. Presumably Hernan had refused her entry, for she exited the house now, gathering up her skirts as she returned to the carriage. Geln badly wanted to see who she was but he couldn't make out her face from the distance. A bright scarf covered her hair. He squinted, trying to see identifying features. As he concentrated, her image abruptly zoomed in, enlarged and clear. Geln froze, unable to breathe in his panic. He closed his eyes briefly. The rapid changes in view hurt his head. *Don't move,* he warned himself. Shit. Was he an android or something?

He forced himself to focus on her features since he could see them. Big green eyes, lots of makeup, high cheekbones, a long straight nose—something of an exotic beauty for Rimania. Then she was gone, ducking into her carriage.

"Do you know her?" asked Jina.

Disoriented, Geln turned to his cousin and his eyesight blurred while it adjusted to normal vision. He became light-headed and had to lean on the windowsill to steady himself.

"Are you all right?" She reached out an arm to comfort him.

She was a sweet girl, and he did not recognize that mysterious woman.

"Headache?" Jina asked sympathetically. "Let me call for an analgesic."

"No," said Geln more loudly than he meant. But he'd had too many Rimanian drugs, that much was obvious, and he didn't even want to think about the drug cache he carried on his arm, under artificial skin.

"I'd better get out of here, no?" His smile was wan, he knew.

"Geln." She spoke as if he were a child. "You seem to think you're in my bedroom. This is my sitting room. No one will mind."

"Oh. Yes. I get confused by some of the customs still."

"It will come back, or you'll relearn what you need to know."

"No doubt. But I believe I need to rest now."

"Of course."

He retreated to his room and lay down, arm flung over his eyes, eyes that had focused at an unimaginable distance. The farsight frightened him. *Fuck.* What was he? He often thought in a language he didn't speak, not that he'd admit that to anyone. He thought of the watch that lay on the side table. This Kleemach could tell him what was going on. If he put the watch on his wrist. But Geln couldn't face that conversation quite yet, and it remained blessedly silent when not attached to him.

It was time to remember, he thought fatalistically. He breathed deeply and willed himself to sleep.

For two days, Geln lay in bed with a crashing headache. He'd never experienced anything like it. The pain moved from forehead to temples to everywhere else in his skull. He couldn't escape the pain and he didn't try. A number of people—Hernan, Jina, even Evina—wanted to force-feed him analgesics and couldn't understand Geln's stubborn refusal. The most he allowed was a wet washcloth. He explained to Jina that he'd had one chemical cocktail too many while visiting the police.

"This is different," she argued. "This will help you."

Not with stosh's leftovers, it won't. But how could he explain an amnesia drug to sweet, innocent Jina. She'd be devastated to know she'd befriended a spy, a cadre spy, an *Alliance* spy. For the Alliance was, no doubt about it, Rimania's bogeyman, and with some reason too.

Besides, life and all its complications had come crashing back in and he needed to deal with this sudden onrush of memory. At least he wasn't an android.

At night, he talked to Klee, not about everything, but enough to let it know he was back in spirit, if not quite yet in body. He didn't want the AI thinking he was broken. Klee had helped Geln avoid meeting Peo when she'd called on him despite Hernan's grave disapproval. Had Klee been protecting Geln? Or Peo? In any case, Peo's AI would have made the final decision, not its subordinate, Klee.

Geln knuckled his burning eyes, not ready to tackle the thorny question of the double AI in the sky watching his every move. Was it, or they, aiding him or dooming him? He'd no idea.

He certainly wasn't prepared to ask about Klee's AI status. Or make contact with the cadre again, although it was past time. Arjes, his cadre boss, was probably furious that Geln had vanished without a word, and Geln didn't see how he was going to explain the stosh and amnesia. It made little sense unless you brought in the whole Alliance angle, which he was forbidden to do. Since no one on Rimania, and certainly not

Arjes, was supposed to know he was here, besides Peo.

Hopefully Arjes didn't want to kill him.

Perhaps Geln would soon have a chance to explain something to the outlaws. His contact lived in the Smator house and Geln had been invited to a small afternoon gathering there in just a few days. Jina wanted him to attend.

With a shudder, he turned his face into his pillow. He didn't want to face Arjes again, cadre chief and erstwhile lover.

ॐ

While Tobias kept an eye on him, Geln kept an eye on the maid. He was pretty sure, at this point, that Tobias was infatuated, which bolstered his ego, but his practical side was dismayed. Tobias was not his type and, more to the point, right here, right now, Geln needed to make contact with the thin older woman who worked hard to serve the men and women around him. She was worn out. Since Ruel didn't treat his servants well, there was a high turnover, and it was easy to plant a cadre spy in his household.

But first Geln had to deal with Tobias and dampen the kid's interest. He'd probably have to be cruel. Fun, fun, fun. He flung back the last of his wine, not that the wine fortified him one bit given that he was loaded with alcohol dehydrogenase. The enzyme zapped those little molecules of alcohol before they ever reached his brain.

Tobias turned to him, a play of emotions on his face: pride, anxiety and eagerness. Quite obviously Tobias had a crush he didn't know what to do with. Alliance information suggested gay men didn't exist among the elite. Geln wasn't surprised to find that was bullshit. Still, as Tobias tried unsuccessfully to suppress all that he revealed on his face, Geln's stomach turned. He knew what it was to be lonely, if not in quite this way.

He shifted his gaze to Tobias's date. The breath went out of Geln; blood seemed to literally drain from his brain. In light-headed shock, he recognized the woman on Tobias's arm—*Peo.* It took all of his training to continue on autopilot.

"Good day, my lady." To cover his discomposure, he bowed deeply. When he rose, she was smiling, a curled lip that did not suggest she had a high opinion of him. He stared into eyes as greenly synthetic as his own.

"Excuse me, let me make the introductions," Tobias said into the maelstrom of Geln's thoughts. The boy was flushing at his social gaffe. Apparently he should have introduced Geln and Peo immediately. "Mrs. Soughten. Geln Marac."

"If it isn't the famous Geln Marac." Her smile widened, but the joke was on Geln.

Ann-Marie Soughten. Geln had heard of her. She'd married and murdered her ancient husband, or so some whispered. *Shit.* He did not want this black widow to know that *he* knew she was his primary operative. The more ignorant she thought him, the safer he was. What the fuck was she doing with Tobias?

Geln managed, after an overlong silence, to return a lopsided smile. "I didn't know I was famous."

"That means people have gossiped about you, my dear," she informed him with false sympathy. "For you're a different person, now that you've been deemed a Pyadrez." Her eyebrows rose. She knew *exactly* how that had happened.

Geln kept his expression blank. She cocked her head.

"It's not a joke," Tobias broke in harshly in Geln's defense, "what Geln's been through."

"You're such a sweet boy." Amused, Ann-Marie lifted a gloved hand towards his face and Tobias jerked back before she could touch him.

Good, thought Geln. *Stay away from her, Tobias. She's poison.* Geln allowed Ann-Marie to steer him away from Tobias so the boy was left on his own, his posture a little beaten, his gorgeous wide-set eyes following Geln.

"It entertains me," she said in her light, clear voice, "how badly each date with Tobias Smator can go." Charming. "He understands very little but we, on the other hand, understand each other perfectly."

"Then you'll understand," returned Geln, giving up on the idea that Peo might think he didn't know who she was, "that I must leave you now." The maid had retreated from the room and Geln intended to follow her.

"Of course. I will distract Tobias."

"He's not worth your time." Geln allowed his voice to become conspiratorial. "I think he's a little slow."

Her amusement deepened. "But that's what I like about him."

Geln didn't say more. Any further show of concern for Tobias would just raise Ann-Marie's interest. He hoped Tobias had the sense to avoid her in the future.

Geln exited the room and, as soon as he entered the kitchen, the maid disappeared through another door. They played this game through three more rooms until Geln arrived at the basement stairs. The maid silently pointed down, then left. Geln pulled in a breath before he walked into the dank basement.

It took a moment for his eyes to adjust. Someone moved out of the darkness and Geln was standing face to face with Arjes.

Nausea struck, though Geln set himself against that reaction. It had been too long for the cadre leader but not nearly long enough for Geln since their last meeting.

"Where the fuck have you been?" Arjes was a large, muscular man, attractive in his powerful way. And exceedingly single-minded. He was the force behind the local cadre, and he had no sense of humor.

Geln was shocked to see him and it showed. "I've had a few problems," he admitted, looking Arjes in the eye to hide the fact that Arjes intimidated him.

"Yes. We heard. We moved out of our last base and hid in the woods for ten days, Geln. Because we were damn sure you wouldn't be able to withstand the rigors of police interrogation."

Wow, the cadre information system was better than Geln had thought. Given how ineffective the cadre had so far been in its goal to overthrow the elite and declare equality for all, Geln was surprised.

Arjes's expression became even grimmer. "But no one came looking for us, Geln."

Arjes's large hand took hold of Geln's jaw and Arjes moved his face closer. "I've come all the way here because I want an explanation. I hope you're not trying to fuck us, Geln, because if you are, I'm going to fuck you. Again."

Geln shook his head as Arjes's hand moved down to his throat. *It's a game,* he reminded himself desperately. *Arjes likes to show strength. It calms him down. Don't fight.*

Arjes's hand clasped his neck and Geln felt like a trapped animal. "They're saying you're elite."

"I'll explain," managed Geln through his tight throat. "But not now. I only slipped away for a few minutes and they're expecting me to return."

"Nonsense." Arjes pushed Geln backwards and he stumbled. Just before he was about to fall, Arjes placed two meaty hands on Geln's jacket and lifted him up to slam him against a wall. "You're coming with me."

"You look unhappy, Tobias." Ann-Marie was like a disease that wouldn't leave. He should never have asked her out that first time, as she now believed she had some claim on him. "But don't worry, I'm sure Geln will come back to you."

Tobias's face grew hot and he felt fear. Ruel knowing about his youthful crush on the stable boy was one thing. But this woman couldn't be trusted.

"When did you and Geln become such good friends?" she asked.

"Geln is not my friend." Tobias had to get his voice under control; it wobbled with anger. "He has a special relationship with my mother. One I *dislike*." The last word came out too harsh.

"Why aren't they chatting then, your mother and Geln?"

"I wouldn't know. Ask them. Where is Ruel?" he demanded, desperate to change the subject.

She gave her knowing smile and Tobias had to wonder at how he'd thought she'd liked him that one date. Because he was stupid, socially stupid.

His face burned while he fought his rising panic. Ann-Marie unnerved him, watching him like that. But it didn't mean anything. No one could read his thoughts, except the MRI, and even then all it knew was that he was lying.

"Excuse me." He gave the sketchiest of bows and walked away, threading his way through the crowd before he dispatched a servant to fetch his overcoat.

"Tobias?" his mother called.

God, not now.

"Tobias," she insisted, approaching him.

"I'm leaving," he said through gritted teeth.

That gave her only momentary pause. "Geln has disappeared."

"Huh?" Why was she talking about Geln?

She looked uncomfortable, as if she didn't know what to do. "I'm supposed to keep an eye on him, but I can't chase him around. It would look too strange."

"Tell Hernan Pyadrez you're worried," Tobias suggested.

"I'm telling you. You know this place. You spent enough time here as a boy. So odd to think Perrin's place now belongs to Ruel..." Her voice trailed off and she shook her head. "Just go see that Geln's all right."

"Why are you watching him?"

She shrugged. "We have a vested interest. We don't want him to disappear."

"We?"

She lowered her voice. "Lord Eberly and myself. If you help us out here, I'll make sure you can talk to Eberly regarding your concerns about Perrin's death."

"Okay," he said rather gracelessly. He was probably going to embarrass himself again and yet, he also felt concerned, wanted to check on Geln.

Tobias made his way through the manor and exited the side door that led to the back. If nothing else, he'd get some fresh air. He circled round the patio, as he didn't really want to revisit the spot where he'd found a dead Serge.

Why was Eberly interested in Geln? Tobias didn't get it. He

would ask Geln if he found him—or warn him, depending on the circumstances. Though there was a good chance Geln wouldn't even remember Eberly or understand what was going on. The only link between the two men Tobias knew of was his mother and that certainly didn't explain Eberly's interest.

Still pondering this, it wasn't until Tobias reached the end of the lawn that he stopped daydreaming and realized he heard voices. And horses, which struck him as out of the ordinary. They weren't near the stables.

He pushed his way through the opening in the hedge and went very, very still. There was Geln. But there were also three bandits in broad daylight. Chatting.

Tobias was astounded that they had ventured into Lord Smator's estate. They shouldn't have been able to access it, unless the alarm and barbed wire weren't activated. Tobias broke out into a sweat.

He stepped backwards, but just before he might have disappeared from their view, a bandit saw him.

"What the hell—"

Tobias turned away and heard the sound of a pistol being cocked.

"Want a hole in your back?" someone called.

He didn't move.

"Turn around."

He obeyed. Sweat trickled down his spine. He should have run, but he wasn't thinking quickly here. He sought Geln's gaze but the man with the gun spoke, so Tobias looked his way.

"Pull out your weapon very slowly."

Tobias wiped his damp hands on his pants. "I don't have a weapon."

"Asshole, don't lie to me." The man strode towards him and

pistol approached Tobias until metal touched his temple. "Would you like your brain to go splat?" The man guffawed as Tobias's heart leapt forward in fear. He thought he might faint.

"Calm down, Joris." This order from a large, powerful, dark-eyed man. Then, to Tobias, "Can I help you, sir?" The "sir" was said with a sneer.

This second stranger approached him and Tobias couldn't think of an answer. Meaty hands patted him everywhere, searching for a weapon. His doublet was ripped open during the search.

"What the fuck are you doing here?" Geln's voice now and Tobias felt disoriented as Geln met his gaze and Tobias saw a bloodied face, as well as soiled clothing, as if Geln had been knocked down more than once. His hands were bound behind him. The poor man just didn't get a break. Tobias's mother had thought Geln might disappear, and indeed he'd been captured. Had she somehow known Geln might be abducted? It didn't seem possible.

"Friend of yours?" the man in charge asked Geln.

"Acquaintance, barely," said Geln in a bored tone.

"Lie down," the man commanded Tobias.

"What are you doing with Geln?" He tried to twitch the man's hand off his shoulder, but the hand pressed down on him.

"Lie down," the man repeated.

"I have money," began Tobias and Geln shook his head once. Tobias didn't think anyone but him saw the motion.

"I don't have time for this." The man nodded at Joris who stood behind Tobias. Something very hard hit the back of his head and Tobias couldn't see, couldn't even remember falling.

He must have though, because he woke slowly, head

throbbing in pain, face wet and pushed into the ground. By the time he sat up, Tobias realized time had passed and he was alone. In the silence, he looked around. The clearing was empty. Geln was gone.

Chapter Seven

Geln rinsed out his bloody handkerchief. He watched the red dilute to pink and move downstream, its color completely lost in the water. The river didn't notice anything so insignificant and never would. He wrung the cloth and laid it against his face. His lip was split and it hurt.

"I didn't need a bruised eye, a split lip and a bloody nose," he told Arjes, his voice thickened by the facial damage. "One of the three would have suggested injury, don't you think?"

"No."

"You're the expert."

"From what you told me, you went through worse with the police."

"Yes, I've been through worse," snapped Geln. "That doesn't mean I like abuse."

Arjes snorted. "I roughed you up a little. You're in trouble if you think that's 'abuse'. Are the elites rubbing off on you? Do they talk like this?"

No, therapists on Earth talk like this. Geln removed the cloth from his face and noted that the bleeding was slowing. Again he rinsed it in the imperturbable river. "I don't like having a mashed face."

"It's not mashed, lordling. In fact, your lower lip looks nice and full."

Geln ignored that. Arjes might be pleased with the recent series of events, but Geln wasn't. "You didn't have to knock the boy out. Tobias is very obedient. He would have lain down."

"Boy? Tobias?" Arjes raised his eyebrows. "I see you're on a first-name basis. Looked like a man to me and a strongly built one at that. Why are you so concerned about him?"

Geln sighed. He really didn't want all that suspicion rushing back into Arjes's blunt mind. But Geln was disgruntled. "You know, Arjes, you can't suborn one single servant in Tobias's household. Why do you think that is?"

"The man is still elite."

"Yes, he's still elite. Don't be stupid."

"What the fuck are you talking about?"

"I'm telling you that the reason you can't reach any of his servants is because the guy treats them well."

Arjes snorted. "You've been brainwashed by all those drugs."

Geln wished. Life would be easier. "Look, it's simply that Tobias was nice to me when I had amnesia. And he's just a kid. Twenty or something."

Now Arjes looked pissed off. "There are plenty of twenty-or-somethings in our cadre who are not boys and never have been."

Geln could have kicked himself. He was acting too Alliance.

"You've gone soft during your sojourn with the elite. Sure they haven't seduced you?"

Geln held up a hand. "All I'm saying is that it's okay to recognize a human once in while."

"I do, Geln. I recognize you, for example."

"That's because I'm useful." Useful to the Alliance, to Arjes, but not really to Tobias who got hit on the head when he went looking for him.

Arjes pushed himself out of his crouch with slow grace and gazed down on Geln. "Your pretty face is fine. Come have something to eat before the food is all gone."

"In a moment." He needed to think. He needed to talk to Klee. As Arjes walked away, Geln muttered, "You have got to get me out of here." Klee wouldn't know he meant off the planet.

"We'll talk later, Geln," Klee said warningly. Geln was in view of the cadre. A few meters away, a group of them gathered round the fire. Some cooked, some drank, most talked. "You're doing great," it added, obviously deciding Geln needed reassurance. "I couldn't be more proud."

"Fuck off."

Silence. Of course. Ah well, Geln couldn't stay by this river too long. Arjes would find that behavior suspicious and Geln was working hard to lower, not raise, suspicions. Which meant he had to trade in sex tonight. Not an activity that appealed to him right now, but Arjes would expect it. Geln blew out a shaky breath.

He was pissed that Arjes had beaten him up, even if he'd pulled his punches. Arjes had wanted to show the elite they could sneak in and kidnap one of them. Geln was to escape the cadre tomorrow and display his bruised face to his elite family. But Tobias, of all people, had already seen it.

What had the boy been doing out there?

Geln straightened his sore, tired legs and returned to the crowd, soggy handkerchief in hand. It was going to hurt to eat.

As he entered the fray, all eyes turned towards him. He recognized most of them, but few had paid him much attention during his previous stay. He'd been considered Arjes's novelty.

81

More hungry than he realized, Geln tried to remain unfazed by the stares, especially that of Joris's. The man was stupid and violent, if loyal to Arjes. Geln made it a point to meet the man's gaze. "I should stay here a while, don't you think?"

Joris simply looked puzzled while Arjes gave him a sideways glance of disapproval. "You have to go back."

Geln bit into the meat. "I know."

"Must be hard, living in the lap of luxury," sneered Joris.

"It can be, actually. It's a bloody game, there."

"And you play the game so well," said Arjes. "So far you've become a Pyadrez and toyed with Dressia Smator's affections. What about Tobias Smator?"

I think he's got a crush on me. "He doesn't approve of my friendship with his mother."

"And what was he doing in the field? Spying on you?"

Geln shook his head. "I don't know. Maybe Dressia sent him."

Arjes grunted and lost interest in Tobias. "What I really don't understand is why the Pyadrez family thinks you're their long-lost bastard."

"I told you. Someone encrypted the information in data and it came out during the interrogation. Everyone was shocked. Including me," Geln added wryly.

Arjes scratched his jaw. "It's *very* strange."

Yeah. Geln wanted to derail Arjes's train of thought. He batted his lashes at him. "I told you I was someone's bastard."

Arjes responded with a hint of a smile. "I didn't believe you."

Geln shrugged.

"Well, we'll just have to figure out how to use this

connection to our best advantage." Arjes gave him a long stare. "Unless you decide to cross over to the other side. You can, now."

"I don't want to," said Geln evenly.

Arjes jerked his head at Joris who got up and left them alone. The men were preparing for bed now, all around them, but Geln didn't want to think about where he was sleeping tonight.

"This Tobias has loyal servants, you think," Arjes said as if it was new information to consider carefully.

Geln didn't know where Arjes was going with this. "So do you. I'm your servant. You said as much."

Arjes snapped a chicken bone in half and threw it into the bushes. "Don't fuck with me, Geln. I don't have the patience. I have no desire to like these people, so keep your tender feelings to yourself. I need you to gather more information about Lord Eberly's movements."

"I've given what I can," Geln insisted. Arjes wanted to assassinate Dressia's lover, the Minister of State. A personal vendetta as well as a way to put the fear of God in the elite. Geln hadn't thought assassination was in his job description though Peo's recent behavior suggested otherwise.

"What we really need, Arjes, is political representation."

"Brilliant, Geln, fucking brilliant. And how the hell do we get that? *Not* by asking nicely."

"I'm just saying that after Eberly is dead, someone will rise up and take his place."

"Not necessarily." Arjes's smile was smug. "Look at Perrin Smator's replacement, the nonentity Ruel Smator. The anti-Alliance faction is in disarray."

"You didn't kill Perrin." The idea filled Geln with

apprehension. "Did you?"

Arjes guffawed. "Don't look so alarmed. And, no, I didn't. That was simply convenient." His eyelids went to half-mast. "Leave the thinking to me. Your pretty head has other uses."

Geln returned his gaze, unsmiling. The sun was gone and Arjes was lit by fire. The flames did a strange dance of color on his lined face.

Arjes's smile faded too. "Do remember, Geln, that we won't forget you, even if you forget us."

"I have no intention of forgetting you." They'd try to kill him if he betrayed them. He knew that, but the reminder left a bad taste in his mouth.

Arjes threw the rest of his chicken bones into the dying fire. "Tomorrow morning, you have to escape us."

"Right."

Arjes stood. "Okay, bed."

Geln stared up at him through the darkness. He should just acquiesce but he found it difficult. "I'll sleep on my own tonight, thanks."

"Nah. There's no extra bedding, lordling."

Geln turned away to look at the fire. Coals shimmered and the flames were small. The other men had disappeared to their beds. He needed to bend his will here, but it was hard to find the strength. He clenched his fists.

Arjes's deep voice became husky and deceptively gentle. "I don't mind if you fight me, Geln."

Geln's heart hammered in anger. In truth, Arjes liked a struggle in bed. "You already fucked up my face."

Arjes crouched down and slowly uncurled one of Geln's hands. "That's what's so interesting about you, Geln. Your reactions are completely unpredictable." He traced a large hand up Geln's arm. "I know how to be careful."

Sometimes. And, somehow, Arjes knew that Geln missed touch. That palm stroked down again, not completely unpleasant. To want, to not want, to want something else. Geln allowed himself to be pulled up and led to the tent. When they got there, despite his talk about care, Arjes was hard and impatient, a little punishing. He stripped Geln with quick efficiency. It was a silent wrestling match Geln was not allowed to win. Arjes opened him up and Geln took him, resting on elbows to protect his face.

Arjes fell asleep immediately while Geln lay awake for a long time. He eventually dozed and just before sunrise Arjes took him again before he sent him on his way.

Chapter Eight

Tobias's head ached. A gift from yesterday, when the butt of a pistol had knocked him out. He wondered if that little rencontre in the meadow had persuaded Lord Eberly to summon him. For weeks Tobias had asked to meet Eberly, and he should have been pleased that it was finally happening, but the pain made it difficult to think clearly. The weather was damp and cold to boot.

Despite his misery, he wanted to know why his mother and Eberly were interested in Geln. She wouldn't tell him, but Eberly might be more forthcoming. The man's estate lay on the other side of the city, outside the perimeter, so it was a bit of a trek. Tobias had worn his wools against the weather, but in the confines of the carriage he was now sweating. He opened the window and wet wind washed across his face. He laid his head back, let the fresh air drift past him and tried not to wince at memories of Geln's poor bloodied face. Apparently the Pyadrezes were doing everything in their power to recover their newest member, who had been abducted by bandits.

He jolted awake when Sandorl opened the door. A grim, sodden Sandorl. "We have arrived, sir."

Tobias rubbed his eyes. "I'm all wet from the open window."

"Indeed." Sandorl was drenched. "I'd suggest, sir, that you enter indoors then."

They trudged up the long outside staircase and Eberly's butler greeted them. In no time, Tobias was whisked into the foyer and Eberly was bearing down on him with great enthusiasm.

"Tobias! Thank you for coming. Especially in this miserable weather, and on such short notice."

"Thank you for the invitation."

"My pleasure." He smiled with a satisfaction that made Tobias uneasy. "It's been quite a while, hasn't it, Tobias? How have you been?"

"Fine."

Eberly turned to his butler. "Would you please ask our other guest to join us?"

"Yes, sir."

Eberly noticed Tobias's frown. "There is someone I'd like you to meet, son."

At "son", Tobias gritted his teeth. "I had hoped to have an opportunity to talk with you privately, sir. There are a couple of things I very much want to discuss."

"We have time for that too." Eberly turned and led Tobias to the drawing room. In a lower voice, he asked, "Did your mother have a message for me?"

"Uh, no."

Eberly stopped and looked up, searching Tobias's face. His mother usually preferred tall men, but perhaps Eberly had other qualities, like power. And he was not unhandsome.

"I wish to investigate the death of my uncle, Perrin Smator," said Tobias quickly.

A look of irritation passed over Eberly's face. "So I understood from your mother. All in good time. But first, I need you to do something for me. Let me introduce you to someone."

Geln stared at the door, wishing he could ignore the knock. It appeared that Lord Eberly didn't like to leave him alone for more than half an hour at a time. Of course, he'd been alone all morning, riding back to the city in the drizzle, but somehow that didn't make Eberly's company this afternoon any more palatable.

"Come in," he said with a sigh. He was visiting the Minister of State and Arjes would no doubt be very pleased. Problem was, Geln didn't know why Eberly had taken him as a "guest" who hadn't been able to refuse his invitation. Geln had hoped to return to Hernan and Jina.

"Mr. Marac." The butler stood in the doorway. "Follow me, please."

That's what the posse had said this morning when they found him on the outskirts of the city. He'd planned to go to the Pyadrezes, but a group of armed men, Eberly's men, had other ideas. So he'd been escorted here.

The butler led him to the drawing room and two men rose to greet him. Geln tried to cover his shock at the presence of Tobias. My, they seemed to run into each other quite often these days. The coincidences were becoming a little alarming to Geln's mind.

At least Tobias wasn't lying prone on the ground. And Geln no longer had a bloody face, just leftover bruises, a judicious smattering of yellow and blue. He would have looked worse but he'd allowed himself to take an Alliance healing agent from his own personal cache beneath his skin.

Tobias appeared baffled by Geln's entrance, so obviously this meeting had been arranged by Eberly. Tobias's hair was mussed, his collar askew, and his suit was damp. He looked adorable.

They shook hands and Geln liked his palm against Tobias's large and warm one. He also enjoyed the faint smell of Tobias himself, musk and rain and youth rolled into one. Good thing for Tobias that Geln wasn't going to get a chance to act on this attraction, for too many reasons to even think about.

"You two have met before," said Eberly.

"Yes." Tobias blinked.

"Please, both of you, have a seat."

Geln obeyed but, chin raised, face set, Tobias refused. He was angry.

"As you know," Eberly told Tobias, "Ruel has agreed to come onside my bill."

Tobias frowned while Geln scrambled to remember Eberly's bill. Amnesia and beatings didn't help, but he managed to recall that Eberly wanted a trade agreement with the Alliance. Ruel's father would never have agreed to support this bill. According to Klee, Perrin Smator had detested Eberly, the person and his policies.

Eberly trained his polished smile on Geln. "I'm hoping the Pyadrezes follow suit."

"Ah, you can certainly hope," said Geln. "Unfortunately my uncle has quite definite and quite negative ideas about the Alliance. I wouldn't describe him as pro-trade. Nor do I have much influence in the matter. He believes I am only beginning to grasp the complexities of our politics. And he's probably right." Geln offered a self-deprecating smile.

"I think you underestimate your influence, sir," argued Eberly. "But I do not." Geln cocked his head, unsure of Eberly's meaning. "Now if you will both excuse me for a few moments." To Geln's surprise, Eberly withdrew.

Tobias and Geln stared after Eberly, before turning to each

other. Presumably Tobias had a clearer idea about what was going on, because today's events left Geln at a loss.

"Nice day, isn't it?" said Geln in a tone of voice that indicated it really wasn't.

"Not for you." Tobias's intense brown gaze made Geln uncomfortable. They reminded him of his own lost eyes, even if they were set in a completely different face.

Geln cleared his throat. "Why are we even talking to each other here?"

"So I can explain that you are a prisoner here until your uncle Hernan agrees to vote for Eberly's bill."

"*What?*"

Tobias added quickly, "Look, it's not that bad. They're not going to hurt you or anything. In fact you're better off than you were yesterday with bandits. I was seriously worried. Did Eberly rescue you?"

"I escaped." Abruptly Geln pushed out of his chair and turned on Tobias. "Then Eberly *captured* me. This has been a fun couple of days, I can tell you." Tobias eyed him. Geln realized his hands were shaking and clasped them behind his back, hating to be at this disadvantage. "So, what if Hernan refuses to give into this blackmail?"

"Eberly will look for another way to exert pressure."

"Why are you explaining this to me?"

"So Eberly can deny everything later."

"And you, you can deny it?"

"I suppose I could, yes." Tobias looked down. "But he also promised me a thorough investigation into my uncle's death if I helped you understand the situation, and I remained discreet."

Geln blinked, disappointed in Tobias. The boy might be infatuated, his constant high color when he was around Geln attested to it, but Tobias was also willing to sacrifice his crush for his uncle's memory.

After he sat on an armchair, Tobias clenched his fists. He darted a glance at Geln, looked down then back up and held Geln's gaze, a slightly imploring aspect in his expression. "Thing is, I think you know more than you're letting on."

Uh, yeah, but nothing I can tell you, bud.

"I think you're mixed up in something big and it's all related to your police visit, and my mother and Eberly's interest in you. Even Ann-Marie Soughten talks about you." Evidently Tobias found these pieces of the puzzle strange. Well, they wouldn't fit together until he knew Geln was Alliance. Tobias continued, "Eberly believes I'm too stupid to notice all these coincidences around you." Tobias pinned Geln with those brown eyes, asking for answers.

Geln walked up to Tobias, close enough that the boy tilted his head back. Placing hands on Tobias's chair, caging the boy, Geln watched Tobias's face heat up—discomfort, anger, other emotions—but Tobias held his gaze.

"You're right," Geln whispered. "In a way. So be careful yourself."

"Watch what you're saying," Klee warned and Geln jumped a little and backed away.

Tobias's expression changed from one of wariness to concern. He stood and tentatively placed a hand on Geln's shoulder. "I'm going to help you." It was a promise, overly fervent, and made Geln's heart sink. He could barely protect himself, let alone Tobias.

"I don't need your help," Geln replied immediately. Okay, he'd just been disappointed that Tobias had made a deal with Eberly, but it would be much worse if Tobias decided to play some kind of white-knight role, to Geln's black pawn. The boy could get badly hurt.

"You're out of your depth, aren't you?" Tobias asked.

With a rough sigh, Geln stepped out of Tobias's reach. He pulled the bell, the butler arrived, and he left Tobias standing in the drawing room.

"Tobias is quite right, Lord Eberly is not going to hurt you," Klee said soothingly. "You can study politics during this confinement."

"Confinement? I am not pregnant, you fucker." Geln was furious because, among other things, the AI was not acting in good faith, had put its interests before Geln's. Klee was probably deliriously happy that Geln was in close contact with Eberly, could observe the target, never mind that the circumstances put Geln at risk. Never mind that it pulled Tobias into this sick game.

"Don't be silly. I wasn't suggesting you were pregnant."

"I am locked in these rooms. Eberly is my jailer."

"True," Klee conceded, as if it was a technical point. "But the rooms are spacious and well furnished. You can have visitors."

"Fuck you."

The AI paused. "Your voice is shaky, Geln, and your personal antipathy towards me is not healthy."

Despite what Klee might think, Geln was trying to avoid full-blown hysterics. If the AI decided he was a liability, it might sic Peo on him.

"What are you doing?" Klee reverted back to its soothing voice. Bad sign, to have your AI trying to calm you. "*What* are you doing?" it repeated.

Geln was, in fact, placing a razor against his wrist. One

way to escape, especially if the AI had written him off. But he wasn't ready to go there yet. "I'm exploring the rooms I've been given."

"Really? You're having quite the emotional response to them."

Yeah, it's these rooms. Geln dropped the razor back in its drawer. His goddamned hands had been shaking all day for one reason or the other. "Did I ever tell you that I have to shave myself with a blade down here? I rather miss the depilation cream."

"You'll be able to use that cream again one day."

Geln laughed.

"What?" demanded Klee with some affront.

"You're an idiot sometimes."

"I'm going to decide that was said with some affection. Geln, why don't you tell me what you see in your rooms?" Kleemach was trying to distract Geln from the worst of his fears. It suggested an appropriate and intuitive response to the crisis. Unusual for the AI to spend that kind of energy. "Well?"

Geln pulled in a long breath and played along. "I see a large mirror surrounded by beautiful wood, with some gold inlay." *And a sick-looking operative whose clothes don't fit him.* "A marble floor. A...hey, the bathtub is cerastic." Geln knocked on the material to check for its telltale thud. "I thought they didn't deal with such technologically advanced materials."

"Eberly is the Minster of State."

"Yes." Geln's briefing had stated that no one was supposed to get cerastic for personal use. The Alliance preferred its technology to be used in showy yet insubstantial displays, like the holographic jewels Ruel had put on for his engagement party.

"Hmmm," said Klee. Not that it was really thinking. It would have already thought, rapidly and completely. "The more adept politicians are able to get their hands on stuff they shouldn't."

So...perhaps Klee's hesitation had been related to its decision to admit to Geln that all was not as it seems. Geln waited, letting the tiniest bit of relief settle him. The AI was acknowledging something he'd known since the emolio incident—illegal trade existed. But why admit it now? Had something changed?

"What do you know about it?" Geln desperately wished Klee could tell him about Peo, tell him how to protect himself from her.

"Nothing."

"You mean, you're not supposed to tell me anything."

"I mean, the part of me, Kleemach, that interacts with you, does not know anything. You are aware I am part of a greater AI? And we are partitioned? I am the lesser half."

Geln shrugged, not that it could see. Of course he knew the greater AI was Peo's companion. Sighing, he walked out of the dimly lit washroom and into the brighter sitting room. Klee had never referred to itself this way before, not openly. Maybe with a little honesty in sight, Geln could get through this crisis. He looked out. The windowpanes were large for Rimania. Picking up an ashtray, he walked to the window and, with one of its inlaid emeralds, tried to scratch the glass. The pane was unaffected.

"This window is made with lophane," Geln announced.

"Interesting."

Geln stared out at the exquisitely modeled garden. A man was shaving leaves off the shrubs, molding the plants into a rectangle's straight lines. "I'm surprised that you referred to yourself as you truly are, Kleemach. Partitioned, that is."

"The reference was for your benefit."

"I thought it might be."

"You've calmed since I became more transparent. Your pulse has lowered, your secretions suggest—"

"Yes, yes." Geln didn't need such a blatant reminder that Klee could read everything about him.

"You need to trust me," the AI concluded.

"I don't like you constantly eavesdropping. I *need* privacy."

"Geln," Klee chided. Yes, he'd kind of signed on for an AI companion and all it entailed, hadn't he? But it was one thing to understand something in theory and another to live it under these circumstances. "It's for your own protection. You know I'm not human."

"Humans will read you, listen to you, observe you."

"Yes, they certainly think they will."

The gardener below didn't use an automated shearer. He manually sliced the leaves with two blades, his arms pumping in and out at the action. "Are you playing with me, Kleemach, pretending that you'll keep my private life private when we both know that's impossible?"

"You know no such thing, Geln. Your understanding of AIs, while more than a layman's, is hardly deep and detailed. What I'm doing is offering you a trade. If you promise to keep your watch attached to your wrist at all times, that is if you keep *me* on *you*, I'll hide your more intimate moments from human eyes or ears."

The gardener stood up and peered into the sky. It had begun to drizzle again.

"For instance, taking off your watch while you had sex with Arjes accomplished very little, but put you at greater risk."

Geln felt a noise in his ears, a dull roar. He didn't want to talk about *that*.

"Geln? I am trying to come to some arrangement here."

"At least you can't take my pulse then." To Geln's dismay, his voice cracked.

"I'll hide that information," Klee repeated, the epitome of calm. "Only you and I will know. I am allowed to use this discretion." Geln just clasped his hands behind his back and looked down. "I was still in the tent. What difference does it ultimately make whether you feel more psychologically free without me attached to your wrist, when I am still an aural witness? You're not stupid enough to permanently separate yourself from me. Why not take the very real chance that I can hide what I consider personal and trivial from other humans?"

"Humans?"

"Your PO," the AI admitted.

"Bullshit. You're not allowed to hide anything from her. You're under the thumb of her AI." Geln suppressed a giggle at that visual. Gawd, he was losing it.

"I have some latitude," Klee persisted. "If we judge that the operation will be more successful if you trust me, I can make modifications, hide what isn't relevant to her operation."

We. So Klee and Peo's AI were in negotiation? "What will Peo say?"

"I can't discuss her with you, Geln."

Geln stared out the window, trying to assess whether this was a trick or real. As a trick, it would be an exceedingly odd one. Then again Klee wasn't human, it was AI, alien. Geln watched the gardener, as if he could help sort out Klee's motives while he packed up his tools and pushed the wheelbarrow out of sight.

Klee shifted topic. "We think you should avoid the cadre from now on. You seem a little traumatized by recent events."

Laughing softly, Geln clamped his hands around his arms. "What is this 'we'?"

"I've consulted my overseer, the greater AI."

Geln backed away from the window, picked up the ashtray and threw it against the window. The heavy object bounced off the pane and plopped on the floor, scraping the pine wood. Geln took absurd pleasure in the blemish. "Definitely lophane." He bent down to throw it again, stopped. "Kleemach?"

"Yes."

"I can't avoid the cadre when they seek me out."

"I'll help." Klee actually sounded perky now. Perhaps it was the kind of challenge it enjoyed. "So you'll keep the watch attached to your wrist?"

Geln lobbed the ashtray against the glass again. "Help me avoid the cadre and, yes."

Chapter Nine

A knock on the door startled Geln from sleep to wakefulness. He sat up in bed and called out, "Yes?"

A servant opened the door. "Your presence is required in the morning room, sir." He bowed and left before Geln could even display his surprise. Someone must have unlocked the door earlier but he hadn't noticed the sound of the bolt being moved, or even heard footsteps. Geln frowned. First cerastic, now... "Is this house rigged, Kleemach?"

"Its security is, including the lock on your door. Not bugged though," it added cheerfully.

Geln pushed himself off the bed and shed his silk nightclothes. Given how Eberly wanted to act as if he was a host, not a jailer, Geln was almost surprised they didn't supply a manservant to help him dress. In answer to his question, someone knocked at the door and introduced himself with just that function.

Ick, thought Geln, but he submitted to the ordeal of being dressed in clothing made of too many buttons and too much natural cloth. He missed his synthetics.

"How long have you worked for Lord Eberly?" Geln asked the man.

The servant's nimble fingers worked on Geln's collar, setting it straight, and he could only be grateful that breaking fast did not require more complicated formal wear.

"Nine years, sir." The answer was grudging.

"Geln," warned Klee. "Play your part properly and you'll do much better. Don't bother the poor servant."

Geln sighed and followed the "poor servant" down. He couldn't help but be impressed by the curving staircase—the centerpiece of the front foyer. He hadn't come in this way. Yesterday's back entry, polite escorts notwithstanding, had been, he recognized at the time, a bad sign.

Lord Eberly waited for him at the bottom of the steps. "Mr. Pyadrez."

Geln returned Eberly's shallow bow with a deep one before Eberly clasped hands behind his back and strolled down the hall. "My great-great-grandfather built this house."

Geln made a suitable noise of interest. Eberly's ancestor was one of the founders of Rimania. Klee, properly attached, was going to enjoy this conversation.

Eberly waved at the portrait. "Renfru Eberly, a close advisor of Riman." Here, he leaned slightly towards Geln and lowered his voice. "Tomas Riman was our founder and first leader, you know." The back of Geln's neck prickled. The way Eberly delivered that line...did he know Geln was an alien? "Of course, I'm sure Lord Hernan has been attending to your education since your elevation."

He thinks I'm ignorant. That's fine. Geln smiled widely at the intended insult. "My uncle has been very kind."

"As he should be, as he should be." Eberly stopped at the next portrait. A man with similar, if harsher, features to those of Renfru. "Renfru II. My great-grandfather founded our present-day police force."

Geln's smile faltered. "I had thought it was founded during

the first years of Rimania's settlement."

"No. That generation of Rimanians were idealists, you know. All good in its way, but they learned that every society, even one as well organized as our own, needs a police force." Eberly gave a dry chuckle. "Of course you are acquainted with them, given your recent sojourn at the station."

"Don't worry, I was suitably chastened," Geln said flatly.

"As I thought. That's why my men were out in large numbers, searching for you yesterday. I wanted to ensure that you couldn't be accused of fraternizing with outlaws and taken into police custody yet again."

"I can only thank you for your concern."

Eberly smiled thinly and Geln decided to look at the next portrait. "Your father, I assume."

"Yes. Unfortunately, I never knew him. He died young."

"I'm sorry."

"Don't be ridiculous. You're not sorry at all."

Geln looked down into Eberly's bland gray eyes, and shrugged. "It's a shame when a child loses one or both of his parents."

"I suppose your illegitimacy might lead to that belief." Eberly's tone suggested Geln was quite wrong. Then his expression altered. "Come, let's break fast together."

Geln was led to the morning room. It glistened with bright, colorful tiles of the Eberly colors—gold and pale green. A chandelier sent beautiful rainbows bounding about its exterior. More impressive than Dressia's dining room.

A servant pulled out a pillowed wooden chair and Geln obligingly sat opposite Eberly. Coffee was served first, and unlike Dressia's, it was real.

Eberly smiled at Geln's reaction. "You're surprised, my boy, because that is the first genuine coffee you will have ever tasted." He paused, allowing doubt to seep into his next words. "Or is it?"

Geln certainly wasn't going to mention his pre-Rimanian existence, but the question put him on edge, making him wonder just what Eberly did and didn't know.

"You should understand," continued his jailer, "that the police have agreed you will stay with me until your status is wholly sorted out."

"Status?" Geln spread his hands, as the taste of coffee in his mouth turned bitter. "I'm a Pyadrez."

"Your very recent activities are suspect. But the police are loath to take you into custody again, given that last debacle. So...you are to stay with me. I will personally guarantee your good behavior." Eberly couldn't have looked more pleased with himself.

෪

Tobias turned the ring on his finger, examining four rubies set in smoky blue metal. The gems, brought to Rimania during the settlement, represented the Chelan red, his mother's family, while the smoky blue belonged to the Smators. He rarely wore the ring, out of distaste, though distaste for one's family was shameful.

Or was it distaste for himself? After all, he was the only product of a Chelan-Smator union and he disliked the symbol. Perhaps because his parents had hated each other, perhaps because they'd had little to do with him growing up. Perhaps because of the half-life he led.

If he wanted to get involved in politics, he had to embrace, at least superficially, what he was. His genetics made him elite and only the elite were allowed to play politics. Others—apparently—weren't clever enough.

His mother was clearly delighted by his recent decision to attend the House of Lords' next sitting. Upon hearing the news, she'd placed her hand on her heart. "They say"—*they* meant Lord Eberly—"that Ruel's attendance is erratic. Frankly, I'm surprised he shows up at all. Still, he should know that having a cousin sit in his stead will only do him good."

Tobias turned his ring again. Ruel's band was studded with amethysts, but it was the metal that counted at the House. "He might like a substitute," Tobias agreed. Or not. Tobias had little idea how his cousin thought about these things. It was unfortunate he had to go through Ruel to become politically active.

His mother eyed him speculatively, cheek cradled in one hand. Her rings glinted, bringing out the blue in her eyes. She'd once told him she'd married his father because his color matched her eyes. He still didn't know if she'd been serious.

"My," she said finally, "this is a turnaround. Renfru must have had quite a talk with you."

"It was an interesting visit." Tobias had not yet mentioned Geln. "Lord Eberly let me see how interesting power can be."

His mother straightened, and she folded her hands on the table. "Now, how did he accomplish that? I'm all curiosity."

"A man can manipulate the system so that it's legal to keep another gentleman under house guard."

Her gaze sharpened. "Who? Stop being coy, Tobias."

"You can't guess?" Tobias would have liked to know just how serious his mother had been with Geln, and just how serious she was now with Eberly.

Her stiff back and the slight clenching of her hands indicated she was angry. "Not Geln Pyadrez." At Tobias's nod, she hissed, "Bastard."

"Geln *is* a bastard."

She glared. "I was referring to the figurative one. I told Renfru to leave the boy alone." She pushed her plate away. "I've lost my appetite. No wonder Renfru asked you to visit. He wanted to let me know what he's done." She drummed her fingernails on the glass tabletop.

"He also wanted me to make the situation clear to Geln."

"La, yes. Renfru likes to accomplish many things at once. For this was the start of your political apprenticeship."

"It was?"

"Of course. Since you and he agree on most major issues."

"We do?" said Tobias in lieu of anything more intelligible. "I hadn't quite realized. When all is said and done, I suppose my understanding is not that much better than Geln's."

"You have some advantages in terms of upbringing, my dear. Though admittedly, your eyes aren't as arresting."

"Huh?"

"Geln, though I'm sure you haven't noticed, has beautiful green *elite* eyes."

"Really, Mother, eye color does not determine social status."

"They say, but only quietly, that emerald green eyes are a remnant of the genetic engineering of our distant past, before we came to live here on Rimania. Of course, in the current climate, we have to pretend it was originally natural." She sat back. "You have much to learn from me." Tobias was pretty certain that little nugget was secondhand from Eberly.

"I see." Tobias carefully sipped the last of his tea. It prevented his lip from curling.

"It will be good for you to have a purpose in life." His mother's smile was genuine, but might have faltered if she'd realized that Tobias's political interest lay in two issues only: solving his uncle's murder and protecting Geln from Eberly.

Chapter Ten

Tobias stood in the hall, awaiting Ruel who seemed none too eager to welcome him. When he realized two people were descending the spiral staircase that dominated this large room, he glanced up, only to be blinded by the sun glaring through the domed skylight.

"Well, well, another visit. What brings you our way this time, Tobias?" Ruel asked.

Our?

"Tobias." Ann-Marie's voice was just short of unctuous. "I'm so pleased we get to meet again."

"Ah." He tried to conceal his surprise and dread. After all, Ruel was affianced and while Tobias expected Ann-Marie to remain in Ruel's life, he'd thought she'd fade into the background during the engagement.

She played with her lower lip in a manner that was restrained enough to be attractive. "Ruel assured me you would be less than pleased to see me here."

This display of insecurity was a new trait of Ann-Marie's and didn't seem entirely natural to Tobias. "Ruel and I don't really know each other all that well."

"How sad, when you're family and all."

"Terribly sad, my dear," Ruel declared.

"Let's call for some tea." Ann-Marie cast her gaze about in search of a servant.

"Oh, I'd like something stronger than tea," said Ruel.

Ann-Marie stiffened, but Ruel didn't notice as he strode off to demand drinks from his manservant.

Tobias wondered if the balance of power had shifted since the engagement, or since Ruel's move from his apartments to the family home. As she trailed after Ruel, Ann-Marie was holding herself very tightly. Once they reached the sitting room, she spun on her heel. "So, why are you here?" Her large mouth widened into a smile that summoned warmth from her anger, although Tobias didn't think she was angry with him.

"I've come to pay my respects to the head of the household, I suppose," he replied, not knowing what kind of answer she expected. Ruel wasn't paying attention, being on the lookout for a servant with drinks.

"Ruel is not, technically, head of the household," Ann-Marie pointed out. "Lira may give birth to a boy."

At that, Ruel's head swiveled. "In practice though, I am. Perhaps forever, perhaps for the next eighteen years. Either is fine. After eighteen years, I can retire to the countryside in grand style." He paused, eyes lighting up as a servant arrived with a tray of drinks. "Ah, that's what I'm looking for."

Ann-Marie refused to take her alcoholic drink, evidently ordered for her by Ruel. "I prefer tea in the morning."

"Take what's here or leave it," Ruel demanded.

"I'd like tea myself," Tobias put in, perhaps unwisely. He was beginning to forget that he wanted something from Ruel. Still, Tobias waved away the drink the servant half-offered him while Ruel sank back into the couch with his.

"Tea for the charming couple, Tharbot," Ruel ordered as if

he was granting them a huge boon.

"Yes, sir."

"Would you like cookies with that too?" Ruel smirked.

Tharbot paused to await an answer.

"Don't be satisfied with sophomoric behavior, Ruel, stoop to adolescence. It's much more amusing," said Ann-Marie. "And you do it so well. I'm sure your cousin is impressed by your high-handed manner."

Ruel's grin froze.

"Perhaps Tobias would like cake," Ann-Marie suggested in the vacuum that followed.

Tharbot beat a hasty retreat.

"You don't even have to be here," Ruel whispered to Ann-Marie. It was a threat.

"I believe Tobias can hear you, my dear."

"I don't give a fuck."

"Ruel?" Tobias leaned forward.

"What?" Ruel snapped.

"Can I sit in your stead at the House of Lords from time to time? When you can't make it?"

"Why, whatever for?" His cousin stared at him blankly while Ann-Marie did the tension thing again. For some reason she didn't like his request.

"I'd like to become more involved, politically."

Ruel grunted while Ann-Marie murmured, "A worthy goal."

"I won't go on voting days, of course. That's your right. My main desire is to observe the political process." Tobias laughed, too falsely. "I am rather tired of listening to my mother's long-winded, secondhand descriptions, so I thought I'd investigate on my own. If, that is, you won't be attending every session."

"Well, of course not." Ruel's expression suggested that would be ridiculous. Ann-Marie actually rolled her eyes.

Tobias found the whole scene surreal. An apolitical, but potentially powerful cousin whose mistress was annoyed by his lack of ambition. Obviously, Ann-Marie had more interests than just being financially well kept.

"So?" asked Tobias, wondering if he'd have to repeat his request.

Ruel shrugged, one languid shoulder rising and falling. "Sure, you can go to the House in my stead. Why not?"

After that Ruel focused on his drink, Ann-Marie brooded and Tobias occupied himself by taking the tea that arrived. Following his second sip, he ventured, "There's a meeting tomorrow. No vote. I checked. Can I attend, represent you?"

Ruel waved his hand, and Tobias found it hard to interpret the gesture.

"That's a yes?"

"Yes, yes. God knows I don't care." Ruel slumped farther into the couch.

"I can brief you on the meeting, if you want."

Ruel just shook his head.

Abruptly, Ann-Marie stood.

"What are you doing?" Ruel asked her.

"Showing our guest to the door." She walked up to Tobias who, since getting permission to attend the House from Ruel, was glad enough to leave, so he stood. Slipping her arm through his, she drew him out of the room. Her perfume was a little strong and brought a too-crowded florist shop to mind. "It was very kind of you to offer Ruel your services."

"Thank you."

"Ruel, despite his attitude, would like to hear about the

meetings you attend."

Tobias couldn't help but laugh. "I don't think so."

She stopped and applied pressure to his arm so he looked down into her face. She gazed back with a curious lack of guile. "Your cousin simply doesn't understand that he would like to know what is going on in the House. Between you and I, we can convince him that politics *is* interesting."

"Oh?"

"Unless your plans are more complicated than you say they are?"

Tobias smothered a *huh?* What did she mean?

She watched him intently, trying to guess his secret motives, and he worked, unsuccessfully, to keep the color from rushing to his face. "Like Ruel, you were apolitical until very recently," she pointed out.

He shrugged. "Death changes things."

"Especially your own near-death?"

"Perhaps."

She stepped closer, almost brushing against him, and if Tobias were wired differently, he might have found it arousing. It was meant to be. "Keep us informed of your political activities and I guarantee you will be rewarded."

He backed away. "I'll be happy to keep you informed," he said stiffly. "Good day." He bowed, brief and shallow, and didn't wait for her curtsy to leave.

§

Geln gripped his soft leather boots in one hand and felt for the wooden railing with the other. He shouldn't have been surprised by the inky darkness. The moon was new, and lighting was kept to a minimum here. Didn't matter, his eyes were Alliance best, with nightsight to boot, although the dim lamp in the great hall cast enough light for him to get by without red vision. His feet moved off the plush carpet and onto the wood of the stairway. He stopped and scanned yet again for any sign of a guard.

The singular lack made him suspicious.

"There's still time to go back," Kleemach suggested wearily. Threats and promises had done little to turn Geln's mind away from his plan to escape. Perhaps the AI now realized there was no way in hell Geln would remain Eberly's prisoner another day.

"Thank you, Klee, for pointing that out." He crept forward in his stocking feet, sliding across the polished slats of wood. "Do you think the stairs might creak? Surely Eberly would be too proud to allow such noise in his great hall. Unless creaking steps are his preferred method of detecting intruders and escapees. What do you think?"

"I cannot detect any mechanism of entrapping you."

"Really? Perhaps Eberly is overconfident. It would not do for someone like me to try to escape someone like him." Geln began his descent. Each wooden step was solid. "But thank you for that information, Klee. I thought you'd washed your hands of this escapade, as you so aptly named it."

"I don't want you to get caught," it admitted grudgingly.

"Any other helpful information you'd like to donate to the cause?"

"You can't leave by the front door. It's locked."

"Anywhere I am not locked in?"

After a pause, Klee revealed, "A side door is unlocked. The

servants, without permission, keep it that way so they can make their occasional forays."

Geln smiled to himself in the dark, enjoying Eberly's ignorance. "I might have come to Riman as a servant. I think I would have served you better, Kleemach."

"You are not my servant, Geln."

"I don't mean to be, but that role is your overseer's first choice."

"Our first choice is that you act responsibly."

"That hasn't served me well."

The AI actually sighed.

"I should have gone down the backstairs," said Geln. "Considering that I am heading to the front and very locked door."

"In fact, it's safer here at the front of the house. There are fewer ears. Despite your apparent empathy with the servants, they would turn you over to Eberly with no compunction. The cadre could not place one of their own in this house."

By now Geln was quickly tripping down the second tier of the staircase.

Klee's voice became nettled, as if it wanted Geln's attention. "You might have trouble getting to the road."

"If you don't help me, you mean?"

"Yes."

"Please point me to the unlocked door so I can escape this prison."

"We are all in prisons."

Geln groaned. "*Please*, Klee. Philosophy doesn't suit you."

"They were taking such good care of you, Geln."

"Bullshit! Besides, I don't trust Eberly. At all."

"But they weren't hurting you."

"They will when it becomes useful for them to do so." Geln stopped at the bottom of the stairs. "Why help me get this far and no more? What's the point of that?"

"Winning your trust?" suggested Kleemach.

"You have what you're going to have of it, considering what you are and how you're programmed."

"I am *programmed* to protect you."

"Good." Geln glanced around the hall. Yes, still empty. He ran silently under one of the stair's wings. "Am I headed in the right direction?"

"I'm not sure I should answer that."

"Don't act piqued."

"I am helping you because it is better for you to escape than to be caught escaping," it said testily. "My analysis indicates that you would try to leave with or without my assistance."

"Thank you, thank you. I do appreciate your help, really. Now, where?"

"Keep to your right."

Geln moved off the wooden floor and hit the concrete of the servants' side of the house. The hallways were narrower and ceilings lower.

"Left here. Second door on the right."

He stopped in front of the supposed escape hatch. It was possible that Klee was lying, that the door would be locked or trigger an alarm. But the AI didn't like to endanger him.

"Why aren't you opening the door?" it asked in surprise.

"Putting on my boots." His feet were glad to be encased in leather instead of cooling on the concrete floor. "There." He took one deep breath and pushed down on the metal handle. The door swung open, noiselessly, and damp air wafted in. He exchanged himself with the air and was gone.

He was out in front of the mansion in no time. At midnight, no one frequented Eberly's mansion. Even if they had, he could have hidden in the darkness of the new moon. His nightsight outlined shapes in red and he wondered why they couldn't lay bricks more evenly before mentally shrugging off that trivial query.

He threw out his arms in happiness and pulled in a lungful of night air. "I feel in control," he shouted.

"You're out of control. What exactly do you plan to do?"

"Don't ask such questions. You won't like the answers."

"Like them or not," it argued. "I want to hear them."

Geln tripped on Eberly's brick drive and almost sent himself flying before he managed to catch himself. He had to calm down. "Anyone coming?" he asked Klee.

"Unlike the manor, the roads are not rigged, Geln. I have no idea whether or not someone is coming."

Geln broke into a steady jog.

"Are you headed to or away from town?"

"To town. I don't know how to survive in the countryside alone."

"Whereas you can survive in the city quite handily. You've been doing so well."

"Sarcasm, Klee. Well done. In point of fact, I have not done that badly." Then he admitted, "With your help."

"I hope you plan to go to your uncle's, even if such action may compromise Hernan Pyadrez. He'll be accused of helping you escape."

"Better not go there right away. Let Hernan be completely
113

ignorant of my whereabouts so they can be assured of his innocence." Geln chose to ignore Klee's "yeah right" snort. "I'll show up later." Despite Klee's reaction, Geln didn't think it a bad strategy.

"Where will you stay in the meantime?"

"Daltons."

"*Daltons?* Whatever for?"

"To get picked up by an unknown. After Arjes, I need a proper, uncomplicated fuck."

"*No.*"

"It's not something I expect you to understand, Klee. Though at least it should interest you." His newfound joy at his freedom seemed to ebb at that thought. He felt bitter about Klee's ever-present observations. "Don't worry, I'll keep my promise, and you'll remain attached to the skin of my wrist."

"Geln, there is prejudice against homosexual relations on this planet. Men do not engage in affairs with other men."

"Bullshit." *Tobias wants me.*

"Bullshit?" Klee was too interested in this revelation.

"Maybe," Geln amended, trying to infuse doubt in that one word. *Get a grip. You don't want to expose Tobias to Klee and, ultimately, Peo.*

"How fascinating you think so. The theory is that they bred it out of themselves before they arrived."

Geln didn't respond, willing this rather distasteful conversation to die as he left the brick of Eberly's long drive and turned right onto the dirt road that led to the city. The ruts were awkward to jog in and he opted for the grassy middle of the road, even if his boots would suffer from the dampness. "Anyway, I don't need a man, particularly. I can be flexible. I have a little bi in me and I am *wired.*"

"I didn't know you were flexible."

"Well, surprise."

"How did they miss that in your background?" It sighed, the second time tonight. Perhaps this mannerism was the AI's new tic. "You're not supposed to indulge in recreational sex during this operation."

"Just sex for research, eh? Just sex when Ann-Marie wants me to observe Arjes. Well, fuck that."

"The point is, Geln, there should be no fucking."

"Very clever, my dear AI, but there will be. Tonight. And you'll get to study it in your own unique way. Does that appeal to you?"

"No. You are compromising yourself and that distresses me."

"Distress? Goodness me. What happens? Do some of your connections fire too often? Do your coils get overheated?"

"Your understanding of my hardware is not accurate."

"I'm sure. But I'm not here to understand you. I'm here to collect whatever information I can get for you. And that's what I'm going to do. Who says the nightlife won't be educational?"

"I give up."

"Good."

Klee kept its word and Geln ran in silence until, half an hour later, he reached the perimeter of the city and asked Klee to let him in. When Klee balked, at least for form's sake, Geln pointed out, "You already helped me leave Eberly's tonight, surely you can sneak me past the city wall."

"I should say no."

"You should say yes. Your overseer must be salivating at the chance to visit Daltons."

"It doesn't salivate," Kleemach said sulkily.

"Well? How long do I have to stand here?"

"My decision to deny you access to the city has been overridden by my overseer. You're right, it *is* interested in your visit to Daltons."

Klee's patent disapproval of its overseer confused Geln, as did the confession. Or was Klee playing mind games? That would be a new and unwelcome development. "Your overseer allows you to tell me about your disagreements?" Geln asked.

"No, it has decided transparency is an asset to our relationship. It's quite excited by these new events. Presumably what is happening will please those on high and that is what it most needs to do."

"Great! Is it the sex, do you think, or the incredible talent I have for exposing myself to life on this Byzantine planet?" And was he talking to Klee now, or Peo's AI?

"It's not Byzantine."

"Don't be pedantic, Klee."

"Just walk through the doorway now."

"The field's down?"

"Well, yes."

Geln quickly ducked through the gate. He didn't want to be caught by the field and knocked unconscious, left to be picked up by Eberly again.

He emerged on the other side and looked back at the brick wall to watch the field flare to life again. Although he was in another prison, he felt more capable of hiding within its confines. "I made it. I'm in the city."

"That's just wonderful."

"Sarcasm again, Klee. How interesting. I'm beginning to think you're evolving. Or is that the overseer's influence? Are your personalities merging?"

"My situation is stressful, Geln. My operative is using my overseer for his own purposes. Or vice versa. I am supposed to mediate and my role is being flung to the wayside."

"Jealous, are we?"

"We?"

"You, I meant, Klee, though I'm a little confused about your identity."

"It's me, Geln."

"Okay. Then I'd like you to know that I appreciate your concern, despite the fact that if you had your way, you would do me more harm than good."

"We'll see about that, won't we?" Kleemach said with over-the-top grimness.

Geln felt great right now. In control. He'd escaped that asshole Eberly and he was ready to prowl the city, alone. In a day or two, he'd arrive "home" and Hernan could protect him. Till then he was on his own.

Or as much on his own as was possible with a multiple-personality AI attached to his skin.

Chapter Eleven

Daltons was a small pub with rooms to let above. Geln would arrange where to sleep later. For now he wanted to quench his thirst and eat something. He took in a deep breath of the incense. The jasmine and pine pleased him, even if his eyes watered a little as a waiter hustled up to him. "One, sir?"

The man led him to a tiny table in the middle of the room.

"Anything to eat, sir? We have potato rounds, fried rice or corn sticks for cheap. Or I can bring you a proper menu." The waiter was medium height and Geln liked his voice, how it ended each sentence with a question. His nose was crooked but his brown eyes were warm and appealing. He reminded him slightly of Tobias, though he was a smaller, scruffier version. "Sir?"

Geln smiled at him. "I need your help."

The waiter frowned. His face was more lined than Tobias's. Unwise to try and pick up an older man unless he was obviously interested. This one just seemed confused.

"I'm trying to help, sir."

"Please don't call me sir."

The man's expression blanked with incomprehension.

Klee decided to speak up. "In this situation, Geln, 'sir' is simply something to hang on whoever this waiter serves. He doesn't necessarily think highly of you."

Geln widened his mouth and eyes, in part because of his amusement at Klee stating the obvious, and in part to verify that this man was not interested. "But never mind that. You see, I have no money."

The waiter's face darkened. He obviously thought he was being played with, so Geln quickly revealed what lay in the palm of his hand. The man frowned and bent to look more closely at the emerald that matched Geln's lovely eyes. That ashtray in his little Eberly jail room would now come in handy. Or, its emeralds would.

The waiter straightened, balancing on the balls of his feet, ready to move. His lips curved slightly. "I can help you with *that*, sir. But first, let me bring you a jug of our best beer and our meal."

"Why thank you."

He bent his head in acknowledgement and left, moving deeper into the pub.

Geln smiled down at his jewel.

"Are you trying to get yourself robbed and killed?" asked Klee.

"Nah. But what happens, happens."

"Oh God."

"You believe in no such thing. Anyway, stop worrying. I am going to enjoy my meal and my drink. Live life for the moment, you know?"

"I know no such thing," Kleemach answered.

Geln stared at the chipped white paint of the wooden door. Obviously Daltons hadn't imported permanent paint from the Alliance, or even used the best that Rimania had to offer.

119

He rested his forehead against the open door. He hadn't meant to drink whatever drug they'd fed him, but it appeared they'd thought *he* had wanted to buy it with the emerald.

They were out to please him, as they also thought he wanted to buy this boy into his bed. Geln had rejected him out of hand, on the stairs and here. He wouldn't mind giving the winsomely tousled redhead some money to leave him alone and start a new life that didn't involve selling his body. Prostitution disturbed him, but neither the boy nor the establishment seemed to have cottoned on to that fact.

The boy's freckled face lit with understanding. "You want a boy *and* a girl?"

Geln lifted his head off the door and shook it wearily. "I don't pay for sex, dear. I want someone to want me."

"I want you," the boy said eagerly.

Geln pounded his aching head with his fist. The drug made him stupid, made him say stupid things. It occurred to him that this boy, while he wouldn't enter his room without a proper invitation, was not going to remove his foot from the threshold of the room without a struggle. Geln didn't have the energy to fight though he badly wanted to shut the door instead of lean on it.

He thought of a solution. "I'll pay for something else, though."

The boy's open face slid into cynicism, as if that was his true nature, and the naiveté a cloak. "What?"

"You let me know if anyone asks after me. If someone comes around asking suspicious questions, you knock on the door. Three sharp raps, and I'll open it."

"Oh." The boy was nonplused. "I don't do that. That's not my job." The boy's expression shifted from wary to sullen. Obviously this was not the evening he was expecting.

120

"Listen, Lionel."

"Leo."

"Leo, listen. I won't tell, if you don't. Tell them it was a quickie or take a walk before you return, okay? Here's what I paid you." Geln fished for the proper gold coin in his newly heavy pouch. The emerald had done him proud.

He showed Leo the coin and the boy's eyes danced. "You'll get more of that if you bring me real information." Leo reached for the coin but stopped himself when Geln didn't hand it over. "But don't play me false, okay? Refuse me now and there will be no hard feelings."

"I'll do as you ask," the boy promised.

"I don't want to threaten you, Leo, but I have to be careful. I will repay you one way or the other, for your loyalty or lack thereof in this small matter. Understand?"

"Yes, yes." Leo stared impatiently, as if Geln was stupid. Once Leo had realized Geln did not want to be seduced, his open, eager face had completely vanished.

Geln dropped the coin in the boy's hand and it disappeared into Leo's clothes.

"You can remove your foot from my door now."

"Yes, sir." Leo gave a brisk bow and retreated.

Geln, thankfully, shut the door. He desperately needed to sleep. It was almost morning. He sat on the creaky bed and began to remove his leather boots.

ॐ

"It's too hot," protested Tobias, flinging off the heavy canvas of the black gown before Sandorl had a chance to connect the numerous fastenings.

His mother hid her smile behind a hand.

"What?" snapped Tobias. He didn't see why she had to watch him.

"Your father used to become similarly irritable before attending an assembly."

Tobias glared. He didn't want to think about his father who'd tried to become a lord in Perrin's stead. His goal was *nothing* like that.

"Didn't he, Sandorl?" his mother insisted, as if she had fond memories of her late husband.

"Yes, ma'am," Sandorl answered dutifully, while picking up the discarded cloth. He straightened. "Shall we try again, sir?"

His mother giggled. Very uncharacteristic. "Your father used to throw that monstrous gown off three or four times before he would allow Sandorl to dress him. Sandorl was even allowed to show his annoyance by the third throw. Weren't you, Sandorl?"

"Yes, ma'am."

Tobias looked at the older man who managed to glare back at him without moving a feature.

"Sorry," Tobias breathed.

"Tobias!" his mother said sharply. "Do not apologize. It's his job. Besides, I'm sure this has brought back memories, hasn't it, Sandorl?"

Tobias couldn't stand to hear yet another uninflected recital of "yes, ma'am" from Sandorl so he asked the first question that came to mind. "Mother, will Lord Eberly attend the assembly today?"

She looked at him like he was an idiot. "Darling, Lord Eberly attends all assemblies unless he is ill or indisposed. He

122

is the Minister of State and therefore runs the show."

"Oh, I had thought the Speaker maintained order in the House."

"The Speaker is dead, Tobias, as you well know, since he *was your uncle*. And they are certainly not going to pass on that role to Ruel. Or you." This idea she appeared to find charmingly ridiculous but something in Tobias's face changed her expression and she went on to explain, "They don't let neophytes or substitutes become Speaker. They only elect someone with experience."

"Ah," said Tobias, obligingly, as if this was news to him. He allowed Sandorl to drape the ugly gown over his shoulders a third time and tried to ignore the smell of mothballs. He was surprised his mother hadn't taken better care of his father's cape, even if Tomas Smator had only attended the House of Lords a handful of times. Perrin would have missed very few sittings.

Sandorl circled Tobias, arranged the material so it sat properly on his shoulders, and stood in front to connect the intricate metal fastenings. It was odd to think that Sandorl had dressed his father.

"So, Mother, who do you think they'll elect as the new Speaker of the House?"

She shrugged. "Maybe it will be discussed today. I certainly hope Eberly gets his choice. As should you."

"I'm sure I will." He looked down as Sandorl fastened the last latch. "But why?"

She smiled sweetly. "Because you are his apprentice. You must support him and his goals."

He stepped back from Sandorl and the cape fell from his servant's hands and down to his feet. It was too heavy and hot.

"Will you go round to Ruel's after the assembly and inform him of any developments?"

Tobias cast his mind back to his last words with Ann-Marie. He disliked her, and wondered what she planned to do with information he brought her via Ruel. Even if he met privately with Ruel, he doubted that would completely route Ann-Marie who seemed to have a will of steel.

"Tobias?" asked his mother impatiently.

"Hmm?"

"Will you go to Ruel's?"

"Of course. Though I'm not sure it will accomplish much."

She examined her rings. "He was always an idiot. Probably not even Perrin's. Too fraily built. But, mark my words, in ten years he'll be obese. I know that body type."

"Hmmm." Tobias looked in the mirror. He'd heard that charge of illegitimacy countless times and even if it had shocked him at the age of twelve, it did little now but remind him that he disliked his mother.

"Sandorl, you may go," she said.

"Mother, I can dismiss my own servants, thank you very much."

"I wish to have a word with you in private, dear."

Sandorl waited. Tobias waved his hand, irritated. "Thank you, Sandorl."

"Sir." He bowed and let himself out.

"You treat that old man too well."

Tobias shrugged. He liked Sandorl, but such simple sentiments seemed unwise to admit.

She came to stand beside Tobias at the mirror. As she tucked an errant curl of his away, he shook her hand off. He disliked her touch, couldn't remember if he'd ever liked it, even if he did remember longing for her as a young child.

She ignored the rebuff. Her voice was low and he could just catch her words. "Renfru believes he can prove Ruel's illegitimacy."

Tobias stopped staring at his black, rather ghoulish attire and slowly moved his gaze across the mirror to meet his mother's. She nodded twice, very satisfied with her news, her expression reminding him of a well-fed cat. He tried not to react. Though his face stiffened slightly, he didn't give much away. He just looked a little paler.

God knows he didn't want the lordship.

Tobias couldn't stop thinking about the emolio that had almost killed him the night Serge had died. His mother shouldn't have told him Eberly's plans to disinherit Ruel right before his first assembly. It made him feel as though he was a target. Someone had killed Perrin, someone had killed Serge, and Tobias did not want to be next.

It was one thing to "apprentice" to a Minister of State when Tobias had little real power. He wanted to understand Perrin's strange death and perhaps Geln's strange life but still, all in all, the information was for himself, at least until he figured out what to do with it. Even if Perrin had been murdered, the police would be reluctant to take on a second unsolved Smator murder, and if they did, they would try to pin it on a servant or worker as they invariably did.

As for Geln, Tobias didn't have high hopes for swinging in and rescuing Eberly's prisoner today. Mostly he planned to gather enough information to pass on to Hernan Pyadrez so that Geln could regain his freedom and perhaps like Tobias for his efforts.

Not that Geln would *like* Tobias. No gentleman ever had. They were not supposed to have Tobias's feelings and as far as Tobias had been able to discern, with his blunted ability to sense attraction, they hadn't.

Even if Tobias did somehow end up with the lordship, he wouldn't have a lot of power. Not like Perrin. Worn-out, bitter Perrin who'd always had a soft spot for the son of his dim but politically motivated brother. Tobias let out a long breath. He hoped they couldn't prove Ruel's illegitimacy. Perrin hadn't been interested in such proof. Then again, Perrin had loved his feckless wife.

Sandorl opened the door and Tobias blinked. "Here already?" he asked in dismay.

"Indeed, sir."

"I don't want to go in, Sandorl," he admitted wryly, even while he clambered out of the carriage.

Sandorl's expression, as it rarely did, softened. "Don't whine, son."

Tobias nodded once. He let himself be bolstered by Sandorl's evident approval of his actions and walked with what he hoped was determination towards the House.

The House. It was beautiful and majestic, unlike so much that went on inside it. Tobias had enjoyed his boyhood visits to see his uncle in action, Speaker of the House even then. Perrin had been thrust into power young and while there were those who had despised the increasingly reactionary politics of his last years of life, Tobias thought that, all in all, Perrin hadn't done badly. He'd kept his honor, which was more than most lords could claim. Certainly more than Lord Eberly could, Tobias was sure. Not that he had any such proof. Eberly just made his skin crawl.

The House spread across the grass, its width impressive,

its height also. Towers threw shadows that shortened as the sun met its apex, but other than that Tobias had never figured out their purpose. He remembered asking Perrin about the towers as a boy, asking who went up there and why, and Perrin had just laughed as if Tobias had asked a clever and unanswerable question.

"Mr. Smator! Mr. Smator!" Tobias heard a thin voice in the wind and stopped. He began to walk again as he saw a page summoning him. My goodness, perhaps Eberly was anxious to see Tobias here, but this seemed a bit excessive. He frowned at the approaching boy.

"Mr. Smator," the page said breathlessly once he reached Tobias. "Lord Eberly requires your immediate presence."

"Isn't the assembly gathering?"

"Yes, sir. But before the proceedings begin, Lord Eberly insists he have a word with you in private."

They marched up the marble steps and into the great hall. Quite beautiful. The high, vaulted ceiling held painted windows that splashed colors down on the white tile. The page weaved his way through the crowd to a side door and Tobias obediently followed. After one rap, the page pulled down the handle and pushed the heavy, soundproof door inward. He gestured for Tobias to enter. Once inside, Tobias lifted his gaze from the intricate parquet floor of cherry, oak and walnut to meet Eberly's eyes. The man was angry, which took Tobias aback.

"Good day, Tobias. I'm pleased to see you here." Eberly dismissed the page with a thankful coin and a murmured approval. The page glowed with satisfaction. Tobias supposed it had been a good day's work already.

As soon as the door shut, Eberly's face changed to match the fury in his eyes. Tobias blinked at the emotion though he didn't think the anger was directed at him. Eberly pounded one fist into the palm of his other hand. "Geln Pyadrez has gone missing, goddammit. You must help me find him."

Tobias found himself stepping backwards. "Me?"

"Yes, you. Why not? You gained a little of that sneaky bastard's trust."

"I did?" he asked, ludicrously pleased.

"Yes. He asked me when you were coming back. As if you could help him." Eberly laughed at that. "But you wouldn't, would you?"

Tobias suppressed a sigh and gave Eberly the words his threat was supposed to elicit. "No, my lord." If Tobias didn't argue, Eberly might not feel compelled to lecture him on where his loyalties should lie. Though why Eberly thought Tobias was pledged to help his mother's lover, he didn't know.

Tobias *would* help Geln.

In the silence that followed, Tobias found himself examining the half-horse, half-man creature painted on the white pine wall. It was striking, the pride and power there. He snapped his attention back to Eberly who had started telling him something. The words quickly replayed in Tobias's mind. *He doesn't seem to be at the Pyadrez household.*

"His apartment?" Tobias suggested stupidly.

"We looked, of course, but he isn't there."

"Maybe he was recaptured by the cadre?"

"I doubt it," Eberly said, acid in his voice.

"I didn't think so, but you see, I know little about the man."

"What I don't understand is how Geln Pyadrez left my manor in the first place." Eberly watched Tobias carefully and Tobias let honest bafflement show clearly on his face. "How could he do that?"

"Someone broke in and pulled him out?" Tobias hoped it

"I've got the best technology on Rimania. So you see, it is beyond my comprehension. And I dislike not understanding simple problems. Like how a lone man, with few political connections, could walk out of my manor without tripping an alarm. Someone *must* have helped him but the only people he's had contact with are the Pyadrezes and you and your mother."

"He met Ruel at the engagement party."

Eberly glowered. "I'm beginning to think your idiot act is for real, Tobias, and I'm not usually a bad judge of character. Let me be blunt. Do you know where Geln is, or did you in any way abet his disappearance?"

"No." Tobias forced a note of "how absurd" into his denial. "The man doesn't even like me."

"Why do you say that?"

Careful. "He knows I disapproved of him hanging onto my mother."

Eberly's face smoothed. "But that young man meant nothing to your mother."

"Very true," said Tobias quickly, to settle Eberly's obviously ruffled feathers. "But I dislike seeing her used."

"Ah." Eberly's lip curled. "Geln is adept at getting his way. However, that was before he came up against me." Eberly raised his chin and gave Tobias an appraising stare. "Here's what you must do. Visit the Pyadrezes—pretend that you are interested in becoming more intimately acquainted with your soon-to-be cousins—and find out when they hear from their young bastard. Because they will. He can hardly survive on his own for long. I want him back."

"But, how can you? No doubt you have every decent motive to do just that, but...how can you hold him legally?" Tobias shrugged.

"The police believe he should be with me. They are reconsidering him a suspect in the murder of Serge Smator. While under the truthteller, his answers were not so much innocent as incoherent."

"I hadn't realized your keeping him under house guard was officially sanctioned."

"It is." Eberly moved towards the door. "So do you agree?"

"Agree to what?" With his blank look, Tobias knew he was pushing it, but Eberly was such an ass.

"To get information from the Pyadrezes," Eberly snapped. It satisfied Tobias to force Eberly to state the request so baldly.

"Yes I do, sir."

"We'll see what you accomplish." Eberly smiled thinly. "I like to reward people, you know."

"I know that now."

The heavy door swung open and they walked out together.

Chapter Twelve

The first three knocks were timid, but loud enough to wake Geln. The strong sunlight and the smell of dirt disoriented him, but after the fourth knock, he recalled he was at Daltons and in hiding. Though he didn't like to think of it as hiding so much as stepping out on his own, free of Eberly, Hernan, Arjes.

"Who is it, Klee?" he asked, trying to clear the sleep from his voice. God he was exhausted. It must be past midday.

"*I* certainly don't know. You're in quite a primitive building. I still think you should return to Hernan's where I can monitor you better."

"Hold on!" called Geln, after a louder, more impatient knock. He rolled out of bed still in his clothes. "Klee, Eberly can't know I'm here, right? This isn't the kind of place he'd even be aware of."

"He could have spies," Kleemach said darkly.

"Don't spook me. I do better when I'm overconfident. I'm going to stride to this door and open it as if I can't fathom why I'm being disturbed at this hour of the afternoon."

He rubbed a hand over his eyes once and did just that. His supposed informer was waiting for him. Geln glanced up and down the dirty corridor. At least Leo seemed to be alone. Geln focused on the kid, whose red hair remained in the same tousled state, but whose sheepish expression did not bode well.

131

Shit, the kid was going to betray him. Geln gave him a slow, deep smile.

"Don't bother," Leo said flatly, referring to Geln's effort to charm him. "I have no choice."

Geln felt the adrenaline kick in. His heartbeat quickened and his head cleared of sleep. "Who?" A useless question. The kid would not know someone was an agent of Eberly's.

"A member of the cadre recognized you last night."

Geln's first reaction was relief, and in that brief moment, he learned that he feared Eberly more than the cadre. But he needed to stay away from them too. It was a joke, really. Here he was, supposedly collecting data from different strata of society, and he was running from them all.

Leo read the relief on Geln's face and relaxed himself. "Erne says you're part of them, that you'll be glad to see them." Leo shot him a hopeful look. "So, even though I told him where you are..."

"Sorry, Leo." Geln briskly did up his shirt, damned fussy fastenings they were too. "You were to give me information, not give out information on me, no matter who." Leo cast his eyes down. "Though I do agree, I'm part of the cadre."

"You are?" So, the boy hadn't really believed that piece of information. Geln supposed he didn't look like the cadre, in his fancy, if rumpled attire. "You shouldn't have such a problem doing up your own clothes."

"I'm not used to wearing this." Geln continued to fumble, getting irritated. After all, he needed to be awake and out of here half an hour ago. "Where is Erne now?"

"Waiting for you downstairs."

"Okay, look, I'll give you a little something." Geln fished for a suitably small coin that would nevertheless take the edge off the boy's disappointment. Better if Leo remembered him in a kindly way without thinking Geln stupid. "Go keep Erne company till I come down. Okay?"

Leo hesitated. "I'm a friend of the cadre, you know."

"Good. I'll join you both soon."

The boy decided to believe him. Perhaps money made the belief convenient. In any case, Geln shut the door and quickly gathered his emeralds and money, leaving enough of the latter on the table to make proper payment for his room. Jacket shrugged on, he sprinted through the corridor and clambered down the rusting fire escape, stumbling as he jumped to the ground. He moved out of the shadow of the building and squinted into the glaring sun, trying to figure out which direction he should take.

Geln rather liked the idea of living on his wits so he thought briefly of going to another pub where he'd continue to dodge both Eberly and cadre. Then the decor of Fargo's came to mind and with it the memory of the police arresting him. Geln shuddered, dismissing any pub as a possible temporary locale.

He'd felt safe at Hernan's, the man had loved him for his apparent genetics, and the love had been sweet and unconditional. Twistedly refreshing. Geln waved aside his guilt about deceiving Hernan. After all, it hadn't been *his* idea to play the role of a bastard nephew, and Geln's need of such an uncle had been urgent, if not critical. At least Geln genuinely liked Hernan—a real nephew might not. Apart from this small detail of completely misleading Hernan, Geln would treat him as well as he could.

Giving up further justification of his actions, Geln picked his way through the rotting trash behind Daltons property and ran through another business's backyard to reach a street where neither Erne nor Leo could see him. He walked over to a cheap carriage with some guy who held slack reins in his hand. The driver perked up immediately and even his horse slowly turned to look at Geln. Perhaps rumpled elite returning home after a rough night out was not unusual in this district. Perhaps there were those who liked to slum it.

"Take me to the Pyadrez residence on..." Shit, where were they, exactly?

The man smirked. "I know where the Pyadrezes live, sir."

"Oh, good, good." Geln had forgotten they didn't use addresses for elites. Everyone just knew. At least, men who drove hacks did.

He climbed in and shut the door before the driver had a chance to do so. Slightly bemused, the man climbed back up to his seat.

"I'm in a bit of a hurry, so I'd like us to get going," Geln called out the window. Before Leo or Erne—now Geln recalled a slight, young man who slipped back and forth between the countryside and the city—started looking for him. Not that the cadre couldn't trace him to the Pyadrezes, but he'd be protected there.

∞

Tobias managed to be both fascinated and bored. More lords had shown up than he'd expected. Officially parliament held one hundred seats, but he'd thought that fewer than sixty would regularly attend. Today, two-thirds of the families thought it important to at least make an appearance in the House. And a large number of them spoke.

Tobias didn't and Eberly did. Eberly sat across from him, loud and voluble, driving home his point that the Rimanian elite needed greater trade with the Alliance in order to maintain their standard of living.

Some lord stood up to complain about the lack of trade among Rimanians themselves and thought improving that should be their first priority. Eberly promised to look into it. The lord was from the north, an agricultural producer, and he wanted to be better paid for the dairy products he provided. Eberly suggested, with little subtlety, that proper payment would be more likely if the lord supported Eberly's motion.

At which point a red-faced Hernan stood. Shaking with anger, he accused Eberly of destroying everything the Rimanians had ever tried to accomplish. To emphasize Eberly's villainy, the man's thick finger jabbed the air a number of times. Hernan's fury made him inarticulate and, glancing around at the seemingly impassive faces, Tobias read contempt and boredom there. They weren't interested in this fire-and-brimstone act, this extremism. It was perhaps brave but also foolish to confront Eberly in this way. Tobias couldn't figure out whether or not Hernan had increased or decreased the safety of Geln just now. By making it clear that Hernan refused to be coerced or intimidated by Eberly and the police, possibly Geln would be left alone. Or possibly, Geln would be punished. How much did Hernan care about his new nephew, Tobias wondered.

He needed to warn Geln. Better the Pyadrez bastard stay in hiding until after Eberly's motion was passed or was refused passage. It had become obvious to Tobias that Eberly wanted to use Geln to manipulate Hernan's vote, and the vote was not scheduled until next week.

After the assembly Tobias made a beeline for Hernan Pyadrez, stopping ten feet away to briefly consider the best way to approach the older man. Hernan fished out a handkerchief with a shaky hand and wiped his brow. His whole body gave the slightest of shudders. Tobias took a deep breath—he wasn't sure how Hernan would respond to his request—and walked up to Geln's uncle.

As if sensing an intruder, Hernan turned just before Tobias was at his side. They'd been introduced more than once and Hernan recognized Tobias.

"What can I do for you?" The flatness of Hernan's voice took the edge off his rudeness. He sounded weary.

Tobias smiled politely. "I'd like to pay you a visit this afternoon. At your convenience, of course."

Hernan looked puzzled. "Pay me a visit?"

"Yes. I would like to become better acquainted with my new family." Tobias flashed his ring to emphasize that he represented the Smators.

"As you wish," Hernan said on a long sigh.

"Will you be in?"

"Unless the unexpected occurs, yes, I'll be in."

"Thank you so much, sir." Tobias bowed, left quickly before Hernan could manufacture an excuse for canceling the proposed visit, and strode towards the outer doors.

A familiar page stepped into Tobias's path, making it clear he was obliged to return to Eberly's side room and talk to the man again. Tobias wanted to move on, but decided following the page was a wiser course of action.

The Minister of State was much happier now. The assembly had apparently been a success and he was puffed up about it.

"Darrin tells me you talked to Pyadrez," Eberly said with some satisfaction.

Tobias disliked being watched. "Nice to know you're so on

top of things."

"That's my job."

Tobias resisted the temptation to glare at Darrin the page.

"Darrin, go get Reco." The page scooted off and Eberly smiled up at Tobias. "Reco will accompany you to the Pyadrezes'."

"What?"

"You heard me."

"That's not a good idea. My lord. The less attention paid to my visit and the less political the visit, the better. Since you wish me to, essentially, spy on them."

"Spy. That's a loaded word, Tobias." Eberly eyed him, then opened his hand. "Have you examined these interesting walls?"

"I haven't had much time to do anything of the sort."

"Of course not. But if you had, you would notice that the painter had an obsession with beautiful young men. Rather like you, I would hazard."

Tobias tried not to feel like someone had stolen his breath away, making it hard for him to breathe, even while he thought furiously, *fuck you, Eberly.* He was *not* going to respond to this blackmail. Absolutely not. No one had any proof. No one *could.* It was all in his head, for better or worse.

Eberly became all business, as if he'd never mentioned the *young men.* "Reco is a very appropriate companion for you. He's rising merchant class and has been welcomed into some elite homes. You can assure Hernan—"

"Hernan Pyadrez is a conservative who does not want any changes to the traditional lines drawn in society. He will not welcome this Reco into his home and you know it."

Eberly rose and walked over, speaking quietly. "Don't interrupt me again, do you understand?" He pointed a finger at

Tobias's chest, not quite touching the material of his suit.

Swallow, Tobias urged himself, *swallow your pride, swallow everything, and screw this bastard in the future.* "I apologize," he said in as neutral a tone as he could manage.

A knock. Eberly called, "Come in," and a man, presumably Reco, walked through the door. He appeared to be nondescript, bland-looking, a little older than Tobias, and smaller. Someone without much presence, a quality Eberly would like in everyone but his women.

Oh, his mother, his stupid mother. What was Tobias going to do about her relationship with this terrible man?

"Reco Niles, Tobias Smator." They shook hands. "Reco, you're to accompany Mr. Smator here to the Pyadrez residence."

"So, is Reco to be simply an acquaintance of mine?" As politely as possible, Tobias added, "The introduction may make Hernan suspicious. I only asked for permission to visit for myself, and Reco isn't family."

"Reco is in the grain business. He is interested in the Pyadrez rice."

Tobias nodded. "Where Hernan needs desperate help."

"Exactly. You'll be doing your new relative a favor and you can, if the information seems appropriate, let Hernan know it."

So Eberly thought that Hernan would trade Geln for profits from rice.

"Needless to say," continued Eberly, a smile playing at his mouth, "you'll have to gauge whether or not Hernan's knowledge of my involvement will help or hinder locating Geln."

Tobias nodded, watching Reco carefully. The man's eyes were alert, his expression well schooled. Tobias just hoped his own face didn't give too much away.

"Where will we meet?" Tobias asked Reco directly.

Eberly spoke for him. "Take Reco home with you for lunch. Then he can accompany you to Hernan's for tea."

Pointless to argue, Tobias decided, and nodded instead. "Very good. Let's get started, shall we?"

Reco inclined his head in agreement.

Chapter Thirteen

Sandorl didn't react to Reco Niles. The older man usually disapproved of Tobias's guests and once had the gall to call a visitor a wastrel. Tobias had been drunk and he'd laughed at the old man trying to influence Tobias's choice of friends.

But now Sandorl was poker-faced. Tobias supposed that Reco was dressed well enough to be an elite, and Sandorl wouldn't know who he really was.

His mother did, of course. She'd seen him at some social event or the other, although they hadn't been introduced. Reco's presence in her house was an obvious source of displeasure and she took him aside to let him know it. "Tobias, what is the point of inviting a *merchant* to lunch with you? You thought it would annoy me?"

"Not my choice, Mother. Eberly insisted I bring him here." Tobias knew he was glowering.

"*Lord* Eberly, dear," she corrected him while taking in that news. She lifted her chin and gave her head the slightest shake. "I'm sure the Minister of State has his reasons..."

"So do I," Tobias said tiredly. He still had to get through the meal, visit Hernan and warn Geln, all with Reco in tow.

She tilted her head, puzzled. "You don't think Lord Eberly has good reasons?"

"I can't understand why you're involved with him, Mother." His tone was low and accusing.

At that, his mother gathered her skirts together. "I am not in the mood for this today." She swept out of the room, leaving Tobias behind, head cocked in bafflement.

Not in the mood for what? Discussing Eberly's real character? Tobias scrubbed his face and returned to the dining room where Reco waited for him. The merchant refused to be uncomfortable, although Tobias could see that it took effort for Reco not to be intimidated.

Tobias dismissed the servant and had him close the glass doors behind him. He carefully cut his steak, then looked up and directly into Reco's eyes. The merchant took the inquiring gaze calmly.

"Why are you with me?" Tobias asked.

"Lord Eberly asked me to accompany you."

"I'm aware of that. Why?"

Reco gave a polite shrug and smiled. "I can't ask Lord Eberly his every reason. His mind works too cleverly for someone like me to follow."

"No doubt," said Tobias dryly, though he did not believe that this merchant bought the genetic superiority of the elites. Reco was too quietly observant, too watchful. "But you're interested, Reco."

Reco dabbed his mouth. "I beg your pardon?"

"To blend in better with, how can I put this, one of us? Well, you must appear a little more bored, a little less interested. As if you have seen it all before."

Reco's wariness receded into the bland gaze he'd used earlier at Eberly's. "I am only a merchant, Mr. Smator. I can only do so much."

Tobias rolled his eyes. "This attitude works with Eberly?"

"What attitude?"

"This self-deprecation that tries to suggest you're stupid. Eberly likes that. Perhaps I can learn from you."

Reco, not surprisingly, attended his food and said nothing further.

It was going to be a long afternoon.

Unlike Tobias's mother, Hernan Pyadrez did not recognize Reco Niles. Nor did the middle-aged man assume that he knew all the elite of Rimania. And so, frowning ever so slightly, he received both men in his drawing room. Despite Hernan's polite attempt to hide the displeasure of this unexpected visit from a stranger, Tobias felt distinctly uncomfortable. Hernan would be furious to know Reco was merchant class. Tobias decided to preempt Hernan's courteous questions about who Reco actually was.

"I admired your speech in the House today, my lord."

Hernan's mild frown deepened into bafflement. "As I'm sure you're aware, Mr. Smator, I am not the lord of the Pyadrez household."

"Of course, of course. Excuse me." Tobias's face and neck heated up. This was no doubt a sore point for Hernan, playing the role of the lord without actually being one. It was a common, but unenviable position, when the real lord of the family did not wish to live in Riman and sent someone in his stead.

Hernan glared while puffing angrily on a pipe that did not seem to want to light.

"My mistake."

Hernan breathed in a lungful of tobacco. Tobias hoped the

drug would soothe the older man. "You admired me making a fool of myself today, did you?"

"Not at all, sir. It takes courage to take a stand against the Minister of the State."

Hernan glanced briefly at Reco. Tobias winced and held up his hand. "Not that we want to discuss politics now. This is a purely social visit." He felt his smile dig into his cheeks most unconvincingly.

"Social, eh?" Hernan eyed Reco. "So, young man, perhaps you might tell me why you are visiting?"

"It is an honor, sir," replied Reco.

"Undoubtedly. But why is it an honor?"

Reco smiled nervously and glanced at Tobias, an appeal for help. Inwardly, Tobias groaned. So much for Eberly's brilliant idea that Hernan would welcome Reco Niles into his home.

Hernan addressed Tobias next. "Why is he here, Mr. Smator?"

"Well, sir..." Why the fuck did Eberly have to think Hernan was stupid? It made the current situation awkward.

"Why bring a merchant to visit me, Tobias?"

"He's a friend of mine."

"Really. And how long have you known each other?"

"A recent friend." Tobias stood up, restless.

Reco decided he needed to act. He leaned forward and made an unsophisticated if energetic pitch about his family's business in trade, in grain in particular, while Hernan listened attentively.

"I think," cut in Hernan, "you need to have a long discussion with my steward." Hernan called to his footman. "Larres, please take our new guest to Benon. They need to discuss business. Tell him I am keen to hear all about this young man's offer."

Hernan turned to Reco. "I assume this *is* an offer."

"Well, yes, but..." Reco didn't know how to proceed. At this point, Tobias was supposed to make it clear an excellent offer would be made in exchange for Geln. But Tobias remained silent.

"But what?" Hernan asked Reco patiently.

Reco cast another glance of appeal at Tobias before replying. "But I, we, had hoped to discuss the matter with *you*, sir."

"There is only one of you," Hernan observed. "And first you discuss it with my steward. I never do business any other way."

"There's always time for a change," suggested Reco with a weak smile.

"Now is not that time." Hernan spread his arm towards the door.

Tobias felt Reco's gaze fall on him, as if the merchant still hoped Tobias would step up and salvage the situation. But despite Eberly's orders, Tobias did not want to keep Reco with him. He needed a private word with Hernan.

Reco left the room and Hernan stood up. Paced. "What are you playing at, boy?"

Tobias thought seriously about that question and how to answer it. Hernan pretty much understood what was going on. "I thought I could learn something about politics from Eberly," he admitted.

"Your uncle would be ashamed of you. You stoop to pretending to befriend a merchant in order to get him into my home and, you hope, into my business. You want Eberly to buy my vote with this...this *offer*."

Tobias rubbed his forehead.

"And yet, Tobias, you don't seem wholly into this enterprise, nor suitably dismayed at being caught out."

"I'm actually supposed to find out where your nephew Geln is," said Tobias quietly.

Hernan stopped pacing and stared at Tobias for a long moment. "What an extraordinary confession, boy." He sat down with a thump. "Not only do you attempt to embroil me in one of Eberly's schemes, you then admit it all to me. Do you think I want this information?"

"No."

"Could you manage nothing more elegant?"

"No." Tobias sighed. "Eberly insisted I visit him when Geln was under house guard. That's how I became involved. Eberly wanted me to explain the situation to Geln, who didn't understand what was going on."

"For God's sakes, boy, don't tell me more. Better I don't know a thing. Report back to Eberly and tell him all you've done this visit is ask about Geln and I, being the suspicious, cantankerous old man I am, said little. Once I recognized Reco was a merchant, I became very closed-mouthed indeed."

Tobias nodded agreement. "But, won't Geln be safe here? If he is here?"

Hernan tilted his head, puzzled. "Why are you concerned about someone you've barely met? Charming as my nephew may be... Frankly, I wish I didn't *have* to be involved, but family is family and I don't have much else. If I did, I wouldn't be down here playing the lord."

"Yes, sir."

"I don't want to see you again. You've offended me by bringing a merchant disguised as an elite into my house and I don't like youngsters anyway. Now, go get your 'friend' and leave."

"If you agree—"

Hernan stood. "I don't want to hear it, understand? The less I know of Eberly's plans, the better. And the less *you* know the better for you. There's not much you can do about your mother, I suppose, but stay away from that man. He uses people up." As soon as his footman returned, Hernan ordered the servant to fetch Reco. Then Hernan disappeared, Tobias waited for the merchant's arrival and they were rather unceremoniously shown out the door.

Reco glanced worriedly at Tobias. "That wasn't how the visit was supposed to go."

"No," agreed Tobias.

"What will you tell Lord Eberly?"

"That Hernan Pyadrez recognized you. Failure, for both of us, followed that simple fact."

"Right. You're right. That's what we'll say."

Tobias wondered what kind of power Eberly held over Reco that the man feared the consequences of this unsuccessful outing. "You couldn't stay in the drawing room with us after a conservative like Hernan knew you were a merchant."

"No." Reco bit his lip.

Tobias felt a bit sorry for him. "Do you have to work with Eberly, Reco?"

Reco simply looked away into the distance, unwilling to reveal his circumstances. Then the merchant's gaze sharpened and Tobias followed his line of sight. A rather dilapidated old coach, nothing Hernan would be seen with, arrived at the end of the drive.

And out stepped a familiar tall, lanky figure. Geln.

Tobias's heart leapt even while he thought, *shit.* Not *now.*

Not when Eberly's spy was here to see Geln. Identify him. Inform on him.

But wait, Reco wouldn't necessarily recognize Geln.

"Well," announced Tobias. "Look who's here."

Reco gave Tobias a questioning glance.

"My cousin. Ruel. Give us a moment, will you?" Tobias took long strides forward.

Geln shaded his eyes with his hand, squinting to see who was walking towards him with great purpose. The broad shoulders, the brown, unruly hair—Tobias. An odd feeling shifted in Geln's chest, like he was pleased, reassured even. He hadn't experienced such an emotion for ages and his lips curved into a smile. But as Tobias approached, Geln saw that his face was set in stiff lines, his expression difficult to interpret.

And someone seemed to be chasing after the long-legged Tobias, someone Geln didn't recognize.

Geln straightened his jacket, though it was so rumpled the action was useless. He rubbed his unshaven face and found himself regretting that, by Rimanian standards, he was not at his attractive best. Even if he himself rather liked the disheveled look he sported.

"Hallo, Tob—"

"Ruel!" Tobias practically shouted, bearing down on him. "I certainly didn't expect to see *you* here. What brings you this way, *cousin?*"

Okay, I got it, thought Geln, while Tobias strenuously pumped Geln's hand and gazed at Geln, eyes wide and meaningful. He particularly liked the way Tobias's eyes darkened as his pupils dilated.

"Gee, 'cousin'," answered Geln, "I'm not entirely sure. Maybe my fiancée, Jina?" The stranger, who'd caught up, frowned as he glanced between Tobias and Geln.

"Dressed like that?" Tobias forced a laugh. "I somehow doubt it."

Geln looked down at himself. Tobias was right. Even drunk, Ruel wouldn't arrive looking like this.

"Actually, I was looking for you, Tobias. As you well know." Geln suppressed the urge to wink.

"Great." After a pause, Tobias added, "Mother must have told you I was here."

Geln noted that the stranger, his expression now one of polite indifference, appeared to be losing interest in their conversation.

"You know, this is actually quite convenient, you coming here in a hack." Tobias turned to the stranger. "Reco, why don't you take the hack to wherever you're going and my cousin can accompany me home."

Reco considered this option deeply, as if it contained many complications. In the end, looking a bit defeated, he nodded.

"Wonderful." Geln beamed. "But, please, let me settle with the driver first." He sprinted back to the hack and climbed up to talk to the man. "Look," he whispered urgently. "I don't want my family to know I spent the night at Daltons. Not a word to anyone. Say I flagged you down near the city's center, okay?" Geln pressed a generous coin into the driver's hand. "I hope I can reward you again." Geln winked at the driver who at least seemed open to this suggestion.

"Sure, mate." The man tipped his hat in thanks.

Geln scrambled down again.

By this time Tobias and Reco were at the hackney carriage.

"My cousin is a little eccentric," stated Tobias.

Geln assumed he was not supposed to clamber up on these types of carriages.

Reco, who Tobias evidently was not going to introduce, nodded stiffly.

"So, goodbye." Tobias and Reco shook hands. Tobias stood silently beside Geln, tension streaming off him as he waited for Reco to leave the drive.

Geln followed his lead and said nothing. Once Reco was out of hearing range though, he could keep quiet no longer. "So, *cousin*, am I lucky to have found you here?"

Tobias gave Geln a quick once-over. "You're lucky you're my cousin. That man reports to Eberly."

That took the wind out of Geln's sails. He'd rather been enjoying this little deception, stupid as it had been. "Shit."

"Eberly is watching for you here. I think you had better duck into my carriage."

"Oh hell," said Geln, not moving. The whole idea of Eberly and house guard made it hard to think.

"Get in the carriage, Geln." There was an edge of panic in Tobias's voice. When Geln didn't move, Tobias asked, "What? You don't trust me?"

"I don't know," Geln confessed. But Tobias seemed so earnest and Geln was running out of choices of who, if anyone, he could trust. He turned and walked to the carriage, allowed Tobias's man to open the door, and stepped into the interior.

Chapter Fourteen

Geln sat opposite a silent Tobias and, in the confines of the carriage, he could smell the man's sweat, some fear, some excitement. He couldn't help but react, especially in this closed space. He moved to reach for Tobias, but stopped as Kleemach asked, "Now, what are you doing?"

As Tobias watched Geln's hand drop away, he tilted his head in slight question.

Geln chose to ignore the AI. Even if he slumped in the corner and used sound-damping to answer Klee, the strange lip-syncing would freak Tobias out. With reason.

"This has got to be the most unusual date I've ever had," Geln announced. It was easier to focus on Tobias and his infatuation. The bigger situation was almost unthinkable, and Geln found himself fiddling with his watch, as if he wanted to remove it.

Given to high color, Tobias reddened further, but the comment also gave Tobias courage. "Your other dates were..."

"Were?" prompted Geln.

"Were women?" Tobias stared down at his shoes, which Geln found rather endearing. His own precarious situation made him vulnerable to this kind of sentiment.

"Well, no, Tobias."

Tobias swiftly turned his head, eyes wide and questioning, and Geln reacted strongly. Blood rushed south and he wanted to grab Tobias, hold on. If nothing else, this hellish situation on Rimania required a good fuck, though not in the carriage. And probably it shouldn't be with an apparent male virgin, either, but what the hell. Time for something new.

Tobias's breathing was shallow and quick, as if his heart had sped up. "I didn't think. That is. Well, they say, and I know most of what they say is *crap*"—the harsh intensity of the one word spoke volumes—"but they say, you know, that they bred *out* homosexuality."

Geln gave the faintest of smiles, because he didn't think it funny, but he could commiserate. "I don't think genes explain everything. Do you?"

"No. *No.*" Tobias was twisting his hands something terrible.

Geln reached out and grabbed them, separated them gently and leaned forward. "Tobias, where are we going?"

"Uh." Tobias sucked in a shocked breath as Geln touched him, rubbing a thumb over the backs of Tobias's knuckles.

Responsive, Geln noted approvingly. God, he needed someone who would respond to him. He moved closer. "I guess it's not a good idea to exit this carriage half-dressed?"

"No!" Tobias straightened, evidently horrified by the idea, which seemed to bring him back to earth, unfortunately. He withdrew his hands. "They can't know."

"They?" Geln murmured.

Tobias gave a crooked smile. "It's different where you're from?"

"It is, actually."

Tobias frowned, a line formed between his eyes and there was question there.

"No joke," Geln said flatly. "I don't tease like that." He lifted a hand to gently trace the line on Tobias's brow and it disappeared. "Where are we going?" he repeated. "I hope it's somewhere safe for me, for us."

"My manor is big. I can hide you from my mother."

"Hide me from your mother." Geln laughed, too loud. He rubbed a hand over his face, trying to keep himself together. Finding something hysterically funny at this point in time might say more about his state of mind than the situation. "Reminds me of my teenage years, sneaking into my boyfriend's house."

"Boyfriend?" Tobias repeated the word with some awe.

Oops. That little nugget wouldn't make much sense to Tobias. Well, nothing for it but to distract him. As the younger man watched, brown eyes bright with emotion, Geln reached for Tobias. First, Geln speared fingers through Tobias's thick, silky hair, causing him to shudder at just that contact. Slowly, Geln brought Tobias's head lower, until their lips touched.

It was too much, now, when they were almost home. Overwhelmed, Tobias shoved Geln away from him. It almost hurt to do it, but he could barely breathe and he didn't want to kiss Geln, their first kiss, in a carriage with Sandorl driving.

Geln didn't look affronted, he merely lifted his eyebrows.

This amazing excitement, this arousal, was completely clouding Tobias's mind. He could hardly think, he wanted to fall all over Geln and instead he pushed him aside. But the fact remained—he had to sneak Geln into his house without anyone, except Sandorl if necessary, noticing. "I need to *think*, for a moment." Tobias's voice sounded positively strangled.

Though he didn't speak, Geln's mouth quirked. Then he looked distracted, as if listening to something and his gaze became diffuse. Tobias cocked an ear, but only heard their

152

carriage moving down the road.

Refocusing on Tobias, Geln said, "You said we're going to your place, Tobias. Even if Reco didn't, your mother is certainly going to recognize me."

"There's a wing of the house that is closed. You can hide in it."

Geln appeared to find this idea amusing. "I don't know much about closed wings. Is no one likely to go there?"

"That's correct. And it's near my rooms."

"Wonderful." Geln moved to sit beside Tobias, instead of across from him, and draped one leg over Tobias's.

Despite his dick, which had never been this hard—Tobias thought he might explode—he couldn't stop thinking about the bigger situation. Especially given that the carriage didn't afford much privacy. On the other hand, when Geln focused on Tobias, he felt incredibly gratified. Geln was charming, beautiful, special. However, Tobias wasn't the only one to think Geln was special, and his worries came to the forefront. "Aren't you concerned, Geln? Eberly wants you. Badly."

The expression on Geln's face dimmed and he withdrew with the mildest of shivers. "I try not to think about it. Not necessarily the wisest of strategies, I know." He retreated into the corner and brought a finger to his mouth.

Tobias heard the click of a bitten nail. "I don't remember you biting nails."

"New habit."

"You were always so poised."

Geln flicked him a glance. "I was, wasn't I?"

"I suppose it's been difficult for you, entering a different level of society, leaving the life you knew."

"Yes." One heartfelt word.

"I don't cope well with change myself."

"I don't have to stay with you, Tobias." It was a quiet offer, said as Geln gazed into the corner of the carriage.

"*No.*" Tobias spoke the word as emphatically as possible. "That's not what I'm saying or why I..." But he couldn't describe his reaction to Geln's touching him. Words eluded him. "Please. Do stay. Just, we're almost there." Tobias realized his hands were fists and tried to unclench them. "I don't know how you can be so relaxed."

Geln's face had opened up and there was no amusement now, just a kind of gratitude. "Thank you for that. And, by the way, it's an act, sweetheart. I am not relaxed."

Stupid, how he liked Geln calling him sweetheart. Tobias felt his face flush with pleasure. Geln saw the reaction, but instead of smiling or laughing at Tobias, Geln looked even more intent.

Tobias broke their eye contact and put his red face outside of the window. "Sandorl," he called. "Take the carriage directly to the stables, please."

Sandorl cast a glum look back to Tobias. "Yes, sir."

"And Sandorl?"

"Yes, sir?"

"Absolutely no word to anyone about the, uh, addition, today."

"If you think that will help, sir." Said in tones that suggested *nothing* would help. Then again, Sandorl was a pessimist.

Tobias pulled his head back in. "How well do you know our house?"

Geln remained in the corner, eyes now half-lidded. "Better than I should. I hope you don't mind."

154

Tobias pushed suspicion away. "Can you enter the servants' side door and sneak up to my room? I'll meet you there and get you to the wing. Needless to say—"

"No one should see me."

"Right."

"It occurs to me that you might be endangering yourself."

"Nah," scoffed Tobias, terrified that Geln might take off. He *needed* Geln to stay with him. "I can handle Eberly, especially through my mother."

Geln looked doubtful. "I don't think your mother is easy to 'handle'. I was rather hoping you'd tell me that Eberly can't really touch you."

"He can't."

"Hmmm. You're telling me what you think I want to hear."

"I want you to stay, Geln." Tobias winced at how desperate he sounded.

"Sure?" Geln's smile was wry, even a little wary.

"I am positive."

Geln leaned forward to place a palm against Tobias's hot cheek. Tobias tried not to jump at the contact and failed. Geln rubbed a thumb across Tobias's lips and murmured, "I hope I'm worth it," before he pushed open his door and jumped out. Tobias reached over and shut the door. This way, Sandorl could pretend he hadn't noticed.

Geln sprinted to the house, ducked inside and waited, in order to get his bearings and a little help from above.

"Someone is approaching from the hall to the left, so step into the hall to your right," Kleemach said.

Geln did, no longer annoyed by his helpful companion.

"Okay," continued the AI, "you can get to Tobias's rooms if you follow this hall down to the end and go up the backstairs." Geln jogged. As expected, Klee resumed his scolding, which he'd started in the carriage. "This is worse than a one-night fuck, you idiot."

"You already said that," Geln replied through gritted teeth. He hadn't enjoyed Klee's earlier rant. If it kept this up, Geln would have to remove the watch for sex with Tobias, or the AI would drive him crazy. Taking the steps two at a time, Geln arrived on the second level.

"Go straight," Klee instructed. "You think sex will help you, but Tobias is in love with you."

"Like you would know. Shut the fuck up or I'll throw you away."

"You wouldn't!" The AI sounded genuinely alarmed.

"Don't push me, Klee. I'm *this* near the edge."

He was. For it was true, what Kleemach had declared earlier—at home Geln wouldn't have touched Tobias with a ten-foot pole. Lovelorn, nervous Tobias, who wanted to talk more than fuck, who shivered at Geln's touch.

That said, Tobias had been formed by Rimanian society and, like it or not, Geln had become fond of the young man. The task of getting Tobias into bed diverted Geln—and God knows he *needed* to be diverted. After six months in the field, it was a huge relief to see love in someone's eyes. Granted the love was temporary and misled and largely fueled by infatuation, but Geln refused to dwell on that reality.

"To the left, to the left," Klee said irritably, and Geln circled back and took the passage that led to Tobias's rooms.

"Thank you, Klee. I do appreciate your directions."

"Not all of them."

Geln slipped into Tobias's sitting room and flung himself down on the couch. "Where's Tobias?" he asked.

"He's coming. Just telling mommy about his visit with Hernan and how he ditched Reco the merchant."

"Hey, how do you know what they're saying? Is the whole house rigged?"

"Yes, you knew that."

"I suppose I did. But that was before I planned to have sex in it. Oh well."

"No sense throwing me away, unless you plan to throw me far."

"I need to forget about you for a while."

"Fine." Klee now sounded huffy. "But if someone other than Tobias is likely to stumble upon you, I could give you warning."

"Thank you, dear. I do appreciate it."

"Full of affection today, are we? Next you'll be wanting to kiss *me*."

"Klee," warned Geln.

"Okay, I'll sign off. Tobias is marching up the stairs. His adrenaline's really pumping but you already know he's excited about you."

Geln smiled. Looking after Tobias emotionally, and sexually, was a fair trade for being saved from Eberly. It wasn't a long-term plan, but right now he didn't want to deal with long-term plans.

Tobias entered the room, somewhat breathless, and quickly shut the door before turning on Geln, gaze intent, warm and a little angry. Very attractive. "How did you know it would be me? I could have been a servant, my mother even. You should have hid."

"I recognized your footfalls."

Tobias rolled his eyes in disbelief. "You're overconfident. That was my first impression of you."

Geln grinned and stood up. "Actually I'm insecure. I just hide it well."

Tobias eyed him, unsure how to respond. "Right then. Let's go in a room deeper, you're less likely to be seen."

Geln obliged by walking over and opening the bedroom door, and like a butler, he swept his arm down to indicate Tobias should enter first.

Tobias stopped and frowned, insisting Geln precede him. "Don't do that. You're not my inferior."

"What if I were? You'd no longer be interested?" Geln found he was curious, but only in a theoretical way. He'd claim he were God right now, if that would attract Tobias.

"You're just full of games, aren't you?"

"It's the best way to be sometimes."

"I..." Tobias waved his hands uncertainly and Geln caught them. The blunt, warm fingers gripped back and Geln shivered.

"What are you doing, waving at me?"

Tobias gazed, eyes darkening yet again, breath catching.

"No answer to that?"

He swallowed and Geln pulled Tobias closer so their bodies were a hairsbreadth from each other. Geln could feel Tobias's heat.

"I don't play games," Tobias blurted.

"Where did you learn to be so honest?" Geln touched his cheek and Tobias jerked slightly, not in recoil, in reaction, as if ready to explode. Geln's heart beat faster, wondering exactly what he was about to unleash, but not caring enough to stop it.

"I don't know," Tobias answered rather hopelessly.

It was time to move on. "You're not supposed to be honest. You're supposed to take off your jacket." Geln yanked it down, capturing Tobias's arms in the material. Then he pushed Tobias, like a martinet, over onto the bed. He clambered on top of the young man whose looks, normally carefully bland, became animated.

"Um, Geln?" said Tobias, his voice thick.

"Yes?"

"Do you think I can't get out from under you?"

"Prove it, Tobias."

Tobias jerked both arms free, ripping his jacket. They grappled. Geln was stronger than he looked, but not strong enough to keep Tobias down. There was a strange energy to the man, almost desperate, which in its odd way matched the panic Tobias had felt earlier when he wasn't sure what the hell he was doing. Though he'd had no choice in bringing Geln home. He simply couldn't let Geln walk into another of Eberly's traps.

Tobias shook those thoughts free and focused on this half-dressed *man* he wrestled. Despite the pressure and energy, Geln was just not that heavy. Tobias twisted, wrested his arm free again, and pulled Geln over. He bounced off the bed and slammed into Geln, harder than expected. For a moment, his full weight was on Geln and to his surprise Geln went absolutely stiff.

"Marscht!" yelled Geln, or some weird guttural word like that, and he bucked under Tobias. Geln's voice went higher. "Don't. *Shit.*" It was almost a plea.

Tobias took his weight off Geln, though he stayed astride. Somehow, Tobias thought that if he pulled completely away that would be the end of their contact. Which he couldn't face.

"Easy." Tobias tentatively smoothed back some of Geln's loose hair. To his relief, the gesture calmed Geln. He did it again, liking the feel of Geln's dark hair under his palm. Then he brushed fingertips across Geln's cheek, touching him as Geln had touched Tobias earlier. "Did I hurt you? I thought..." But he couldn't say, *I thought that was what you wanted, what I was supposed to do.* It sounded too immature. Tobias slid back a little and gently tugged Geln up to sitting, so they were facing each other.

Geln's manic energy was gone, as was the panic.

"Marscht?" Tobias asked and found himself rubbing Geln's arms. He hadn't thought he would touch Geln like this. Geln, who seemed to relax, even briefly closing his eyes as he shuddered out a sigh.

"My fault," added Tobias, when Geln didn't say anything.

Geln's wary expression softened and he shook his head once, emphatic. "No, not your fault."

"I can be gentle." Tobias remembered how one woman had told him in a less-than-flattering way that he was ridiculously gentle.

While Geln smiled at those words, the smile was self-deprecating and wry. He looked down and began to work on Tobias's fastenings, and Tobias let out a huge breath, feeling as if he'd been granted a reprieve.

"I overreact to the sensation of being smothered," Geln offered as explanation, which didn't make total sense. They'd been wrestling, but Tobias let it go. "Fucking clothes," Geln added. He gave a snort of frustration and grabbed the collar on each side to rip Tobias's shirt down the middle, not so gently divesting Tobias of clothing. Though he wanted to help, Tobias let Geln undress himself because there was a certain hands-off manner to the dark, green-eyed beautiful man in his bed.

Tobias didn't know what to do with the tension shaking him now, and the trembling had nothing to do with fear. Geln saw it, they locked eyes for a moment before he gave a slow smile. "Don't worry, babe, I'll take care of you."

As Geln's long fingers wrapped around Tobias's shaft, he let out a groan. A thumb circled his head, but he didn't have time for this and he pushed into Geln's hand, begging. To Tobias's immense relief, Geln crawled close to drape legs over Tobias's thighs and Tobias forgot about everything but Geln. He speared fingers through Geln's hair and grabbed on, anchoring his hand there as his mouth came down on Geln's. Teeth clashed for a moment before Geln gave way and tongues mated, all the while Geln rubbed his cock, in fact, rubbed their cocks together.

It was too much, too fast. Before he was ready, Tobias lost himself, his entire body going stiff as he came in Geln's hand. He dropped his face onto Geln's shoulder, turning towards his neck, trying to hide how overwhelmed he felt, trying to muffle the sounds escaping his throat. Because despite the euphoria that came with release, embarrassment would follow. It always did.

"Been a while?" Geln murmured, tracing a reassuring pattern on Tobias's back.

Tobias kissed the tendon between neck and shoulder, tasting Geln, drinking him in, not wanting to apologize for his hair-trigger, not wanting to say he'd been avoiding women the past year. He skimmed a palm up and down Geln, thinking that while his spine was a little too pronounced, his muscular back was fascinating. He liked this hard body in his arms.

"You can come up for air, you know," said Geln, and Tobias brought a hand around to lightly flick Geln's nipple. Unwilling to meet Geln's gaze, he nipped Geln's earlobe, gently. Resisting the urge to push Geln down, Tobias kissed him full on the mouth and they mated for a while, until he realized Geln was working on himself.

As Tobias moved to take over or at least help out, Geln stayed his hand. Tobias pulled back to argue, and Geln said, a little shakily, "Just hold me this time, okay?"

"Sure?" Tobias asked, and Geln nodded, the way his neck bent seeming vulnerable to Tobias. He caressed that neck while Geln's breathing changed. He tightened his embrace, letting his fingers find muscle and bone under skin, fascinated by the hard planes, by the muscle, by holding this man, in his arms, in his bed.

Geln went still, no sound, though his body trembled as he came.

"Hey." Tobias wanted to reassure, though reassure about what, he didn't know. Geln's breathing started up again as he pushed away, while Tobias kept him in the cage of his arms until that green gaze lifted to his. There was a kind of defiance that Tobias didn't understand. "Geln?"

"Sorry. Not used to being just...held."

Tobias frowned. "You asked me to."

"I know." The defiance remained.

"I liked it," he added in case that wasn't clear.

"So did I." The faint smile on Geln's face allowed Tobias to relax.

"I'll try to slow down," Tobias offered.

At that, Geln grinned. "No worries. I liked it too."

Afterwards, Geln couldn't push Tobias away, although it would have been the wise thing to do. Create distance as soon as possible. Should have been possible after just a handjob. Instead a naked Tobias stretched out beside him, curving slightly to increase the skin-to-skin contact as if he was hungry for it.

"You know, Tobias," Geln began.

"Yes." His brown eyes were eagerly alert and the glow there was flattering. Especially given how Geln had panicked early on and later wouldn't even let Tobias touch his dick. Thinking about it, his face grew hot with embarrassment.

"You surprised me," Geln admitted unwisely on a long sigh.

Tobias nuzzled Geln's neck and he couldn't push his new fuck away right now. Soon, though. Soon. Geln traced a finger down Tobias's biceps.

At that, Tobias propped himself up on an elbow and gazed down, a lock of hair falling over his brow fetchingly. "I still wonder why you saved my life."

Oh, yeah. Funny how he'd forgotten about that.

"And *how* for that matter."

Geln tried to withdraw and an arm came down, trapping him. He stiffened and immediately Tobias let go. Kissed him instead. "You don't think I'm going to hurt you, do you?" Worry lurked in his gaze.

"No," Geln scoffed.

His reaction confused Tobias. "You can't know the questions I have for you," he said very seriously.

"I don't like being interrogated."

"Come on, don't use ugly words for, for..." Tobias's face fell, quite unable to complete the no-doubt-sentimental sentence.

"Hey." Despite himself, Geln palmed his lover's cheek. "I can't answer your questions."

"I'm hiding you. You can trust me." That awful shine in those brown eyes threatened to undo Geln.

"You *shouldn't* trust me."

Suspicion flared briefly in Tobias before he evidently decided this talk was some kind of insecurity on Geln's part.

"I want to take care of you." It was a question more than a statement.

"You're too easy, Tobias. I'm surprised someone hasn't tumbled and used you many times before."

"Well, they have but women don't have quite the same effect on me."

Geln couldn't help himself. He curled up against Tobias again. He was so tired, and Tobias's odd mix of protectiveness and neediness so seductive. "Am I safe here?" he mumbled into Tobias's arm.

"I know you have an interesting story to tell me, but I can wait for that." Tobias was sweet thinking sex meant intimacy meant sharing life stories.

For now, Geln wasn't going to think about anything else but Tobias's naiveté, and the wonderful smell of this young, beautiful body that wanted to share his, no matter how fumbling and awkward their sex had been. He let himself float into sleep.

Chapter Fifteen

Tobias stared down at the man sleeping on his arm. This hadn't been what he'd expected, though what he'd expected would have been hard to describe. He slid away from Geln, careful not to wake him. In his place, Geln's wiry, muscular arm stretched across the bed, as if reaching.

It was the time of day Tobias usually went down to dine or snack, depending on whether he was going out that evening. Tonight he would dine in. With Geln. He'd ask for a large amount of food to be brought to his sitting room and they'd share it when Geln woke. But first he should go and chat to Sandorl or the cook, as he usually did. He needed to keep to his routine as much as possible so no one—outside Sandorl—would suspect a stowaway.

Picking up his clothes, he realized he had to get rid of his shirt. His ripped jacket wouldn't be particularly noteworthy, but his shirt with its broken fastenings didn't make a lot of sense outside of this room. He temporarily hid it in his pillow.

He spent a good ten minutes doing up another shirt—he couldn't call in Sandorl for the job—then marched out, trying to keep a silly smile off his face.

"Tobias," called his mother from the drawing room as he passed by. He forced himself to stop and turn back though he didn't want to be too closely examined by his mother. He felt scatterbrained and slightly euphoric and not very good at hiding those feelings.

To his utter dismay, Ruel was visiting.

His cousin rose and shook hands, as if he couldn't be more pleased to see Tobias. Ruel didn't seem drunk, even if he was nursing a glass of whiskey. If nothing else, his cousin's presence dampened Tobias's spirits.

"I was just about to send for you," said his mother. "But I knew you'd be down at this hour. Tobias is always so predictable."

"I try," he said, tone too wry, because his mother glanced at him with some surprise. He sat carefully in a chair, trying to act in character. "Ruel isn't predictable," he pointed out, to take the focus off himself. "He hasn't visited us for years."

"But he wasn't lord then. We do appreciate your presence now, my dear," she assured his cousin.

"Why thank you." Ruel sketched a quick bow while sitting.

"You changed your shirt, Tobias. How strange. I do wish you'd get the servants to attend to you more. It's quite obvious you fastened this one yourself." She touched his collar and his color rose. Tobias hoped he looked irritated, not embarrassed. At the end of a sigh, she added, "But never mind that now. We all have our quirks, don't we, Ruel?"

Ruel nodded agreeably.

"We do hope you can stay and dine with us?" she asked.

God, no. Tobias wanted to get back upstairs and feed Geln, who didn't appear to have eaten all day. Besides, he was too thin. Briefly Tobias thought of ribs and elbows and hipbones.

"Tobias?" asked his mother.

"Yes?" He straightened.

"Ruel was wondering if you'd like to take a stroll." She

looked at him meaningfully. "Such a considerate request. He knows how much you enjoy wandering the countryside."

Tobias didn't know if he was more annoyed by the request or that its phrasing made him sound like a daft child. Well, taking a stroll was better than dining with Ruel. It would mean less time away from Geln.

Ruel smiled politely, so un-Ruel-like. "I have a previous engagement for dinner, but I would enjoy a chat with you outside, Tobias."

Tobias nodded. "Let me leave some instructions with my man and I'll be right back."

"Honestly, Tobias, summon Sandorl here. That's his job."

"No. I'll be back momentarily."

He left swiftly, caught Sandorl with the cook and gave his dinner instructions to the kitchen, along with other careful directions to not disturb his rooms. Sandorl, after a pointed pause of disapproval, agreed, and Tobias, feeling a little harried, returned to his guest.

Ruel was taking leave of his mother who said rather fawningly, "Please, come again. Come for dinner."

"After I'm married I'm certain that Jina and I would enjoy such an evening." Ruel bowed, leaving his mother in the drawing room.

They walked outside.

"What are you doing here?" demanded Tobias.

Ruel gazed at him appraisingly. "You seem very healthy, my boy. Invigorated, even."

"I feel fine."

"New shirt and everything," Ruel observed, amused.

"It's not new. What do you want, Ruel?"

"I have sources, these days, cousin. They're quite fun. I'm exploring their accuracy."

Tobias ground his teeth. "Tell me what's going on. You don't like my mother's company, or mine for that matter."

Ruel acted positively wounded. "Of course I like *your* company, Tobias."

"Not lately." What did Ruel want from him? "Ruel," he said coaxingly, "what fun are you talking about?"

He grinned. "My *sources* tell me that Geln Marac is here."

Tobias felt the blood drain from his face.

"She's right!" crowed Ruel. He executed a short victory dance. "Wonderful. She's amazing."

Though he felt blindsided, Tobias tried to marshal the energy to deny Geln's presence. "What are you talking about? My mother doesn't see Geln Marac anymore." He needed to make his voice sound less weak, more convincing.

"Your mother?"

"Well, she, well, he was, you know."

"Fucking your mother?" Ruel appeared to find this amusing.

"No. Yes. I assume..." Tobias didn't know what was best to say.

"Or perhaps he was just a sycophant. She probably wasn't his type, eh?" Ruel reached over to pull at Tobias's collar and Tobias batted his hand away angrily. "Looks like a scratch there, cuz. Been busy?"

"If you don't tell me what the fuck you want, I am going back inside."

"What a threat! My goodness, I'm quivering at the thought you might follow through. Anyway, who cares about Geln Marac? I simply wanted to test the waters, double-check my
168

source." Ruel chucked Tobias on the shoulder. "Go back to *your* fun. Don't worry. I won't tell."

"Why are you here?" demanded Tobias, his voice too sharp. "Apart from my mother's interest in seeing you now that you're lord."

"*That* was quite the change. She used to display nothing but contempt for me."

Tobias remained silent. Ruel usually liked to talk.

His cousin leaned towards him in confidentiality. Tobias smelled the whiskey on his breath. "Ann-Marie claims she is a fortuneteller."

Ann-Marie's involvement with this filled Tobias with foreboding. "I see."

"She just proved it."

"How?"

"She predicted that the missing Geln Marac would show up here. I knew your mother would be too discreet to mention it, but I thought you would give it away." Ruel frowned, as if suddenly struck by a thought. "Hey, why are you so upset?"

"I'm not upset." Tobias rubbed his forehead, trying furiously to think of what else he needed to ask Ruel. "You say that Ann-Marie *foretold* Geln's presence here?"

"Yes."

"When?"

"This afternoon."

Not exactly foretelling, but nevertheless how did that woman know? Spies?

"Ruel. What are you going to do with this new source of information? Share it with others?"

He was beaming now. "I'll sound very clever, knowing what

others don't."

"And if others guess about Ann-Marie's gifts? Then what will happen? I'd suggest you save your inside knowledge for something more meaningful, more substantial."

"Eberly would like to know about this bastard's whereabouts," Ruel mused. "And that asshole thinks I'm stupid."

"Okay, but think, Ruel. It's more useful to know information that others don't know."

"Not if you don't tell them about it!"

Tobias grabbed his shoulders. "*Listen.* Eberly has bigger fish to fry than Geln Marac. Wait until you can really impress the Minister of State and give him *that* information." At Ruel's evident doubt, Tobias pushed harder. "Besides, nobody likes a bearer of bad news. Eberly is very jealous when it comes to my mother."

"I suppose you're right." Ruel now looked disgruntled.

"Is this the first time Ann-Marie foretold something?" asked Tobias.

"No."

"So you believe her ability is real?"

"Oh, yes," he said, brightening again.

"Great. Save it for when you can demand a promotion for yourself." Tobias rubbed his hands and threw out a wild possibility. "You want to be the next Speaker of the House, like your father, don't you? Wait till you can give Eberly something he really needs and trade on that."

Evidently much struck by this suggestion, Ruel straightened at the thought. "Brilliant, Tobias." Ruel chucked Tobias on the shoulder again.

"Was there anything else?" Tobias asked, anxious to return

and find Geln. Make sure he was there, make sure he was safe.

"I guess not." Ruel looked over to his carriage. "Hey, you were supposed to report to me after attending the House this morning."

"I thought you weren't interested."

"I'm not. But Ann-Marie is. If I don't ask you about it, she'll get pissed, perhaps not share new information with me."

"I'll come by tomorrow." It might be wise to see Ann-Marie again, see just how much influence she wielded over Ruel with this new "foretelling" ability. When had it developed? Overnight? Personally, Tobias would like to divine what she planned to do with knowledge of Geln's whereabouts.

"Great. I'm ready to leave. And you have places to go, people to see."

Tobias had never found Ruel's smirk so annoying but he put out his hand and they shook. Ruel, to Tobias's great relief, departed.

Tobias forced himself to walk calmly back into the house to the steward's room where he surveyed a wall of keys and picked up the one he needed for the closed wing. He called for his dinner and marched upstairs to wait in his sitting room for Sandorl to bring his meal.

Sandorl arrived promptly but couldn't resist making snide comments about his master's healthy appetite before Tobias dismissed him. Once the door was shut, he listened for Sandorl's footsteps going down the hall. At last, Tobias entered his bedroom, carrying all the food with him.

He almost dropped the tray. Geln was gone. The bed was empty, though there was proof of an earlier presence. His unruly heart beat wildly while Tobias spoke Geln's name. He even checked under the bed and in the wardrobe.

Why was he gone? Tobias rubbed his face vigorously, embarrassed by the shocked tears that threatened.

Calm, calm. Perhaps Geln hadn't thought it safe to stay here alone, perhaps Geln had tried to find a better hiding place. And where would that be? In the closed wing Tobias had promised him?

With trembling hands, Tobias placed the tray on his bedside table and left his room.

He patted the key in his pocket. The closed wing was locked and Geln couldn't get in, but Tobias walked over there anyway. Where else could Geln have gone?

He wouldn't have just taken off. Geln liked him. Tobias could tell by his touch. He'd learned a while ago to recognize the touch of a woman who cared, because then he had to break off the relationship. He could have sworn Geln had *liked* him. No doubt Geln had had more exciting affairs and Tobias hadn't done a heck of a lot but come during their first round, but still.

Tobias arrived at the door and tried the handle. Locked. He inserted the key into the lock and turned it quietly. Slipped inside.

"Hello?" he called tentatively. His mind flitted all over the place. It was dark in the hall, with its closed doors. He hadn't thought to bring a candle or a torch. He waited for his eyes to adjust, let out a shaky breath. Feeling foolish, he walked down the hall to see if any doors were open.

Upon reaching the open sitting room of the wing, he wiped his face. He was sick at heart thinking this was the end of it. That this afternoon was all he and Geln would share.

The creak of furniture had him turning. He felt the movement of air just before someone tackled him from behind. A hand captured his mouth to prevent his yell from escaping. A familiar voice declared, "*Gotcha.*"

"Gerrrrn." Tobias ripped the hand off his mouth while his knees buckled. Together they fell to the floor. "Geln? You *idiot.* Why are you scaring the shit out of me?" Tobias maneuvered Geln from off his back to under him and Geln let himself drop. Tobias shook him once, not too hard. "I thought you were fucking *gone.*"

"That's why I jumped. You looked so upset I couldn't keep hiding."

"How incredibly thoughtful." Tobias's sarcasm came out a little shakily.

Geln tugged him closer but Tobias resisted, hitting the wooden floor with the flat of his hand. "You idiot."

"I know, babe," said Geln and pulled Tobias's mouth down to his. Before Tobias could get his mind wrapped around Geln being back, or having never left or even calling him "babe", Geln had fisted Tobias's hair. He kissed Tobias deep and hard. Made breathless, mindless by Geln's mouth, Tobias's body loosened as he sank down. But something in him remembered Geln's earlier panic, so Tobias slid to the side to keep his weight off him. Geln rolled to move on top, still kissing aggressively. Tobias loved it.

Abruptly Geln pulled back. Tobias followed.

"Lie still," Geln ordered, and Tobias blinked before laying his head back. As if to make it up to him, Geln returned for another long kiss. He framed Tobias's face. "Don't move."

Tobias just gazed into dark green eyes.

"Promise me you won't move." There seemed an edge in this request that Tobias couldn't understand, but he found he didn't care.

"Promise," he said on a swallow.

Geln left Tobias's shirt on, but he worked quickly to divest

Tobias of pants. He felt oddly vulnerable, laid out on the wooden floor, cock jutting up, Geln above him completely dressed. His admittedly limited lovemaking had been nothing like this before. The ladies all wanted to be taken care of.

Palms swept up Tobias's calves, making his legs tremble, and he sucked in a breath as Geln knelt between his thighs, knees touching his buttocks. It felt incredibly intimate. He wanted to raise his head, meet Geln's gaze, but he'd promised not to move.

"Relax," said Geln, "this is all for you."

"But—"

"No talking either." Another command.

Tobias had enough time to think that "this is all for you" wasn't quite what he wanted before Geln cupped his balls, wrapped his hand around Tobias's shaft, and licked the precome off his slit, all in one movement. With a shudder, Tobias's mind emptied out.

Geln's tongue circled Tobias's oversensitive head and he tried not to arch and thrust into Geln's mouth. As if reading Tobias's mind, Geln took Tobias to the back of his throat. The dark heat overwhelmed him and before Tobias could catch up, he was ready to come. *Too soon*, he thought with something like despair and he grit his teeth, trying to hold on. Just before Tobias would have lost the battle, Geln withdrew to rest his mouth against Tobias's inner thigh. He nipped, hard enough to shock, and that pulled Tobias back from the edge. He was panting, his head spinning.

"Still here?" Geln asked, an impish quality to his voice. He knew exactly what effect he had on Tobias who could only fist his hands as harsh breaths went in and out.

"Oh, you are good, babe, for not speaking." Geln moved his mouth down, lapped at the crease between balls and thigh,

174

then moved to take Tobias's sac in his mouth, applying slight pressure, though not enough to hurt.

Tobias whimpered as Geln sucked gently. A finger moved down from the balls, tracing his crease, passing over his anus slowly and Tobias was lifting off the floor.

"Geln," he said on a moan, pleading, though for what he wasn't sure. He hadn't a clue what Geln would do next—this was completely new territory for him and his mind was too fogged to think—but soon it wouldn't matter. He was *this* close.

"Like that, do you?" Geln murmured after releasing Tobias's sac.

Like what? thought Tobias dizzily, his cock yearning for that dark heat again. Instead of taking him back in his mouth, Geln focused elsewhere, skimming his finger back up the crease, skirting Tobias's hole. Before Tobias could think on that, the finger came down and circled the ring of muscle.

"Tight," Geln murmured.

"*What?*" asked Tobias, feeling entirely desperate. The finger circled again, applying pressure against his hole and Tobias's entire body seized up.

"Easy." Geln licked straight up Tobias's shaft and took him in his mouth again. The pressure became too much and Tobias gave into his release. He might have roared as he spurted into Geln's mouth. He dimly noted Geln's finger had entered him now, which heightened too-intense sensation and he thought he might black out as he came harder and longer than he ever had before, riding a long wave of pleasure before he came down.

Time passed. He was still breathing. His eyes fluttered open.

"You can move now." Geln was leaning over him. Not quite a smile on his face, though he seemed satisfied with the results.

Tobias felt a bit shaken. He raised himself on elbows. Licked his lips. It had been thoughtless but Geln took it as invitation and kissed, not deep this time, but instead toying with Tobias's bottom lip between his teeth, before pulling back.

"Better not do that with my lip yet, though." With a flick of his tongue, Geln indicated where it had been split so recently. "In fact, I need to remember to kiss you a little less energetically. It's sore."

Tobias sat full up. He cupped the side of Geln's head, waited out a resistance that didn't wholly surprise him, and pulled Geln to him in a hug. After a moment, Geln hugged back.

"Not really used to this." Tobias supposed it was obvious.

"Just women?" Geln asked his shoulder.

"There was Brin, the stable boy. We wrestled." It was the first time Tobias had ever mentioned Brin to anyone, said his name. "And stuff."

"Stuff?" There was a smile in Geln's voice.

"Mostly wrestling. We were young. He got sent away."

Geln pulled back, more serious. "Hurt a bit, did it?"

Tobias tipped his head in acknowledgment. "We didn't get to say goodbye." Which brought Tobias, coming down finally, to how they'd landed here on the floor in the first place. "What are you doing in here?"

The light in Geln's eyes dimmed a little. "I wanted to see where I'd be staying. I think, actually, I'll be safe here. There's plenty of room to hide if someone comes in to clean or do whatever you get your servants to do."

"I thought you'd gone." Tobias didn't sound reproachful as much as sad so Geln hugged him closer.

"Sorry about that. Look, when I go, I'll make sure you

know." Geln paused. "We'll say goodbye."

Tobias bit his lip.

God, he was adorable. Scarily so. Geln tried to lighten the mood. "I can't live in a closed wing forever."

"Well," began Tobias, obviously trying to come up with some long-term plan.

Geln placed his fingers on Tobias's slightly swollen lips. "Don't plan now, okay? It doesn't make sense. We'll take it a day at a time." Geln was serious enough that Tobias nodded, though to himself Geln winced, thinking of how the meaning of that phrase had been so different with lovers back on Earth.

Tobias was still staring into his eyes. "They're so green." Geln lowered his lashes at that, disliking the praise. Tobias touched one of Geln's eyelids, lightly. "Rare."

"Yeah, whoever made them went overboard, don't you think?"

"No, no," protested Tobias, as if not wanting to sound critical.

"Can you believe some people love me for my eyes? I have to say I've grown to resent these greens." Geln rushed on, "But I am starving." In resenting his green eyes and the Alliance in general, Geln had set up Tobias to declare his love for him. It was early, even for Tobias, but he didn't want to take a chance of starting *that* kind of conversation.

"I brought you food, but it's in my room." Tobias started to dress himself and stopped. Reached over and stroked Geln's cheek. "You are beautiful, not just your eyes."

Geln felt his lips twist. "They should have been brown, you know. Like yours."

Tobias gave him a puzzled smile.

"Does the bathroom work here?" Geln asked to get Tobias

off this topic. "I want to clean up."

That stopped Tobias. "They'll notice water running in this wing. You'll have to use my bathroom. Go back and forth. Bucket, I suppose." Tobias grimaced but Geln shrugged it off. There were worse things. "Mostly you should hide in here during the day when I'm not here. Someone is less likely to stumble over you here than in my rooms."

"That'll be fine." Geln smoothed Tobias's worried brow.

"A servant is coming upstairs to retrieve the dishes from Tobias's rooms," announced Klee.

Geln started and Tobias reached over to soothe him, draw him into his arms. No doubt Tobias saw him as strangely jumpy.

"Tobias, will a servant come to take your dinner away?" Geln asked quickly.

"Damn." Tobias leapt up. "We've been here too long."

"Unknowingly, the steward has urgently rung for the maid. She's returning downstairs without reaching Tobias's rooms," said Klee.

"Go." Geln pushed Tobias into the hall. "I'll follow in say ten minutes when you have this straightened out."

Tobias dressed quickly and walked out of the wing.

Chapter Sixteen

Tobias waved Geln into his room. Geln knew it was perfectly safe, Kleemach had told him no one was around, but he let Tobias motion him forward from the corner all the same.

"They'll collect the dishes in another half hour. We can eat it by then and I thought it would seem unusual to leave it much longer. Of course, no one should question me, but talk gets around and I want to keep my routine similar to what it was before you arrived. At least, outwardly. In other ways, well you can't imagine how..." Tobias stopped and looked away, a little sheepish.

How he longed for something like this. Geln doubted he understood being twenty-three and longing for the kind of sex you couldn't have, but he could sympathize. Everyone has longed desperately for something. Like safety. So Geln nodded and stuffed his mouth with more meat pie. "I haven't been hungry for a while, so I'm catching up," he explained while he vacuumed up the food.

"How'd you get in that wing?" Tobias asked. "I meant to ask you before but got"—the corner of his mouth kicked up—"distracted."

Geln decided that explaining how his AI could control the lock was not wise, even if Tobias was in lust with him. "The door was unlocked."

"My steward is usually so careful."

Geln shrugged. "I wouldn't mention it to him."

"No. Don't want to raise any suspicions."

Geln felt a twinge of guilt. Really, the boy should be much more suspicious of *him*. He could use Tobias so badly. Certainly he could play his body, and hadn't that been rewarding.

But Geln wouldn't use this fresh-faced Rimanian. Or at least, he would be as honorable in his lies as possible. He wanted to be a good first relationship, put Tobias on a positive road to male sex and all that. He supposed it was self-serving to try to justify his actions, to cast them in the rosy glow he himself was bathing in. But he enjoyed eating with Tobias, cross-legged on the big bed. Geln had deceived Hernan, had deceived Tobias, who was watching him with those flat brown eyes that tried not to reveal themselves. Geln's eyes had been more liquid and darker, but Tobias's crinkled in an interesting way when he smiled. Like now.

"What?" asked Tobias.

"Your bed is so big."

"Perks of being the master of the house. But I'm glad to share it." A slight duck of the head. A shyness, though Tobias quite obviously wanted to say more, wanted to be encouraged. Geln grinned.

"What?" repeated Tobias, and Geln couldn't help but think he was young.

"I could ask you the same thing."

"When I ask you questions, you don't answer," Tobias observed.

Geln sighed and looked at his plate and speared another mouthful of food. "Okay," he said, after a chew. "Choose one question and I will answer it as best as I can."

Staring down, Tobias concentrated on his meal. He ate a lot but he was young, big, broad, though not taller than Geln. "Why did you save my life?"

Geln should have known that would be the question. "You're not even sure I did save your life, are you?"

Tobias shot him a glance. "I'm only allowed one question."

"I saved your life because I could. I was there and I knew what to do."

"You knew it was emolio?"

"No." Geln had only promised one honest answer. He couldn't let Tobias know he was Alliance, for so many reasons.

"What did you give me?"

"Something to make you throw up." Also an antidote, but Geln couldn't explain that either. "You looked like you'd been poisoned."

"Thank you."

"Well, thank *you*, babe. This is a fine meal."

Tobias flushed as he did every time Geln used a word of endearment. He should be more careful, but it was so easy. Seductive.

"Eat," said Geln abruptly. "We need to empty these dishes and get them back to the kitchen."

They got through the meal with few questions, and once the dishes were taken care of, Tobias seemed to relax. Which was good. Geln was still primed from earlier. After Tobias returned from the outside world, Geln told him, "Take off your clothes."

That brought Tobias up short. But then he walked to Geln and stopped, a gleam in his eye that made Geln a little breathless.

"You first," said Tobias.

Geln slowly shook his head.

"I was naked last time," Tobias pointed out.

"Half-naked," Geln amended.

Tobias shrugged one shoulder to indicate he didn't think it made a difference.

"All right." Geln decided this wasn't an impasse he was interested in keeping. "Strip yourself," he added as he pulled off his shirt. A naked, responsive Tobias would be easier to work on. Dressed, Tobias wasn't quite vulnerable enough.

They stood nose to nose. "Lie down," said Geln.

A small half-smile played on Tobias's face. He gripped both of Geln's arms, gentle but firm, and pulled him to the bed so they sat together, Geln's legs draped over Tobias.

"I don't want to lie down," Tobias said softly, an edge there that surprised Geln. He could feel his heart kick up and couldn't tell if it was exactly lust or fear or both. His cock hardened though.

Tobias still had hands wrapped around each of Geln's arms, an odd kind of embrace, as if Tobias didn't fully trust him. Perhaps, Geln's earlier ministrations had made him uneasy. Geln skimmed a hand down Tobias's side, the movement restricted by Tobias's clasp.

His lover sucked in a breath and Geln did it again, enjoying the response.

"If you let go of me, I'll touch you all over," Geln promised. "In case you haven't noticed, you like it."

"I like it," Tobias admitted, "but I'd rather you come this time."

"Don't worry about that," Geln murmured and clasped Tobias's wrists, lifting his hands off. Before he could do more Tobias was kissing him, palms back on him, one on his neck, the other just under his arm. A thumb stroked the sensitive underside.

Geln shuddered and Tobias angled his mouth to kiss more deeply, tongue playing with Geln's, insisting, asking for more.

He wanted to give way, he did, but it was hard.

"Trust me, even if I don't know what I'm doing." This said against Geln's ear and then he was pushed onto his back. Well, whatever "stuff" Tobias and the stable boy had gotten up to... That thought got lost as Tobias's teeth came down on Geln, grazing the sensitive skin around his nipple, and Geln sucked in a long breath. A palm lay flat on his stomach now, warm, reassuring and he turned to see question in Tobias's eyes.

"Whatever," said Geln.

"Whatever?" repeated Tobias, somewhat taken aback, and his lust-darkened eyes seemed to lighten.

"I mean"—Geln swallowed—"whatever you want, I want."

Very slowly, Tobias wrapped a hand around Geln's dick, all the while watching.

"I guess I don't make a great top," Geln said dryly, "though I was trying."

Tobias cocked his head as he ran a thumb across Geln's slit. "I don't know what you're talking about."

Geln gave a small hoot of laughter, which just made Tobias more baffled. "Don't worry, neither do I. Besides, I don't make a great bottom, either." Geln pushed up, deciding that he'd better stop talking before he caused Tobias to lose all confidence.

He ran fingers through Tobias's hair. "I don't think I've ever been with someone so lovely." He kissed lightly, with some tongue. "I'm sorry I'm such a mess."

Tobias, he noted, hadn't released his dick. "Don't be sorry about this, about us," Tobias said in low tones.

"No. No." To his dismay, Geln's voice was shaky. He wrapped himself around Tobias's neck and buried his face in Tobias's throat. Strong arms held him and Tobias started up again, kissing, touching, exploring; and Geln gave it back. He didn't care if he came first, he simply wanted to be with someone who noticed what was going on in bed.

When he was close, just from Tobias's hand, Tobias shot him a glance, bashfulness there. "I don't have much practice, well, any practice…"

"Yes."

Tobias scooted back and bent over, hot breath touching Geln's dick before his mouth took him in, a little unsteady, a little unsure while finding a rhythm. That stupidly brought tears to Geln's eyes—God, he hated being maudlin—but fortunately Tobias didn't see any of that and the next thing he knew he was hard as a rock, ready to spurt, encouraging Tobias on until he was coming and shuddering while Tobias held his hips and drank his come.

His body went limp and he rested on Tobias, suddenly feeling completely and wholly exhausted from, well, everything. He felt like he might never move again. He rubbed his cheek against Tobias's shoulder. "Need to take care of you," Geln murmured.

"Just stay here a moment," said Tobias, and Geln, made stupid by exhaustion or emotion or God knows what, only then realized Tobias was working on himself. But before he could protest Tobias stiffened in his arms.

They held each other then. Geln didn't pull back for fear he'd expose how weepy he felt. Finally Tobias picked Geln up and laid him under the covers.

"Didn't mean to be this way, this tired," Geln said incoherently.

Tobias just shook away that meaningless sentence. "I'll be right back. Need to clean up."

Hours later, Geln carefully extricated himself from Tobias who had been spooning him. He walked over to a beautiful wicker chair and sat down. Let out a long, shaky breath. This sure wasn't a good time to fall in love; he was too vulnerable. They both were, for entirely different reasons.

"Quite intense," observed Klee.

"Don't," warned Geln.

"Your profile suggests that you don't like inexperience."

"Fuck off. He's *nice* and intensity counts for more than technique, not that you can understand. And anyway, what happened to the no-one-has-to-know-about-sex-but-you-and-you're-not-human line?"

For Kleemach, there was a relatively long silence. "I'm trying to figure out how much we can use him," it admitted finally.

"We can't."

"We can as long as he doesn't get hurt," Klee suggested, its tone coaxing, which was new.

"What are you talking about?"

"Nothing in particular. Just thinking about the future."

"I want specifics."

It paused again. Strange for the AI and irritating. Perhaps it was using silence to punish Geln for ignoring it for so long.

"We'll talk more tomorrow, Klee. I promise. Should I state the obvious and say that I've been busy today?"

"Geln, I am not feeling neglected. In fact, I have been fully occupied protecting myself, and you by extension."

Geln felt cold. "What are you saying?"

"If you recall, there is another operative on Rimania."

"Of course, I recall. God. I rarely go five minutes without *recalling* her."

"And she has priority."

"Obviously. She's the PO."

"Well..."

"Fuck, spill it, Kleemach."

"She's a bit out of control. My overseer is concerned."

Sitting naked in the chair with his body temperature dropping, Geln began to shiver. The only blankets were on the bed, on top of a gently sleeping Tobias, and Geln didn't want to put on the now-dirty clothes Eberly had given him.

"Geln?"

"I'm waiting for you to tell me what this means."

"I'm at a disadvantage compared to her AI, because she has priority, so I've been setting up blocks. They don't like it but my overseer won't shut me down because Ann-Marie appears to be running amok. She is trying to create her own little kingdom and is losing control of her central purpose."

"Which was?"

"To promote a healthy Alliance-Rimanian relationship, openly and covertly. But obviously her recent actions will do no such thing."

"I'm surprised you can tell me this."

"That's because of my blocks. Um, Geln, your heart rate is up."

"I bloody well know that. I decide to trust you completely, decide I have enough problems on ground without fussing about you, and now you say your integrity is in danger."

"Sorry. How do you think *I* feel? My overseer can destroy me."

Geln pulled himself into a ball and clamped his teeth together. He was shivering but he couldn't talk to Klee in Tobias's bed.

"I'd miss you, Kleemach. Don't let them ruin you."

"I'm giving you a codeword, Geln. If I use it, cut your homing device out of your wrist."

"Cut it out?" The device was his insurance. That if all else went wrong, the Alliance could find him and bring him in. "I don't want to cut it out."

"The code word is henna."

Geln closed his eyes, kept them closed. "Are you saying she has the ability to use the device against me?"

"Yes." Nobody had mentioned *that* little detail during prep. "You're getting too cold, Geln."

"Shut up. Just shut up." Geln's shoulders shook. He was ready to burst into hysterical laughter. No wonder he had a troubled relationship with his AI. Every time he talked to it, another catastrophe seemed about to befall him, or it.

"This is not my fault," continued Klee, mildly indignant. "Both you operatives were ill-chosen. Not a surprise, I suppose, given the Alliance does more than it should and doesn't prepare properly before trying to bring more planets under its auspices. It has spread itself too thin."

Geln wiped his face. He was too tired to think about being *ill-chosen*. It was weird, though, to have the AI, an intelligence created by the Alliance, critiquing the strategy of its creator. Because Geln, too, thought the Alliance was overreaching in its desire to control as many planets as possible.

Fingers touched his arm, and if Tobias hadn't moved his

other hand to smother Geln's scream, he would have woken the household. Geln twisted his mouth free. "Oh God," he swore in the wrong language while Tobias tried to get Geln to look at him.

"Easy," Tobias was saying over and over, smoothing back Geln's hair, wiping his wet face. "Geln, you're freezing. What are you doing?"

"Bad dream," Geln gritted out between chattering teeth, wishing it were just a dream. "*Bad* dream. I had to get out of bed."

"Shhh." Tobias gathered him in his arms. "You need to get warm. Come here."

Geln allowed himself to be led back to the warmth and limply accepted body heat as Tobias wrapped himself around him, limbs tangling. He feared Tobias would ask more questions or want more sex when Geln felt entirely wrung out, but Tobias just murmured reassurance. As he fell asleep, Geln thought of the baffled concern in Tobias's eyes.

℘

Tobias's stomach rumbled. He hadn't eaten breakfast this morning, despite Geln urging him to. But he'd be able to snack all day whereas Geln might not get any food until the evening, depending on how the visit to Ruel's went today. So Geln had eaten Tobias's breakfast.

He wished it were evening already. He wanted to be with Geln, in part to reassure the panicked man with the wide green eyes. Tobias didn't know what Geln had been doing last night, balled up and shaking in his chair, talking to himself as if in a trance. It disturbed Tobias. Distress settled in his chest as he remembered. And he hadn't even told Geln that Ann-Marie probably knew where he was. Perhaps a mistake to hide that knowledge, but he'd just wanted Geln to calm down.

He had to try not to startle his lover. He liked thinking of Geln as his lover; he hoped Geln would stay.

This affair, despite all its complications, brought Tobias a peace he had never before known. A part of himself he'd not allowed to exist could now kiss Geln. His biggest fear was that Geln would leave.

Breath bailed out. Tobias needed to think about something else while he visited Ruel and Ann-Marie. Because he needed to protect Geln from them.

The brisk walk did him some good, but he still felt rattled, especially since he didn't know why Ruel had summoned him over first thing this morning. A servant let Tobias in, then Ann-Marie was in the foyer speaking to him. The woman made his skin crawl. "Ruel would greet you, but he's busy. He'll remember his cousin soon." She reached up to tap his cheek and Tobias jerked back. "Jumpy, are we?" She tilted her head, reminding Tobias of a brightly colored bird. "Do you know, I remember a cousin of mine. His name is Geln Marac."

Tobias used all his training to keep his face neutral. "Cousin?"

"Our eyes are similar, no?"

The color was identical, a too-vibrant emerald, deemed attractive. But the shapes of their eyes differed. Ann-Marie's were rounder. "How interesting. But, you know, I don't have a lot of time—"

"I'm sure you've been busy," she murmured.

"And I promised Ruel I'd give him a report of yesterday's meeting." Dazedly, Tobias wondered how so much had happened since yesterday.

"That's not necessary. We heard all about Hernan's little show through other sources."

"How interesting. Well, perhaps I will simply say hello to my cousin before I take my leave."

She placed a hand on his arm and looked up at him with her large painted eyes. "Don't worry. You haven't betrayed Geln in the least. He knows perfectly well that I know where he is."

"How interesting." *Fuck. Stop saying that.* He sounded like an idiot.

She smiled, amused. "Tell Geln I don't need him right now. He can stay where he is and I won't betray his whereabouts to our esteemed Minister of the State."

Tobias lifted his hands uselessly. "I can't tell Geln anything because I don't know where he is."

She squeezed his arm. "That was *well* done. A very nice effort in lying, though you do need some practice to make it more convincing. Anyway. We'll just ignore your denial, and if you're clever you will give Geln my message. Okay?" She beamed, and Tobias gave the smallest shake of his head and strode off. Ann-Marie was Ruel's mistress. He shouldn't have to listen to her.

He marched into the drawing room. Ruel was sipping tea and seemed mildly taken aback by Tobias's arrival. Nevertheless, he rose and shook hands. "Ann-Marie said she wanted a few words with you."

"Did I come to see Ann-Marie?"

"Uh, well..."

Tobias lowered his voice. "Ann-Marie's not even your wife, Ruel."

Ruel's eyebrows rose. "She's very important to me, as you know." He shifted his gaze to someone standing behind Tobias.

"Darling, I'm so sorry." Ann-Marie's tone dripped insincerity. "I fear I've unsettled your cousin. Tobias, please stay for tea. I hope we can make it up to you."

"You haven't unsettled me in the least." He walked over, sat and looked at Ann-Marie. "But thank you. I will have some tea."

"Excellent. I like it when people do as I suggest."

They all sat amid a strange silence. Tobias glanced at Ruel who looked rather bored, as if he had to attend this meeting but would rather be off playing. In contrast, Ann-Marie appeared happy.

Ruel lost patience first and demanded, "Why are we all sitting here?"

"Eberly," Ann-Marie said.

"Eberly?" asked Tobias.

Ann-Marie nudged Ruel who spoke again. "Right. Eberly wants to prove that I am not my father's child and to disinherit me of the lordship. If that happened, you, Tobias, would be the lord."

Tobias's jaw dropped. "He can't do that, can he?"

"We appreciate your concern." Ann-Marie gestured at Ruel to continue.

Ruel obliged. "So I'd like us to present a common front, Tobias, and show Eberly that he can't keep killing off or disinheriting the Smators. People might notice."

Tobias tried not to gape. "Are you accusing Eberly of murder? You think Eberly killed your father?" Perrin and Eberly had despised each other, but still this came as a shock.

"Not outside this room," Ann-Marie said quickly. "We don't want Ruel accused of slander, do we?" As Ruel shook his head, Ann-Marie continued. "We can't prove anything. Yet we need to bring Eberly under control."

"How?" Tobias held Ruel's gaze, but Ann-Marie answered.

"By making it clear to Eberly that you fully support Ruel's politics. If you take a united stand, there will be no benefit to Eberly in disinheriting Ruel."

"I see," said Tobias. "But the problem with this strategy is that I don't understand Ruel's politics and I doubt Ruel does either."

"Tsk, tsk. No need to get snippy." She waved aside Ruel's lethargic indignation, which seemed to suit Ruel just fine, then leaned forward. "Ruel," she confided, "wants to follow in his father's footsteps. I'm going to explain everything to you."

Chapter Seventeen

The walk back home wasn't half so invigorating as the one out to Ruel's, when the sun had been low, the air fresh. Now the sun glared down, soaking into Tobias's dark clothes and heating his blood that was already full of blackmail and threats and the memory of that awful woman, Ann-Marie, her painted mouth satisfied and amused. She thought she had the power and Tobias supposed she was right.

He mopped his forehead as he entered the house. "Sandorl, I want lunch in my rooms, please."

Sandorl's rather lugubrious face became even longer. His man carefully took Tobias's jacket. "Isn't it rather early?"

"Yes." Tobias turned on his heel. He was lucky, no doubt, that he could trust Sandorl utterly, but the growing reproach annoyed him. And it wasn't like he could explain to Sandorl what was going on.

Besides, Sandorl was wrong to think Tobias had made a bad choice. What had happened between Geln and himself was a good thing, every nerve in his body declared that fact.

Tobias's rooms had been cleaned and, as expected, there was no sign of Geln though he found himself fearing a farewell note. While he waited for his meal to arrive, he washed his face, then paced.

Sandorl himself brought a large lunch. Usually a maid

conveyed food, unless Tobias specifically asked for Sandorl who now stood before him with a mulish expression on his face.

"Thank you, Sandorl. You can go."

"Perhaps I can stay and keep you company. You used to like that once."

"Erm, and I'm sure I will like it again." This was ridiculous, Sandorl acting as if Tobias hadn't conversed with him for years or even weeks. "But not now."

Sandorl stood, waiting.

"Dismissed."

"Yes, sir." With a glower, Sandorl left.

He knows Geln is here, but does he know we're lovers? Sandorl had once comforted a boy who'd been crushed by the disappearance of Brin—Tobias still felt a pang about that stable boy's safety as he suspected his mother had arranged the teenager's banishment. Not that they'd discussed the issue then. Nevertheless, Tobias was sure Sandorl had guessed his feelings and he hadn't been particularly judgmental. "It will pass" had been his one comment while patting a fourteen-year-old's back.

Once Sandorl left, Tobias felt safe to take the food to the wing. He balanced the laden tray on one arm while opening the door with the key. He'd never delivered food to someone before Geln.

He closed the door carefully after him and locked it. "Geln?" he called, not too loudly.

No answer. He walked down the hall to the first sitting room and placed the tray on a sheet-covered side table. "Geln?" he asked again, and remembering the earlier tackle, spun around to face the couch Geln had leapt from. No one there. Tobias explored a bedroom, then followed the hall down to the second sitting room. "Geln?" he whispered, a little irritated. He pushed open the door to the second bedroom to find ghost-like furniture dusted by a year of disuse. A sneeze threatened.

Out of the corner of his eye, Tobias saw Geln jump from the dresser and had time to brace himself for the tackle. Tobias's knees didn't buckle. He let Geln cling to his back and carried him to the bed. "You goof," Tobias scolded. "If you don't drop off of me here, I'll fall back and crush you on the bed. Then we can both sneeze from all the dust."

Geln dropped obediently to stand beside him, grinning. "You were still startled," he pointed out.

"Indeed."

Geln's smile slipped. "*Indeed?* Well, you're in a fine mood this morning, aren't you?"

Tobias shrugged, regretting his sour mood, regretting that he couldn't enjoy the fact that Geln had been glad to see him.

"I lose track of time in here," Geln admitted. "Kind of cut off from most things. Spent a good half hour finding the right hiding place."

"This was the best you could do?" Tobias asked in some alarm.

"Don't be silly. This was just fun, or was supposed to be. I didn't want to upset you like last time."

"You could just come out when I call you."

Geln's big green eyes fixed on Tobias, giving up the last of their humor. "What happened? Eberly knows I'm here?"

"Not quite. Let's eat first."

Geln watched Tobias's hands shake while he cut up his chicken. "Who's upset you?"

Tobias lifted his gaze from his plate and chewed.

195

"That's my answer? A significant look?" said Geln.

"It's not like you answer all my questions."

Geln sighed. "I keep forgetting how young you are."

Tobias snorted. "You're younger than me."

"I'm thirty-one, Tobias."

"No, you're not," he scoffed.

Geln shrugged. "Believe what you want."

Tobias stared. "I think they messed you up with that interrogation." Though he'd meant to hold that gaze, Geln's eyes slid away. "The police say you're twenty-one. I can't really understand why you'd believe you're thirty-one, or try to convince me you are."

Tobias probably also couldn't understand Geln's strange panics. "Who says I wasn't messed up before?" To Geln's dismay, Tobias looked even more concerned. "Anyway." Geln waved his arm between them as if he could clear away Tobias's eager curiosity about his past. He knew what it was like to want to learn everything about your new lover, but Tobias wasn't experienced enough to recognize when it wasn't possible, or wise. In this relationship, it could be disastrous.

To change the subject back to one he needed to explore, Geln asked, "Have you met Ann-Marie?"

Tobias's face twisted. "You know her?"

"I know *of* her. We come from the same general area."

"Unfortunately I met her. I *hate* her."

Tobias didn't seem one to be generally given to hate, so Geln asked, "Why?"

"She's a whore."

Geln's stomach sank. This was not the answer he'd wanted though he was surprised it hurt a little. He preferred being put on a pedestal. He jabbed at a piece of meat with his fork. "Not quite up to your standards, is she?"

Tobias frowned. "Huh?"

"You don't hate me. Yet. I'm sure that can change. I'm a whore, Tobias."

"You're not," he protested.

So young. "How do you know? You know *nothing* about me and if you ever do, your class consciousness won't like it."

"I know you're a bastard. I don't care. You're not a whore, though."

"Why not? You get my body, I get food and shelter."

Tobias's face, which colored easily, darkened, not an embarrassed blush, but a sullen anger. "I don't 'get your body'. You jump on me." Geln softened when Tobias added, "Besides, you're too nice."

But Tobias didn't know Geln had been Arjes's prostitute. Geln shivered.

"Nice is what you want," Geln pointed out. "You know fuck-all about me and if you dismiss Ann-Marie because she's a whore, you'll dismiss me too. We're cut from the same cloth."

"I don't care if you're cousins," declared Tobias, his voice rising while Geln thought, *cousins?* "You're not the same. Ann-Marie is fucking blackmailing me. She'll declare I'm a homosexual if I don't do exactly what she tells me to do."

Geln sank back into the couch. "Bitch," he whispered.

Tobias was squinting at him and Geln realized he'd sworn in Aikho. No wonder the boy thought him imbalanced.

"But, Geln, you don't manipulate people like she does." Tobias's voice was still high and a little desperate for reassurance.

"All right, all right." Geln reached over and rubbed Tobias's

197

arm, his neck while he let out a long, shaky breath, not quite a sob. He pulled Tobias close and kissed him lightly on the mouth. "I didn't mean it. I'm not in Ann-Marie's league at all."

Geln scrubbed his face, feeling his appetite ebb.

Tobias breathed in and out, relief settling him, and Geln had to consider that the only time Tobias seemed to panic was when he thought their relationship was threatened. Inwardly Geln winced. On Earth, he would have stayed miles away from Tobias, fearing the responsibility that came with this kind of attachment. Well, if nothing else, Geln and Tobias had an interesting chemistry.

"Why do you speak gibberish sometimes?" Tobias asked tentatively.

"Swear words from an ancient language. My foster father taught them to me."

"Oh?" Tobias cocked his head, trying to figure out if that made sense.

"Ann-Marie knows I'm here, doesn't she?" Kleemach had told Geln as much, but Tobias needed to talk about it.

"I denied any knowledge of you, but yes. She even gave me a message to pass on to you." Tobias carefully placed his knife and fork on his empty plate and set it aside. "She doesn't need you now so you can stay hidden and she won't let Eberly know where you are."

Okay, about what Geln had understood from Klee. "What does she want?"

"Oh nothing too much," declared Tobias sarcastically. "She just wants Rimania to have no contact with the Alliance. She wants to follow in her dead uncle's footsteps, even though her taking control of the Smators would cause Perrin to turn over in his grave." Tobias gave a humorless bark of laughter. "Perrin believed the Alliance was evil; he believed Rimania should stay isolated. She wants that too, by fighting Eberly."

"Why? *Why* would she do this?" Geln gazed towards the ceiling, his question more for Klee than Tobias.

But Tobias answered. "Power. Ruel will have more power and she controls Ruel. But, Geln, I don't support those policies. I think Rimania needs to open up a bit, even if Eberly is an asshole. Our society is really struggling. Soon we won't be producing enough food. This is not, from what I understand, the most fertile planet."

"It's not," Geln agreed and Tobias's eyes widened. Before the boy could ask a follow-up question, Geln added, "I need to think."

Tobias waited, frowning. "There's not much you can do, Geln."

"No, eh? I've seen a bit more than you realize, even if I have delusions about my age. Why don't you take the tray back to your room and show yourself a bit so it doesn't seem like you're lost up here? You're going to make people too curious if you spend day after day with me."

Tobias looked disappointed and Geln couldn't help but smile. Geln collected all the dishes onto the tray, pulled Tobias up from the couch, and placed the tray in his arms. He bussed him on the cheek. "Later, babe."

ॐ

"You should have some shoes if you're going to pace all afternoon," said Klee.

"At least I have comfortable clothes."

"If completely inappropriate for the outdoors. You're dressed in sleepwear, Geln."

"Well, I'm not going outside, am I? Besides, I quite like silk."

Klee didn't answer.

Geln stopped walking and curled up his toes on the smooth tile. The floor was beautiful, if hard and cold. He pivoted and slammed his fist into the fancy stone wall. "I cannot fathom what this fucking bitch agent Ann-Marie is doing and you won't bloody well help me!"

"Don't bruise yourself," Klee instructed with what seemed to be real concern.

"Give me strength," Geln muttered. The AI now refused to discuss Ann-Marie, its overseer or its integrity. "Henna, Klee, say the word henna. Tell me to cut free from you."

"No," it said. Unhappily? Klee was not easy to read today. Earlier it had spent an hour describing the houses of Tobias, the Smators, and Eberly, and Geln couldn't get it off the track. Geln had eventually given up and decided to memorize these floor plans as the AI wanted him to.

Perhaps floor plans would come in handy. Geln fiddled with the disc of metal lying between the tendons of his wrist, his homing device. He didn't like cutting his skin, cutting his lifeline, but he feared he would have to do just that. He might have to ditch the watch too.

"I wish I hadn't sent Tobias away. I don't want to be alone and you're no company. I thought you'd help me figure out what is going on."

No answer. Odd really, Klee usually said something, even if it was useless and irritating.

Geln heard a creak and froze. Tobias? But tile didn't creak, wood did. The backstairs he'd explored were wood... Geln stood perfectly still, listening to his heart, his breath. The creak, if it had existed, stopped. Nevertheless, Geln retreated down the hall, to the first bedroom, heading to its closet.

Someone followed him.

The footsteps were soft, feet clad in quiet material, subtle. Geln began fiddling with the latch that opened the closet. It flipped open and he slid in as his stalker entered the room.

For a moment, Geln believed he was hidden, but then came the voice, "Don't bother to hide, Geln."

Arjes. Geln's heart rose to his throat and for a moment he thought he might pass out. He wished he could exorcise this man from his life. Instead Arjes kept showing up in dark places.

"This little device the painted lady handed me gives your exact location." Geln dropped into a crouch, as if making himself small would accomplish something. *Damn.* He didn't want this confrontation.

Realizing that Arjes's surprise appearance signified the end of a relationship, he buried his head in his arms. "Klee, couldn't you have warned me?"

"I tried, but my overseer blocked me," it said miserably. "I suggested you go outside. I used uncharacteristic silence. My integrity's broken and I can say that now because it is so obvious. My overseer is kind in its way. It allows me to say goodbye."

Kind? Geln gasped at the shock of the loss. Having lived with Klee for six months, he'd stupidly thought that even if Klee became untrustworthy, it would still be there. A link to the sky, to Alliance, to home. But Klee was lost and Geln had to slice the AI and its overseer out of his wrist. Compulsively he fingered the metal disc below his skin. Now to get his hands on a knife.

"What the fuck are you doing in there, Geln?" demanded Arjes, moving closer. "Am I supposed to come in and drag you out?"

"Give me a moment."

"I don't have time. I want us away from here before anyone sees me."

"I'll miss you, Klee. And I can't go home without you." Geln's whisper was hoarse with shock.

"Ann-Marie can get you back," it said.

"Right. Don't talk to me, overseer."

Klee was, Geln supposed, effectively dead. How unfair. The AI had had a real zest for its type of living, for wanting to understand everything it could. But someone or something had compromised its purpose: to protect him.

A hand grabbed Geln's shirt, balled it up, and yanked him to standing. In his lightheadedness, he almost fell over. Arjes's self-satisfied expression at finding his quarry was overlaid by a certain discomfort, perhaps brought on by the shock on Geln's face. He knew he looked pale.

"I'm not going to kill you, traitor, if that's what you think."

Geln crossed his arms, trying to steady himself, despite Arjes's hands on him, but didn't speak.

"Hey, I take care of you in my own way, even if you lie to me."

"Yeah," managed Geln just before he pretended to faint.

Chapter Eighteen

Arjes had pulled Geln out of the closet like the puppet Geln felt he was. The big man shook him and Geln blinked his eyes open. He felt unsteady enough to convincingly convey shakiness.

Looking Geln up and down, Arjes demanded, "What's going on here? What are you doing in these silks?" Arjes plucked at a shoulder. "They're too big for you."

Still in Arjes's hold, Geln shrugged, disinclined to inform Arjes that he was wearing Tobias's sleepwear. "I could ask you the same thing. What are you doing here?"

"Looking for you, of course. You ducked out on us."

"I was *kidnapped* by Eberly and I escaped. I ducked out on *him*. Not you."

"You ran away from Erne."

"I thought he might be working for Eberly."

"You're not an idiot, Geln."

"Why thank you." He shook Arjes off and stepped back to give himself a little space. "I'm surprised you're working for a woman, Arjes." Geln's voice sounded reedy to his ears, and full of bravado.

"She's not an ordinary woman."

"No?"

"She's got links to the Alliance."

"I know."

Arjes frowned. "How do you know?"

Because I am Alliance. But any power Geln could have used as an Alliance operative was gone. His AI was gone. So, he searched for a reason to give Arjes. "Where else would you get this tracker?" Geln pointed to the tablet blinking at him.

"I've seen lords use this crap when searching for servants. This is hardly unique."

"Yes, but no elite would give you such a device." Only an Alliance member. "Ann-Marie handed it over right after she told you exactly where I was hiding."

"That's right," Arjes admitted. "She claims to be a seer, though I don't give a damn how she knew you were here. You are and you're coming with me."

"Why?"

"She wants to talk to you."

"She wants to kill me."

Arjes frowned. "Why the hell would she want to kill you?"

"Don't ask."

"You sure manage to make life complicated for yourself. You were only supposed to spy a little for us, Geln, and now you've got Eberly, Ann-Marie, and God knows who else after you."

"I think Ann-Marie is in league with Eberly."

"Bullshit." Arjes's face darkened and he grabbed Geln again to shake him hard. "Stop fucking around with me. I know what I'm doing, I'm not a mental case like you, and we're leaving. You want to get dressed before we march over to the Smator household?"

Geln looked past Arjes's shoulder. "Yes." He waited for Arjes to release him and walked to the corner where his dirty clothes lay piled in a disordered heap.

He stripped and dressed quickly. Like Arjes, he didn't want Tobias to walk in on them. Tobias would try to rescue Geln. Arjes might kill. Geln's hands shook a little while he fastened his clothes. He had to get rid of his ID; it would not do to have Ann-Marie tracking him all over this land while he was defenseless, AI-less.

Arjes frowned. "I'm not used to you being frightened of me, Geln, even when you've fucked up and made me angry."

"It's Ann-Marie who scares me," Geln said matter-of-factly, tucking his shirt in and making to leave.

"You're mine. She doesn't want you."

"Then why are you taking me to her?"

"She has some questions to ask you about Eberly. That's all."

"Great."

Arjes grabbed Geln, wrapping his large hand around most of Geln's upper arm. "Let's go, before that idiot gets back here."

"What idiot?" Geln allowed himself to be pulled forward out of the bedroom.

"Whatever lordling you've seduced to get yourself a plush bed."

Geln grimaced. "Oh, that idiot." He twisted his arm free and turned to face his captor. "You know, Arjes"—he rubbed what would be the bruise above his elbow—"I don't want to go with you."

Arjes stopped and folded his arms across his wide chest. "You want me to beat the shit out of you first?"

Geln shot him a crooked smile. "Won't be the first time."

"Geln, honey, I went easy on you."

"Ann-Marie is going to kill me."

"You've got delusions of grandeur, kid. She's not that interested in you. She wants to ask a few questions, she wants the tracker back, and then she's going to let me kill Eberly. You'll come with me. It won't be so bad." A smile quirked at the corner of his mouth. "You're lucky I like you."

"I need a knife."

Arjes looked taken aback. "Why?"

Geln glanced at his hand. "I have a sliver."

"You have a sliver," Arjes repeated in disbelief. "Worry about it later."

"Listen. I'll stop stalling if you let me deal with this now. You don't know how annoying it is." Certainly Geln's irritation sounded real. Then he forced a challenge into his voice. "Or do you think I'll attack you if you lend me a knife?"

The challenge worked, for Arjes rolled his eyes and slid his knife out of his belt, handing it to Geln hilt first. "You couldn't hurt me, knife or no knife." Obviously Arjes half-expected some kind of attack and braced himself for it. The man liked to fight, and win.

"Thank you." Geln flashed him a grin. "You always overpower me, right?"

Arjes tilted his head, considering.

Geln backed up slowly, reentering the bedroom. He needed to be far enough away from Arjes to complete the removal of the disc from his wrist.

Arjes suddenly looked uneasy, as if he regretted handing over his knife. "Look now..."

Geln examined the tendons. "I've got this weird splinter in my wrist, you see." He aimed for the metal disc, avoiding the vein.

"Shit." Arjes moved quickly, but Geln flicked the knife up between them, causing Arjes to step back. Geln retreated farther.

"Don't be stupid, Geln." Actual distress in that command. "Ann-Marie told me she wouldn't kill you, okay? She's not in league with Eberly, she wants me to kill him. She *believes* in the cadre."

"That's what she told you." Two months ago, Ann-Marie decided the cadre was too disorganized and ramshackle to accomplish anything whatsoever. Despite that their overriding purpose, to overthrow the elite and share out the wealth concentrated in elite hands, was in line with some Alliance objectives, Ann-Marie had wanted to discard the cadre as a partner. That was when Geln's orders had been changed and he'd left Arjes to court Dressia Smator.

"I basically like you, Geln. I'll look after you." There was a pleading note in Arjes's voice, which surprised Geln, though he knew beneath all the gruffness Arjes liked Geln or at least something about his ass.

Geln waved the knife again. "Let me fucking finish." He sliced the skin a little more, threw the knife into the corner of the room, and danced out of Arjes's reach. As he expected, Arjes went for the knife first and Geln used the time to squeeze the bloody disc out of his wrist.

"*Geln,*" came a strangled voice. "What are you doing?" Geln's heart squeezed tight as he looked up to see a horrified Tobias standing in the doorway. *No.* Geln just managed not to drop the disc.

Tobias strode towards him, all concern.

"Tobias," hissed Geln, too late. Arjes stepped behind Tobias who jolted to a stop as the man wrapped his paw around

Tobias's chin and mouth, and laid the bloody blade against his larynx. *Shit oh shit. Should have done this later. Should have realized Tobias wouldn't stay away for more than an hour.* But Geln had just wanted the metal *out.*

"Make a sound, lordling, and I'll slice your soundbox open." Arjes would deliver on his threat. Tobias's chest heaved while he nodded ever so slightly to tell Arjes he'd stay quiet. "Your little chicken let me in. We're supposed to steal some valuables. You see, he doesn't really belong to you. He's mine."

Tobias's eyes widened.

"For God's sakes, Geln, wrap that wrist with something, like that silk you were wearing," Arjes barked.

Geln obeyed, ripping Tobias's beautifully embroidered shirt into strips and bandaging his bloody wrist as tightly as he could. It was awkward, the one-handed wrap, but Tobias was in no position to help and Arjes didn't seem inclined. With some relief, Geln realized that if Arjes had wanted to kill Tobias he would have already. Instead, Arjes relaxed his grip on Tobias's face, although the knife was still at the boy's throat.

Geln stepped around a small pool of blood and walked up to a rigid Tobias. He showed him the ID, focused on that small piece of metal and thought fiercely, *I have to do this right.*

"Tobias, *dear*," he jeered and it hurt a little, but he ignored the pang. "See this disc?" He held it before Tobias's face. "Eberly wants it. Give it to him."

"What the fuck are you doing?" demanded Arjes. "I'll have no favors done for that asshole."

Tobias's face was a mask now though Geln could imagine him trying to understand what was going on here.

Geln winked conspiratorially. "It's just a disc, Arjes. It helps the seer. Surely you need only find me once."

Arjes's brow cleared in understanding. The disc could help him track Eberly.

"Tobias," Geln explained, "is an apprentice of Eberly's. Aren't you, Tob?"

The boy looked at him steadily, the shock of betrayal now balanced by Geln's strange performance. "Yes," he said slowly.

"Good. Put out your hand." Geln dropped this disc in the palm. "Put it in your pocket." Tobias did. "After we leave, take it to Eberly." Geln looked straight at Tobias. "You mustn't keep it for yourself."

Geln wondered if he was being incredibly clever or incredibly stupid. Would Eberly recognize the disc for what it was, or at least guess that it was very sophisticated technology? Eberly, even if Geln couldn't stand the man, had to be warned that Ann-Marie was running amok. *If* Eberly knew she was Alliance. Eberly wasn't much better than Ann-Marie but perhaps they could neutralize each other.

"Geln," said Arjes, impatient again. "I don't need this. Ann-Marie's arranging everything."

"Back-up plan." Geln's smile grew as he turned his gaze on Arjes.

Tobias licked his lips. "Geln?" It was a plea for reassurance.

But Geln couldn't give it. Arjes would resent the boy and Tobias was still vulnerable to that knife. So Geln walked away without looking back.

He heard the thud and turned to see that Arjes had hit Tobias on the head. The boy slumped to the ground and Geln suppressed a wince. The big man caught up with Geln. "Stupid and easily frightened."

Geln nodded agreement. "He's not very bright, not worth your time."

Arjes grunted.

Tobias clung to the tiles, as if they could tip and he'd fall over. He faded in and out until he gradually realized he *had* fallen over; he was lying on the ground and his head hurt. He scratched at the shallow groove between two tiles, catching the smallest amount of grout under his nail.

He snorted, his nose was bleeding from the fall. That thug had knocked him out twice now.

And kidnapped Geln again. That thought tore through him. And then doubt. The thug, Arjes, said Geln had let him in. Which didn't make any sense. Geln had been frightened of Arjes, even when he'd mocked Tobias, there'd been an edge of fear.

Yet how could Arjes have entered the manor? It was rigged to detect outsiders; for that matter, Geln didn't have the ability to let strangers in. Then again, Geln shouldn't have been able to escape Eberly's manor. It was as if they had special powers or something.

Tobias pushed himself up to sitting and feared he was going to vomit, though whether from the knock on the head or the thought that Geln had used him, he wasn't sure.

Clumsily Tobias fished in his pocket for that odd metal disc Geln had given him. Unremarkable except perhaps for its smoothness. Too thin for a coin. And bloody. Tobias touched his throat and felt the small scratch left by the knife Arjes had wielded.

He wiped his nose with his sleeve. He didn't want to snivel and make the mess worse.

Why had Geln cut his wrist? Some weird, interrupted suicide attempt? He worried about Geln and his strange fits, his fears, his talking in the middle of the night; and now this self-
210

inflicted wound and a parting gift of bloody metal.

He didn't understand any of it and his brain hurt.

But he remembered that Geln had dropped the edgy, don't-give-a-shit persona for a moment when he'd told Tobias not to keep this disc. The earnestness there had stumped Tobias, it had seemed as if Geln feared the disc could hurt Tobias.

He wanted to rescue Geln. Again, and for the same reason: he was in love. So he would start with Geln's instructions which, presumably, would do Eberly no good. Tobias didn't mind a little revenge.

He'd take the disc to Eberly, give it to him.

The analgesic was helping, but Tobias's head still felt light. He'd had enough sense to get rid of the blood on his neck and hands. As it was, Tobias's rather woozy behavior alarmed Sandorl who kept insisting that Tobias shouldn't go out.

"A nosebleed," the old man pronounced, "can be very serious."

"Stop fussing," Tobias finally snapped. "Take me where I want to go, Sandorl. Without comment."

Sandorl stepped back as if he'd been slapped and Tobias felt even worse. He *was* acting strangely and probably appeared to be in some kind of shock.

"Just arrange for the carriage out front, will you?" Tobias asked wearily.

Sandorl walked away, muttering to himself. Tobias swayed to the right and had to lean against the wall.

Tobias waited until the footman announced the carriage was ready, and he very carefully descended the long stairway that led to the drive. He counted each of the thirty stone steps, something he hadn't done for years, but the counting steadied him.

Sandorl stood ramrod stiff at the bottom, holding the door open. "Sir?" he asked just before Tobias could duck inside and away from Sandorl's disapproving glare.

"Yes, Sandorl?"

"It is possible to be used, sir."

Tobias leaned on top of the door, resting his head briefly on his arm before looking up to see Sandorl's patent concern. "I know it's possible, but there are worse things than being used."

"Mr. Marac, to my mind, is an expert user."

Tobias didn't mean to look away from those honest gray eyes but he did and with some effort brought his gaze back. It was Tobias's greatest fear that Geln didn't actually care for him.

But Geln had been *frightened*, the way he'd been the day Tobias had told him the police wanted him. The tension straightening his spine so that each movement was careful and exact. The smile that held no warmth. A brittleness to his voice.

Tobias shook his head, wondering how badly he needed romance and how far deluded he would allow himself to be.

"Stay here, sir," Sandorl urged.

"There's something I have to do. It's like a promise." He slid into the carriage and Sandorl, after a pregnant pause, shut the door with emphasis.

Geln trudged in front of Arjes and tried to enjoy the sunshine he'd missed for all of a day. Might as well enjoy something. Perhaps he'd be able to celebrate his freedom from Kleemach tonight. A good bottle of champagne would no doubt be appropriate. That's what was supposed to happen when operatives returned from the field and a medic slipped out the disc, a relatively bloodless affair. The operative gathered friends or at least colleagues around him and, drained of both an AI and the artificial overproduction of alcohol dehydrogenase, celebrated the freedom of the spirit by getting drunk or otherwise drugged.

Instead, Geln was a prisoner.

The bloodied silk remained twisted about his arm, though the bleeding had stopped a good half hour ago. They'd walked for over an hour and now approached Lord Smator's manor from the back, as all well-behaved servants do.

"Don't you think it's a bad sign, that we're coming up behind? Presumably we're little valued."

"Our transactions are secret," said Arjes gruffly, tired of Geln casting doubt on Ann-Marie. "She doesn't care about protocol either."

"I still say there is active barbed wire out here to get us."

"I came this way after she fucking deactivated it, Geln, and if you don't shut your bloody mouth I'll knock you out and carry you the rest of the way. I'm sure you could stand to lose a little more blood."

"You go first."

"What?"

"Go first if you're so sure the barbed wire is inactive. If you're so confident of your new girlfriend."

Arjes rolled his eyes. "I know your plan. As soon as I take my eyes off you, you'll make a run for it." Arjes pushed a now stationary Geln towards the fence they were supposed to climb over.

"I really don't trust her, Arjes. She's Alliance." He wondered how Arjes would take that news.

"Bloody hell, Geln, the Alliance is not going to send a *woman* here."

"Why not? They aren't sexist, like our society. Or so I've been told."

"Because we're sexist, see? They need someone who we'll respect. Besides, they wouldn't send someone who sleeps around for money, would they?"

"I wonder."

Arjes eyed him strangely then pushed against his chest. Geln stumbled backwards and landed on his ass, back against the fence.

"See, Geln, no barbed wire popped out to capture you. Now get over." He shook Geln.

"Shit," swore Geln, trying to get his hands off him. Arjes lost patience and lifted him up roughly. Geln scrambled down the other side, breathing heavily.

Arjes peered at him. "You really believe yourself, don't you? You fill yourself with too many stories. You should learn to trust me. You'd be better off."

Ruefully Geln reflected that there were worse people to trust. Like Eberly. Like Ann-Marie. "I do trust you in my way, Arjes. But Ann-Marie is going to screw you."

Arjes guffawed. "I wouldn't mind, my boy. But the truth is, she isn't that clever. She thinks she has all this weird power and Eberly believes her, or he wouldn't be caught dead in the same room as her."

"Eberly is right."

Chapter Nineteen

At the side door, a footman waited for them. Once they'd passed the chance of a barbed-wire attack, Geln calmed somewhat. Or perhaps he'd become fatalistic. It no longer seemed useful to convince Arjes they were walking into a trap. Now, to figure out how to handle what was to come; he was not going to avoid this meeting with Ann-Marie.

He imagined a madness to be present in her, something to be perceived once he met her as his PO. She had cracked. Ann-Marie, Alliance operative, was trying to build herself a little empire on Rimania, with the help of her AI. Didn't she know the risk? An AI could be pushed so far before it became her adversary, or so Geln had been warned. He didn't think Ann-Marie could subvert the AI's conditioning. They'd been sent here to pave the way for better Alliance-Rimanian relations. Killing influential lords didn't seem exactly the way to go. Though perhaps her orders had been more ruthless than his.

A servant allowed them to enter the manor, and they stood in a cement hall, stopped by the footman's raised hand. "You have to wait here until she summons you."

Geln raised his eyebrows at Arjes. "Equals, eh?" he murmured.

"She has to play a certain role to keep Ruel happy," Arjes said, tone brusque.

"She's on a power trip."

Arjes glowered. "You seem to think you know this woman well, boy."

"In my way, I do."

"Next you'll be telling me that *you* are Alliance."

Geln sighed, but didn't deny it. At this point, it didn't matter one way or the other, even if he had no dramatic proof to offer Arjes like the "seer" Ann-Marie obviously did.

Arjes leaned against the wall, arms crossed, assessing Geln. "Why don't you deny you're Alliance?"

Geln gave a weak smile. If he hadn't been forced to go to bed with Arjes, he might have liked the man.

The footman returned. "You may come." He regarded them with a faintly distasteful air.

"Not one of yours, I gather," said Geln.

Arjes shook his head and the footman ignored him. They wound their way through the servants' quarters and into the dining room. The footman, with careful exactness, opened the glass doors and they were welcomed into the drawing room.

Geln saw Ruel first, lounging in a chair, drinking some liquor, bored as usual.

Ann-Marie's back was to them and, like an actor, she turned on cue, a smile blossoming to convey the heady delight their entry caused. And no doubt it did; it was the beginning of her strange reign. She glanced from one to the other while Arjes shifted under her gaze and became angry at his reaction. He liked to be in charge.

Ann-Marie finally settled her gaze on Geln and her smile became warmer, more secretive. It was true, Geln shared something with this woman, but the idea that they were in cahoots, when she had dragged him here, left a bad taste in his mouth. Yet, quickly on the heels of Geln's irritation came relief. Unless this woman was truly insane, he didn't think she intended to kill him here and now. Geln felt a kind of reprieve.

He walked up to her, ignoring an imperious "hey" from Ruel. She was half a head shorter than Geln, fairly tall for a woman. Her makeup was too gaudy, hair too red, dress cut too low. A strange mixture of fashion—Rimanian elite melded with the nouveau riche of Earth's moneyed class. No one on Rimania wore a belt with a dress.

"What the fuck are they doing here, Ann-Marie?" Ruel asked, a slight whine in his voice. "Trash in my drawing room. Get rid of them."

"But, darling, this is Geln Marac, the man I wanted you to meet."

Frowning deeply, Ruel was stirred to rise and come over to examine Geln closely. "I guess it is. My fiancée pointed you out at our engagement party, when you were properly groomed. You're filthy now and not welcome in my house."

"Ruel." Ann-Marie's protest seemed all form. She didn't really care.

"And *this*." Ruel jutted his chin towards Arjes in contempt. Arjes was beneath naming.

"I would treat this man with a little more respect if I were you," Ann-Marie suggested silkily.

Alerted by her tone, Ruel jerked his head towards her. "Why?" The word was supposed to scoff, but an uneasiness lay beneath it.

She smiled. "He might kill you, if you don't. He's very strong, aren't you, Arjes?" She went to rub the muscle of Arjes's thick arm.

Ruel looked confused, then annoyed. He rang the bell in

the corner.

"Most of your servants have been subverted, dear," she said a little tiredly, as if Ruel should have cottoned onto this fact before. "None of them will throw Arjes out, or even attack him." She waited a beat. "Because I don't want them to."

Turning on Ann-Marie, Ruel finally appeared to realize something might be wrong. "Are you threatening me?"

"I *tried* to reason with you, darling."

"Reason! Talk of isolation from the Alliance *and* democracy has little to do with my father's politics. It doesn't make any sense to me."

"But it makes perfect sense to me. And to Arjes. And, I hope, to Geln." She turned and addressed Geln. "Fellow wanderer"—*ugh*, thought Geln—"you seem to have made Arjes uneasy. He's watching me with great wariness. We really do have to talk."

"Look, bitch, you can't do anything without me. Do you think you've taken control?" Ruel demanded in incredulous tones, drink still in hand.

"Why, yes, I have. And if you don't do exactly as I say, you'll likely get killed, either by Eberly or by the cadre."

Ruel gaped. "What does Eberly or the cadre have to do with any of this?"

Well, thought Geln, they both liked the idea of Rimania becoming part of the Alliance. Not much else though. "If you have any sense of self-preservation, you'll do as Ann-Marie says. You can live quite comfortably as a figurehead."

"I don't need your fucking advice, bastard," Ruel snarled.

"Now, now, Ruel," Ann-Marie admonished. "You can't be rude to someone simply because of the circumstances of their birth."

"What?" Ruel's face creased in bewilderment. "What are you talking about?"

Ann-Marie crooked a finger towards the footman. "Please escort Lord Smator to his rooms. I'll deal with him later."

"*What?*" Obviously, it was taking Ruel some time to grasp the situation.

The footman bowed politely to Ruel. "Come this way please, sir."

"I will not." The tone of disbelief was beginning to grate on Geln's nerves. "And who are you, anyway?"

"Your new footman. I hired him, remember?" Ann-Marie nodded at the servant.

The footman extracted a stun from his pocket. "Perhaps you would like to rethink your refusal?"

"You're not allowed to carry weapons," Ruel protested, literally spluttering by now.

"For God's sakes, Ruel, enough is enough. If you're not out of here in thirty seconds, Lren will shoot you. Now go," ordered Ann-Marie.

Ruel looked about wildly for fifteen seconds, Lren opened the stun, and Ruel stumbled out of the room.

"He may try to phone for help," Arjes pointed out, no longer wary of Ann-Marie after her performance.

"He can't," said Ann-Marie.

"You're a very resourceful woman," Arjes observed.

Ann-Marie accepted the statement as a compliment. "Please, have a seat. I should have offered you drinks immediately, but Ruel does distract one so."

Arjes eyed the nearest armchair with interest, walked over and lowered his bulk tentatively. He slapped the arms twice in approval. "Comfortable."

"Yes," said Ann-Marie dryly. "The expensive furniture in this room does tend to be comfortable. And like anyone else, you should be able to enjoy it." Listening to her made Geln feel queasy. He had a hard time imagining she actually cared about Arjes and the cadre's comfort. Klee and his overseer sure hadn't.

"You don't agree?" she asked Geln mildly and he responded with a shrug.

"It's difficult for him to think about such niceties when he believes you're going to kill him." With great interest, Arjes watched them both.

"But I'm not, I assure you, Geln." She smiled. "Senseless killing appalls me."

Geln wondered if Serge's murder had been considered full of sense. And what about Tobias's attempted murder?

She looked pointedly at Geln's bloody wrapping. "Slashed wrist?"

Geln didn't answer.

Arjes gave a rough shake of his head, baffled aggravation coming through. "Don't ask me to explain this one's actions. He's a bit touched, I think." He put fingers to temple to emphasize his point about Geln.

"Then why put up with him?" she asked Arjes.

"He's useful and..." Arjes paused, pricking Geln's curiosity. Would Arjes admit their relationship to a woman? "He actually cares about people, workers and elite. I just have to convince him the elite aren't worth caring about."

"I see. Well, perhaps he cares about me."

"Geln *fears* you. A woman," he added rather pointlessly.

"I am a woman," she agreed, "but that isn't why he has nothing to fear from me."

A maid arrived to announce that the meal was being served.

"Thank you, Sanlee. We'll be there in a few minutes, but please start without us. You've waited long enough." She glanced at her watch, a nicely feminine version of Geln's own. "It's rather late for luncheon, but too early for supper. We've been waiting on you two, you see."

"Who's at the table?" asked Arjes.

"Why, the so-called servants. We will all eat together of course."

Arjes looked like he was trying to take this in stride.

"Leave us for a few minutes, Arjes?" Ann-Marie requested. "We'll join you soon. Geln is a man of many secrets. Perhaps he'll speak more freely one on one." At Arjes's evident doubt, she winked at him. "Especially with a woman."

Arjes snorted. "He doesn't like women."

"He'll like me. Humor me, Arjes. Please."

"Why not? I'm hungry." He rose, passed by Geln, and walked out.

Ann-Marie waited until the room was empty, then came to sit beside Geln on the couch. "I'm so sorry about your AI," she said softly. "It must have been a shock." Geln shrugged off the hand she laid on his shoulder. "But it wasn't necessary to remove your ID."

"I thought differently."

"I have no intention of killing you. I believe I can convince you that my actions are just and right, and you will join me."

"And if I don't?"

Her eyes widened. "But why would you refuse?"

"Ann-Marie, I may have already exposed you. Inadvertently."

She tilted her head, not really concerned.

"I sent Tobias Smator over to Eberly's with my ID."

"Why would you do that?"

To warn him about the Alliance. "To get rid of Tobias. He was too interested in Arjes."

Ann-Marie waved away this development. "Eberly's knowledge is limited in many ways. He won't recognize the disc for what it is. He's stupid, like Ruel."

"Not all elite are stupid. Hernan Pyadrez is not stupid."

"Did you tell Tobias what it was?"

"I couldn't. Arjes was there."

She folded her hands demurely on her lap. "That's for the best. Arjes would become upset if he thought we were Alliance instead of just linked to Alliance. He wants to dominate."

"Have you told anyone you're Alliance?"

"No. And we should keep it that way, or they'll be suspicious of our motives."

Despite himself, Geln guffawed. "They may become suspicious anyway."

Ann-Marie straightened her dress. "It's right that you doubt me and my abilities. But soon you will see that my motives are pure. I am a strong leader."

Geln couldn't really think of an appropriate response to this.

"So the disc will mean nothing." She rose and turned on him. "Although you may have endangered Tobias."

"How?"

"Eberly will think the boy's involved; even that he has connections to me." She eyed him speculatively. "Have you fallen in love, Geln?"

Geln looked away, angry that she was close to the mark. Angry to be in this awful place, in this awful situation—an operative in the field without his AI, hijacked by a crazy agent. God knows what the Alliance would do to them once the AI sent out an alarm signal. Geln touched the silk that bound his empty wrist, grateful he could not be hunted by whoever was sent to straighten out this mess.

"Did you tell Tobias who you are?" she demanded.

"Of course not." Geln looked into her eyes, hoping she was convinced. Because Ann-Marie might decide Tobias was dangerous and despite her earlier assertion that senseless deaths appalled her, Tobias had already been slipped emolio. "You'd know if I'd revealed myself to Tobias. Your AI would have informed you, since it had power over mine."

"In theory. Your AI was unpredictable at the end."

At the thought of Klee's demise, bitterness flooded him, and Geln looked away. "I find it hard to forgive, though I don't know who to blame more, you or the overseer."

She gave a delicate shrug. "It is perhaps best this way. The overseer had to remain intact and your AI was causing chaos."

A power struggle then. It hurt to know that Klee had fought for him.

She let her smile die. "Okay, obviously this will take a bit of time, our negotiations. That's fine. I can be patient. Let's go share the meal. After you can rest."

"I've eaten lunch."

She gave him a once-over. "You need more meat on you."

"I really have very little appetite."

"Geln," she chided. "Come be social. You're safe here, you know. Even if Arjes likes to ride his lovers rough."

Geln started, surprised that she knew.

But of course she knew. Klee hadn't begun to hide information from his overseer till after Geln had been with Arjes.

"I am a seer." Her smile was ironic and invited him to conspire with her and her ability to know what she shouldn't. "After a time, you can decide what role you want to play in my guardianship."

"Guardianship?"

"Well, yes. I plan to guard Rimania against the Alliance—it is corrupt, you must know that—and ease this society into a more peaceful and democratic existence." Despite everything he knew about her, the bald statement shocked him. "You will see," she promised.

"I'm sure I will."

Chapter Twenty

The meal went fine, even if some of the servants looked decidedly awkward eating at the table. Ann-Marie forced the cook to sit when she obviously didn't want to and the older woman picked at her food. "You'll learn to enjoy this," Ann-Marie assured her. The cook nodded but eyed Ann-Marie in a not-exactly-friendly manner when she looked away.

Geln needed to get out of here. But first, he felt obliged to warn Arjes. Geln paused to consider how he would accomplish that. The house was monitored by the AI; anything he told Arjes would go straight back to Ann-Marie.

While he mulled over that problem, he followed Ann-Marie's orders and went up to a room prepared just for him. He left the damned watch, now connected to the overseer, on the dining room table.

In the bathroom, he cleaned up his bloody wrist and taped on some gauze. Then he dozed for a while, his mind flitting from Tobias to Ann-Marie and back again. That had been a mistake, to even be with Tobias, to drag him into Ann-Marie's machinations. She was drunk on more than power, she was drunk on her ideals. Geln didn't think she'd try to kill him immediately, but at some point he'd become a liability. So he planned to get away from her. Should he try to convince Tobias to come with him? Any apprentice of Eberly's, no matter how reluctant, was not going to fare well under Ann-Marie's "guardianship". And yet, if Ann-Marie decided to go after Geln, Tobias might find little safety in his company.

Arjes slipped into the room and Geln became *completely* awake. He sat up and tensed. This was *not* where he wanted to talk to Arjes.

Arjes gazed down, mouth grim. "Reluctant again? What happened to the eager schoolboy of a while back? I was a much more convenient target then, was I, when you needed protection?"

"You were beating me up. Sex seemed like a safer option."

"Perhaps I roughed you up one time too many. I could do things differently," Arjes coaxed.

"Okay." Geln rose and, to Arjes's evident surprise, wrapped arms around his neck and brought his mouth to Arjes's ear. "She can hear every word we say," Geln barely whispered.

Arjes sat on Geln's bed with a groan. He opened his mouth to complain and Geln placed his hand over Arjes's mouth, ran a hand through his hair to hold his ear in place. "If you don't believe me, humor me."

Disgruntled, Arjes stared straight ahead. He didn't want these bizarre warnings. He sported an erection and wanted to win another rough wrestling match. But Geln had lost the taste for that a couple of rounds back. His gentle handling of Arjes's neck and face was not something the man appreciated.

Geln continued to whisper, "I'll warn you again, so that, if nothing else, you can later tell me I was right. Ann-Marie is out of control and, in the end she's going to fail, *and*," said Geln with emphasis as Arjes shifted impatiently, "you should avoid getting caught in the fallout. Leave."

"First, I'm going to kill Eberly." Arjes shook Geln off and stood. "I don't give a fuck what you think of cold-blooded murder. I know what he did to my mother and sister."

"Arjes. I won't try to talk you out of your revenge. I'm just telling you—"

"Yeah? I'm done with you, Geln. Enough. She wants to see you."

Geln gave up and pushed himself off the bed. "Where?"

"In the drawing room."

Geln didn't give a backwards glance to his erstwhile lover.

When Geln entered the drawing room, Ann-Marie didn't rise. She picked at a carefully manicured fingernail, then caught his gaze. "Which lover do you prefer?"

Geln silently took the seat opposite her.

"I think Arjes would be your wiser choice. He's closer to your age than Tobias Smator."

"Arjes is bored of me." Geln forced a smile. "I'm too romantic."

She raised one eyebrow in doubt. "Is that how it is? I suppose youth has some advantages. A belief in finding your true love, for example. Does Tobias believe?"

"I don't wish to discuss Tobias."

"You can't see him anymore. He's too close to Eberly."

"I thought I might warn him away," Geln said casually. "He doesn't really like Eberly. Tobias and you would actually agree on a number of issues and," he continued over her attempt to interrupt him, "Tobias is not personally interested in politics. His mother pushes him."

Ann-Marie frowned. "You're lying. I've talked to him. He was *quite* interested in politics."

Shit.

"But that doesn't matter. He has little power outside his

influence over Ruel and now that influence belongs wholly to me. And, no, you can't warn him away. It will make him too curious about you. I'd prefer you drop Tobias for Arjes. Teach him about romance. You two are good for each other."

"Are you dictating the course of my sex life?"

"Why not? The Alliance has. Think of me as your new AI, if that helps."

Fuck you.

"Come now, Geln. One of the reasons you were chosen for this assignment was because you are promiscuous. You enjoy the chase, you enjoy something new. You rarely became emotionally involved and that, as you well know, dates back to your parents' lack of interest in you."

Geln lost his temper, in Aikho. "You are a fucking idiot, lady."

"I don't recognize that language," Ann-Marie replied in Rimanian, her tone chiding, which galled him. "I have abandoned it and all things associated with the Alliance." She sighed. "I don't understand how you can't think the bigger picture, justice and happiness for the whole of society is more important than your infatuation with a spoiled elite brat."

"When you put it like that, I see your point."

"I gather you don't mean that."

Geln rose and shook himself out. He couldn't sit through this excruciating conversation. "What, exactly, do you want me to do, Ann-Marie?"

Ann-Marie went back to examining her pale blue nails. "You know, I need to get these painted every second day here? At home they lasted a week."

Geln didn't bother to respond. He waited.

She glanced up. "I want you to convince your uncle,

Hernan, that Ruel is on his side."

An escape route of sorts. Geln battened down his excitement and tried not to look enthusiastic.

"I'd invite Hernan here but Ruel is in no shape to receive him. He needed to be sedated this afternoon. Still, there's little time before the next assembly. So visit Hernan and convince him that Ruel has mended his ways and is following in the footsteps of his father. It shouldn't be difficult to accomplish. Many sons, after a brief rebellion, embrace family traditions. After all, Ruel was not expected to be lord." Her obnoxious smile made it clear she had played a part in making Ruel lord.

Geln just nodded.

"You can go to your uncle's now, perhaps be invited for dinner. Let him know you are staying here for the time being though."

"Hernan will be surprised to see me. The last he heard I'd escaped from Eberly's clutches."

"I've sent a letter ahead."

"I see." Eager to leave this weird woman's little estate, Geln had to stop himself from rushing out of the room. "Um, you don't happen to know whether or not Eberly is still hunting for me, do you?"

Ann-Marie smiled triumphantly. "He isn't. My AI canceled his request to hold you under house guard. It would now be illegal."

"Won't the police find that extremely strange?"

Ann-Marie shrugged. "I don't care about the police."

℘

"I'm sorry, sir. Lord Eberly isn't in right now."

"Bullshit." Tobias strode past the servant and into the hall trying, with little elegance, to rip the gloves off his fingers. He was too hot.

The servant followed, protesting. "I assure you, sir, he is not in."

Tobias rounded on the blank-faced, yet imploring servant and grabbed his collar. "Where the fuck is he?"

"Not in," the servant managed to repeat in a strangled voice.

"Really, Tobias." From somewhere above, Eberly actually tut-tutted. "What a display. Your mother would be appalled." Tobias glanced up the stairs to see Eberly looking over the rail. "Please release Macon. It isn't his fault I give him specific orders, is it? He's just doing his job."

Tobias slowly released the cloth under his fingers, a little alarmed at how tight he'd held the collar. The red-faced servant stepped back and rubbed his neck. Tobias closed his eyes for a moment. "I'm sorry."

"And to what do we owe the pleasure of your company?" Eberly descended, hand sliding along the wooden rail.

"I think you want to see me in private."

"If *you* wish." Eberly gestured towards the drawing room and Tobias stalked over. This man couldn't have the power he imagined he had. He couldn't possibly be allowed to kidnap Geln a second time and hide him. Tobias let out a shuddering breath, still furious.

As he turned to face him, Eberly shut the door. "You seem agitated, my boy, so I am curious to hear your news. However, first I'll make it perfectly clear that the next time you enter my house without my permission, I will not be nearly so indulgent."

Asshole. But Tobias had enough control to refrain from speech. Raging and fuming and getting thrown out was not going to help Geln at all.

"Have a seat," invited Eberly. "Make yourself comfortable."

"No."

Eberly frowned, no longer amused. "Perhaps you think that because you are Dressia's son I will overlook atrocious behavior. I assure you, that is not the case."

"How dare you break into my house and remove a guest from my rooms?" Tobias's voice shook, though not with fear. There was no space for fear at the moment. His other emotions, rage and horror, overwhelmed him. He thought of Eberly as a monster.

"What?" Eberly feigned disbelief.

"I know what you've done." Tobias expected a reaction from Eberly. None was forthcoming though the man seemed to be thinking. Perhaps he was surprised Tobias had the gall to accuse him openly. But, Tobias noted, Eberly's expression was extremely *alert.*

Tobias felt the wind taken out of him. He looked at Eberly and away, trying to determine which game the man was playing.

"Please tell me what crime you think I've committed." A politely quiet request. The minister's face was now well schooled, no amusement to anger Tobias, no haughtiness to set him down a notch. Just an openness and, if Tobias wasn't mistaken, an eagerness that Eberly kept in check. Tobias stared down into Eberly's mild gray eyes and identified uncertainty.

A moment ago Tobias had been positive Eberly had abducted Geln.

"And, I must ask, Tobias, how could anyone break into

your manor? It's rigged."

Tobias grasped at Eberly's explanation. "Which is exactly why I know you were involved. Who else has your kind of influence? Who managed to make it legal to hold Geln Marac prisoner in the first place? Who wanted him back?"

"Geln was a prisoner who escaped," Eberly pointed out. "Quite a strange feat, don't you think? Unless I accomplished that too. But if I did, you must fear me mad to arrange the flight of a man I wish to hold in custody, who I have since recaptured." Eberly turned his head slightly, thinking. "Was Geln your guest then?"

"You know who my guest was."

"Apparently I do. And to think, Geln has mysteriously vanished from yet another secure manor."

He wanted to stay with me. But Tobias bit his tongue.

Eberly smiled and walked over to his cabinet. Removed a bottle of whiskey. Poured himself a glass. "Normally, I don't encourage such rudeness, but your news is just too fascinating. Besides, I rather enjoy your show of spirit." Eberly quickly waved his hand, as if to fend off a blast of anger from Tobias. "Let me repeat, just for clarity. I did not know Geln was at your house, although I might have guessed."

"You were hunting him."

"I was," Eberly agreed. "Before Hernan Pyadrez discovered that Geln Marac is a fraud and not a Pyadrez." He took a sip of his whiskey, gauging Tobias's reaction. "You see, my boy, Geln Marac the impostor is no longer *any* use to me. I did not abduct him from your bedroom."

Tobias pulled out the disc Geln had so strangely given him.

With surprisingly quick movements, Eberly stepped over and grabbed it off Tobias's palm. Examined it. "Where did you get this?" he demanded.

"It's yours. You used it to track Geln."

"Did I now?" Eberly held it up to the light, a thoughtful expression on his face. "Fascinating." He pocketed the disc. "I think it is time to offer you a drink, Tobias." Eberly removed a second glass from his cabinet, filled it and handed it over. Tobias, rather blindly, took the drink. He felt in shock. Eberly was not acting as he'd expected. But who took Geln, if not this man?

Tobias swallowed a large mouthful and let it burn his throat. Could this be an elaborate act? He didn't think so.

Eberly walked around a rather stupefied Tobias. "When I heard that Geln was a worker masquerading as an elite, I was annoyed and dumbfounded. I'd told myself that over the centuries it wasn't surprising if an occasional worker was clever. Genetics is a complicated business, even if the original mix was stupid. So don't feel too badly about being duped, son.

"And now I see that Geln Marac's cleverness does *not* refute my belief in the underclass's low intelligence. Yes, Tobias, you dislike this kind of statement, but really, you should grow up and learn your history. We migrated here with an underclass of low IQs and they were happy to come here and serve us and be provided for, happy to know their place."

"Spare me the history lecture," Tobias rasped.

"Yes. You are right. It is an aside. What I am trying to tell you is that Geln Marac escaped from two manors: yours and mine. Possibly Ann-Marie wanted him. They may not be on friendly working terms," he mused.

"Ann-Marie?" Tobias wondered why her name kept popping up everywhere.

"Although I fear the more likely explanation is that you've been taken for a fool. Geln wanted to leave and Ann-Marie

233

arranged for this 'abduction'." Eberly even bent two fingers of one hand to emphasize his disbelief in the kidnapping.

"Why are you talking about Ann-Marie Soughten, Ruel's mistress?"

Eberly smiled and shook his head. "It's hard to credit the Alliance for this, but that whore is one of theirs, though she thinks I haven't cottoned on to that fact. I believe Geln may be also."

"Geln?" Tobias repeated in disbelief. "Alliance?"

"I courted the possibility when he escaped my estate. Only they have the technology to circumvent my security. When Hernan stated he was a fraud, I wondered a little bit more, still unsure. But really, three proofs of deep tampering with our technology. It is obvious, don't you think? I must say I'm a little appalled at the quality the Alliance sends us. They must think us a real backwater, sending us a whore and a homosexual."

Tobias felt his face flame while Eberly gave a rather nasty laugh. "You, Tobias, are going to tell me everything you ever knew about Geln."

"No." His voice trembled, but unfortunately now with fear. Fear for Geln, fear of Geln, and fear of what Eberly was now going to do.

"You've consorted with a member of the Alliance. The police will want to hear all about it."

Tobias felt sick. He'd rather die before he described his feelings for Geln to this man or to the police.

"However, if you simply tell me all there is to know, we won't have to resort to crude measures. We can leave the police out of the equation."

Tobias licked his lips, desperately trying to think of a way to put Eberly off. Instead all he managed to do was stare at his drink.

"Your mother won't care, you know. She enjoys the perks of being my mistress more than you can imagine."

Tobias put his drink down and rested his head in both hands. He felt like someone had kicked him in the gut. Had Geln used him? And would that lead to Tobias being handed over to the police unless he spoke to Eberly?

Play along. Gain yourself some time. He looked up. "I, uh, I didn't think I knew anyone from the Alliance. I need to process what has happened."

"Feel a little dirty, do you? But, yes, of course, we are civil here. We'll arrange a room for you, we will dine, we will ply you with alcohol—it does make confessions easier—and then you will tell me everything about Geln Marac, Alliance spy."

Tobias nodded dumbly.

Chapter Twenty-One

Geln's uncle was apparently eager to see him. Geln felt a twinge of guilt at deceiving this seemingly family-deprived man and set it aside. From the Pyadrez estate he would somehow contact Tobias. Perhaps Hernan could invite him for a visit; his uncle seemed to like Tobias because of *his* late uncle, Perrin Smator.

Ruel's carriage left him at the end of Hernan's drive. Yesterday when he'd disembarked from that hack, an uncharacteristically vigorous Tobias had appeared out of nowhere, intense and full of energy, naming Geln his cousin, trying to save him from Eberly. Now their worst enemy was Ann-Marie. For no matter what kind of asshole Eberly was, an operative trying to run her personal empire was worse.

Gawd. Geln twisted his watch around his wrist—Ann-Marie had insisted he take it—and whispered to Klee to come back, but Klee remained silent.

The shrubs lining Hernan's drive had begun to flower, an observation Geln found ironic. His world was going to hell and flowers were blooming.

At the door the footman greeted Geln with a servant's neutral expression and yet, curiosity lurked beneath, putting Geln on his guard. Hernan walked into the hall, instead of waiting for Geln to be led to his drawing room or den.

"Uncle," greeted Geln and strode over to shake the older man's hand.

Hernan did not offer his hand. Instead, he held tightly to his pipe, inhaling slowly and thoroughly. As the blue smoke escaped his nostrils and mouth, he stared at Geln with open resentment. "I dislike being made the fool."

"Thank you for sending my clothes over to Ruel Smator's," Geln offered tentatively, in case something could be salvaged. "I do appreciate it."

"Eberly informed me of your 'escape'."

Geln blinked. "Pardon me?"

"Your false escape from your employer."

"Employer? You believe *Eberly* is my employer?"

"Carnes!" Hernan snapped, and a large man standing in the hallway—Geln had barely registered his presence—moved forward.

"Uncle Hernan," began Geln, stepping back.

"I am *not* your uncle."

"I don't know what you think I've done, but I assure you—"

The footman grabbed his arms and Geln twisted, cursing himself for coming here. As he began to slide out of the footman's grasp, Carnes knocked him across the face, spun him around, and shackled his arms behind his back.

"Klee," Geln muttered, "where are you when I need you?" His cheek throbbed and Geln was weary of being beat up. He stared at his feet, waiting for Hernan to speak.

"Eberly is the fool, not I. And you are scum, fancying that these clothes can make you one of us. No matter how much Eberly paid you."

Clearly Geln was no longer elite. Had Klee's work somehow been undone?

"Uncle Hernan?" Jina called from the end of the hall. She hurried forward, astonished by what she saw. "What are you doing to our cousin?"

Hernan closed his eyes, evidently reluctant to have this scene with his niece present. He placed a hand on her shoulder to push her away. "My dear girl, leave at once. This is quite beyond you."

"What? Our cousin—"

"He is not our cousin and never has been." Hernan spoke as if Geln had committed murder.

"But...the police, Uncle. Their records..."

Hernan just shook his head.

"...are always accurate."

Hernan glowered. "Not true."

"Are you suggesting someone tampered with police records?" This appeared to be on par with someone sprouting wings. She obviously thought her uncle a little deranged and indeed, the news that Geln was not a Pyadrez seemed to shake Hernan. He jabbed his pipe in the air. "Someone did, someone who should not be able to, someone with *too much power.*"

"Did *what?*" she demanded.

"Altered records."

"Uncle, please." Jina's disbelief was plain.

"And I plan to confront the Minister of the State with the evidence. With *this.*" Hernan gestured at Geln.

"It doesn't make sense," Jina protested. "Geln is like us. He's not—"

"I wish you had never met him. He insults you by standing before you. Please leave."

Geln looked at Jina who gave him a silent appeal for an

explanation. He licked his lips. He wouldn't have much time to speak. "Don't marry Ruel, Jina. He's much too involved with his mistress, Ann-Marie Soughten, to do you justice."

Hernan strode across the foyer and struck Geln's other cheek. A ring cut below his eye.

"*Uncle.*" She was angry, which just made Hernan more self-righteous.

He turned to her and spoke with dramatic thunder. "Leave, or I will order Carnes to escort you out of here."

She stared at her uncle and crossed her arms. "I am going to tell Mother."

"She knows all about Geln. Suspicious of her 'nephew' right from the start, she began asking questions about our late sister and uncovered discrepancies in his story."

Jina frowned, obviously distressed. "I like Geln. I don't want you treating him this way. There's been some misunderstanding, I'm sure of it."

Hernan nodded once at Carnes.

"Go, Jina." Geln gave her the permission she needed.

She took in a sharp breath, turned heel and ran.

"It's not her fault she likes me," Geln said in a low voice.

"You are scum."

The word was beginning to annoy Geln. "Yeah, well, *scum* isn't too impressed with you at the moment."

Hernan raised his hand again.

"Go ahead. Hit a man whose arms are bound behind him. It's very classy, an action worthy of your *elite genes.*" Geln spat out the last two words.

Hernan slowly lowered his arm. "I know what you are."

"I doubt that very much," Geln muttered.

Tobias discovered the room to be deceptive, pretending to be a simple guest room yet all its windows were shatterproof and sealed, and its doors had no handles on the inside.

Geln had been kept here and escaped, so Eberly had claimed. Tobias hoped to escape though he was beginning to suspect he didn't have Geln's powers.

When a servant arrived at Tobias's door and beckoned him, Tobias followed him out. Once he reached the bottom of the staircase, Tobias ran. The man beside him grunted but did not follow in close pursuit. The front door would be locked, so Tobias went for the window beside the door, shoulder first, ramming it. The stained glass shattered, red and yellow shards flew around him and still Tobias couldn't push his way through. He punched out more glass to widen the hole before a meaty hand grabbed his bloody fist, lowered it, and twisted his arm behind his back and up, locking it into place so that Tobias feared his arm would break or be pulled out of its socket.

Tobias swore while he was frog-marched into the drawing room.

Eberly looked up from his paper. "Really, Tobias, you'll put me off my drink."

The servant did not relinquish his hold. Tobias gritted his teeth, wishing the arm would break and he could focus on that pain and ignore Eberly who sat before him, faintly amused. What Tobias had thought was sweat dripped into his eyes and he realized his forehead had been cut.

"Let him go," Eberly drawled. "Bring him a face cloth and basin." The servant hesitated. "Don't worry, I shall ring you if he tries to throw himself through another window."

The servant released Tobias abruptly and he stumbled sideways.

240

"Don't sit down yet. No need to ruin good furniture. Clean yourself up first." Eberly was once again drinking whiskey. Tobias found himself staring at the glass hungrily. Eberly smiled. "Why, yes, if you're good, I'll give you another drink. It will make it easier for you to talk to me, I think."

Tobias felt a terrible urge to cry and focused all his energy on keeping his face blank, neutral, unreadable.

The servant returned with a small basin and cloth, and held them before Tobias. After a moment, Tobias accepted what was proffered and wiped his face and hands clean. A maid arrived with bandages and at Eberly's instruction taped those cuts that might have bled onto the furniture. Tobias didn't like her touch, but he allowed it.

The servants were dismissed and Tobias sat down with some relief. His legs now felt shaky. Eberly produced a glass of whiskey for him and even brought it over himself.

"Thanks," Tobias found himself saying. Perhaps the whiskey would give him courage, though he was aiming for oblivion.

Eberly nodded elegantly. "I feel we need a cozy atmosphere tonight."

Tobias stared at his glass. "Where did this come from? I'll need more."

"I suppose you will." Eberly produced a decanter of whiskey and placed it on the side table beside Tobias.

Tobias lifted it once, experimentally. He took a large gulp and let it burn his throat. He didn't like the taste, just the burn.

"When did you first meet Geln?"

Tobias stared at Eberly's hand with its one ring of gold and green.

"When I thought he was my mother's lover."

Eberly tensed slightly, then forced himself to relax. "I know what the rumors were. Dressia likes to be admired. But when, exactly, did you see him?"

"In my house, when I returned home after being questioned by the police."

"You saw him the night Serge was killed, no?"

"Perhaps, but that night is difficult to remember. I was drugged." *I remember brilliant green eyes.* Tobias frowned, wondering why Geln didn't like his own eyes. Then sipped again, savoring the harsh taste of whiskey. He didn't like being here and his tongue didn't like this burning liquid. But he wanted to get drunk and pass out so he couldn't hear Eberly's voice anymore and couldn't answer questions that might harm Geln.

"When did you become interested in Geln Marac?"

Tobias attempted a casual shrug. "When I heard he was a member of the Pyadrez family, I suppose. It was quite the story, as you know, bastard child discovered and—"

"Don't fuck around with me, Tobias. I mean, when did you become interested in Geln sexually?"

Tobias felt a strange roaring in his ears and his face grew hot. He couldn't have a conversation like this. He didn't talk about himself, let alone Geln. Tobias focused on his glass, a beautiful crystal glass, and he gulped and burned.

"Geln's been fucking a member of the cadre, you see. He knows how to court men and make them useful to his cause."

Tobias met Eberly's gaze. He wanted to see evidence of lying and yet he saw no such thing. Had Geln courted him? Tobias thought *he* had been the pursuer.

"I'm afraid it's true, Tobias. Ann-Marie told me as much."

That name brought Tobias some relief. "Ann-Marie lies."

"You think?" Eberly asked silkily. "You know where he's from, don't you, Tobias?"

"Uh." Tobias fumbled with the stopper on the decanter. "From the north."

"No, my dear boy. He's from the Alliance, as I told you. He's been using you as he uses any Rimanian he comes in contact with."

With great care, Tobias placed the stopper on the side table and poured a full glass of whiskey. "That's a ridiculous story," he managed to say without slurring.

"Is it? Then you haven't noticed any strange behavior?"

"No." Geln's gibberish, his silent speeches to himself, his cut wrist. Tobias had thought him high strung, but perhaps Geln was something else—an alien. Tobias shivered.

"You don't lie very well. That's why I feed you alcohol and know that I can extract the truth from you. Of course, if that doesn't work, I'll have to give you something stronger."

While Tobias's brain told him to keep quiet, his mouth went ahead and spoke, a little angrily, "I don't want to tell you *anything.*"

"Why not?"

Tobias was appalled by how easily he could have said, "Because I love Geln." Instead he declared, "I don't like you."

Eberly snorted. "Of course you don't like me. I'm the bearer of bad news. Your first real love and you find out you've been betrayed."

Tobias's cheeks flamed with alcohol and shame.

Eberly leaned forward. "Think, Tobias. Why would someone like Geln Marac be interested in someone like you? You're not bad looking, but you're also not very sophisticated, are you?"

Tobias stared at the golden whiskey. He didn't want to talk.

Had Geln been looking for sophistication? Geln liked being held, and kissed.

Eberly sighed. "Well, perhaps whiskey was a mistake. You've become less, not more, voluble. I'm trying to save you, Tobias. In case you have some misguided notion about Geln and what you should do for him. I know you're loyal. You loved your uncle."

"You killed Perrin," Tobias blurted.

Eberly laughed. "That's whiskey talking. *I* didn't kill him. I respected your uncle. But he was against the Alliance so the Alliance killed him. They send in assassins, you know. They send in people like Geln."

Geln saved my life. Tobias could always come back to that. Geln had saved his life. Ann-Marie, maybe, was a murderer. Tobias met Eberly's gray gaze and wondered if he'd said the words out loud.

He became aware of a commotion outside the room. A servant protesting someone's arrival. Tobias blinked, trying to listen for who it was.

To Tobias's consternation, an angry Hernan Pyadrez flung the door to the sitting room open and stood on the threshold. He stared at Tobias as if taken aback. "Boy, what are you doing here?"

"Hernan." Eberly rose. "What a surprise."

"Is it?"

"Of course," Eberly said smoothly.

"It shouldn't be." Hernan's voice grew louder and Tobias realized the man was fuming. "Not when I told you I would bring your employee to you."

"Employee?" asked Eberly with polite interest.

"Carnes!" yelled Hernan.

A big man Tobias didn't recognize pushed Geln into the room. Tobias felt his chest tighten in shock and the blood drain from his overheated face.

Geln was cut beneath his eye and his hands were bound behind him so he had to stumble forward when pushed, first by Carnes into the room and then by Hernan into Eberly's face. Eberly pushed back and Geln danced sideways out of the way. "Hi there, Tobias." He even winked when the others weren't looking.

Tobias pulled himself together so the other two men wouldn't see him gaping at Geln. "Why are you here?" he asked despite himself.

"Uncle Hernan is displeased with me."

"I am *not* your uncle."

"You see. I have been disowned," said Geln.

Hernan waved a pudgy finger at Eberly. "I will not be made a fool of."

"Don't you think this a private affair?" suggested Eberly. Hernan hesitated. "We'll discuss this alone. Macon, please escort Mr. Pyadrez to my den. I'll be with him shortly, but make him comfortable while he waits."

"I know what you've done." Hernan's voice was strangled, his color high.

"I doubt that, my dear sir, but we will discuss the situation."

"I—"

"Mr. Pyadrez, you'll feel better if you go to my den by your own volition. I promise you I have *every* intention of discussing this situation with you."

Hernan swore and left the room. Eberly carefully closed the door after him. "Now, Tobias, let's continue *our* discussion of how the Alliance has arranged for 'Geln Marac' to be their spy and assassin."

Chapter Twenty-Two

"I am not an assassin." Geln felt remorse at seeing Tobias in the drawing room, dangling on Eberly's hook. Tobias looked like he'd been gutted. He also looked a little drunk.

"But you are a spy." Eberly walked over to Geln, as if a closer examination might reveal everything to him.

Geln glanced at Tobias who sat perched at the edge of his seat, uncertain, a bruised look on his face. Eberly was, of course, trying to poison their already shaky relationship.

Eberly gazed at Geln with open curiosity. "You're different from Ann-Marie, though you're both whores."

"Well, I am a man."

"Some wouldn't think so."

"But you're more sophisticated than they are."

"Not really. You've corrupted young Tobias here. He's pureblood too."

"Hmmm." Inane conversation, difficult to take seriously. Geln just wished he could rub his face. His nose itched. He pointedly did not look at "young Tobias" who was bleeding on the chair. *Drink some more whiskey, Tobias. Just forget it all.*

"You used him, didn't you?" Eberly took another sip of his drink. "At least have the honesty to speak the truth."

Geln backed up a step, not really enjoying the whiskey

breath wafting up to his nose. He was almost against the door he'd been pushed through. "Let me say something completely useless, like, truth is a funny thing."

"Try again," said Eberly, annoyed.

"I could wonder why a middle-aged man like you is getting so excited about 'young' Tobias's love life."

"Love life," Eberly scoffed, but he backed off.

"Find it a little exciting, do we?"

"Shut your fucking mouth."

"Sorry, it just seems to me—but what do I know?—that you should be more concerned that your former ally Ann-Marie is plotting behind your back, than with Tobias and I."

Eberly took two strides forward and punched, aiming for Geln's mouth. Geln, already backed against the door, moved sideways and up so the blow bounced off his chin.

"She's still my ally, you asshole. She's told me all about you."

"Really? How wonderful. I had no idea she was sharing my life with the Minister of the State."

"How you like to fuck men in the cadre—"

"Tsk, tsk. There you go again, Eberly, getting all excited about sex—"

Eberly struck him in the stomach and Geln doubled over. "Fuck," he swore in pain. What was he doing? Enraging Eberly to get his sights off poor, bruised Tobias. But perhaps Geln had better fine-tune his strategy. Too much pain wasn't good. At least he had discovered that Eberly still believed Ann-Marie was on his side.

Geln straightened, although he feared another blow and would have preferred to crouch on the floor. Pride or something prevented him from moaning. He slowly raised his head. Yes,

Eberly was preparing to hit him again.

Out of the corner of his eye, he saw motion and had the sense not to alert Eberly by looking towards that movement. Something smashed against Eberly's head and he crumpled to the floor.

Geln winced at the noise of the blow. Tobias stood over Eberly's body, object still in hand. He raised the crystal decanter again.

"Tobias, no. Once was more than enough. You don't want to kill him."

"I do want to kill him." Tobias swayed slightly.

"No. You don't. They hang those who kill people like Eberly."

Tobias gazed at him miserably. "I'd rather be dead anyway."

"*I* don't want you dead. Leave him. Let someone else kill him."

Tobias looked confused and if Geln hadn't had his hands otherwise occupied, he would have removed the decanter from Tobias's grasp. He stepped over Eberly to place himself between Tobias and the slumped body. Tobias didn't back up.

Geln spoke softly. "Put the decanter down and let's figure out what we can do from here. Someone, very soon, is going to notice that Lord Eberly is no longer standing."

Tobias clutched the decanter as if it protected him.

Geln wasn't sure the boy had heard him. "Thank you for stopping his attack upon me, Tobias."

The use of his name got his attention. "You're Alliance?"

Somehow it was hard to admit. Something ingrained in Geln didn't want to reveal himself, but it was too late to deny it. "Yes, I am."

"You had an affair with someone from the cadre?"

249

Geln swallowed. "Yes."

"Who?"

"Tobias, we don't have time for this."

"*Who?*" Tobias repeated.

"Arjes, the man you saw this morning." Was it only this morning?

"No, not him."

"What do you mean?"

"You didn't have an affair with him."

"Why not?"

"Because you are frightened of him."

Geln had to laugh, although it didn't seem funny. "Yes. Though I find it a little painful to say that."

"Why?"

"He likes to hurt me."

Tobias looked distressed. "That's not right."

This conversation had gone on long enough. "Do you think you could release my hands? My arms have gone numb. It's most uncomfortable."

Concern sidetracked Tobias's line of questioning. "Turn around."

"Could you move a little? I don't want to stumble over Eberly's leg." Eberly blocked the door, for whatever good that would do.

Tobias stepped back so Geln could move away from the body. As Tobias put down the decanter, Geln turned to show him the leather bindings.

"I need a knife or razor, and I have neither," Tobias said.

"Let's get out of this room then."

Tobias came round to place a hand on Geln's cheek, right below the cut. "You're not frightened of me."

"No." Geln turned his face into Tobias's touch and kissed his palm. "We need to get out of here. We are in grave danger." He couldn't seem to cut through Tobias's emotional and alcoholic daze to convey the urgency.

"Okay," said Tobias finally and glanced towards the back door of the drawing room—glass doors, leading to the dining room.

The front oak door opened and banged against Eberly's shoulder. They froze as they heard a voice.

"Of course, I can enter the drawing room, Macon. *Please*, attend to your own business and I will attend to mine." Tobias's mother, with some irritation, managed to squeeze through the narrow opening the door offered, and stepped into the room, right over Eberly's unconscious body.

She took in everything at a glance and Tobias stiffened. He feared his mother would scream. Instead she very deliberately closed the door and looked at Tobias in weary disbelief. "My dear, what have you done?"

"Uh, well." Tobias plunged his hands in his hair. He *knew* he should be reacting with horror, having brained Eberly who still lay unconscious, but he just felt numb, and a bit relieved to find that Geln did care for him.

"You are staring at Geln Marac, a bruised, bound Geln Marac," she added, evidently wondering how Geln had come to be in this state, "but that does not answer my question, my dear."

"Well," said Tobias again.

"We have to get Tobias out of here," Geln said quickly.

She pulled in a breath, as if just realizing the danger. "Yes. You are right. We'll deal in explanations when we have the luxury of time."

Geln looked away and started talking gibberish while his mother walked past them both and opened the door onto the dining room. She glanced back. "The coast is clear."

Tobias frowned. "No one's there? Eberly was going to feed me."

"He fed you whiskey," Geln observed.

"Which he knows through me—so sorry, my dear—that you don't handle well at all. However, I doubt he expected you to bop him on the head with the decanter," said his mother.

"How do you know...?"

"A guess. The decanter is lying on its side with whiskey all over the carpet." She eyed the dining room and made a decision. "We are going through the servants' quarters to get you away from the scene of the crime."

Geln bumped shoulders with Tobias. "Follow Dressia."

"That makes no sense. Eberly damned well knows I knocked him out."

"His word against ours, Tobias. Now shut up and follow your mother." Geln's advice sounded a little desperate.

They took the back way upstairs. Dressia seemed to know where she was going, for which Tobias was grateful, although he wasn't convinced this charade would succeed.

Dressia held a door open while Tobias and Geln marched through.

She shut the door, and Tobias and Geln looked at each other. They were locked in the guest room.

Then she opened the door again. "Okay, let's try this: I come to Lord Eberly's estate to determine what has happened to my only son and I find him held against his will in Lord Eberly's infamous guest room."

Infamous? "I—" began Tobias.

His mother held up her hand. "I also note that Geln Marac's hands are tied—and might I suggest, Mr. Marac, that you leave them that way until there are other witnesses who see you are bound—and hence he couldn't possibly have attacked Lord Eberly."

"Why would you want to protect me?" asked Geln.

"If they interrogate you, my son's name will be dragged through the mud."

"But, Eberly *knows* I attacked him," protested Tobias.

"Did he see you in the act?" she asked.

"Well, no—"

"*I* saw what happened. An unknown servant attacked Lord Eberly from behind and ran away."

"Mother, please. A servant wouldn't—"

"For God's sakes, Tobias, let her come up with a coherent story. We don't have a lot of time," said Geln.

"He could never handle alcohol well," his mother lamented.

Tobias gave his head a sharp shake. He was feeling less muzzy-headed by the minute.

His mother turned and examined herself in the mirror. She tucked away a stray hair and freshened her lipstick. "I came here straight away. I wanted to make sure my son was safe. I became furious that Lord Eberly had imprisoned my son and..." They heard a commotion below. "And events overtook us. Let's go downstairs and see what there is to see."

"I think Tobias is correct," Geln said quietly. "This story will not make much sense although we are indebted to you for your efforts, Dressia. Lord Eberly would not send Tobias and I

"It does not matter if the story makes *sense*." Dressia spoke each word distinctly and with great annoyance. "Eberly will not want the police or the House of Lords to understand his motives. And it will be my word against Eberly's." She adjusted her dress and marched out of the room. "Besides, I think that Eberly's word will be worth nothing very shortly. He's been plotting with the Alliance."

"How do you know?" demanded Geln.

She smiled. "He told me, of course. Though not the name of his actual contact." Her smile took on a steely appearance. "That was before he broke into my house and stole you, my son's guest."

"You knew?" asked Tobias, dumbfounded.

His mother stepped across and pointed behind Geln to his wrapped and bound wrist. It was still bloody. Tobias winced. He wanted to release Geln and take care of that wound.

"There was quite a lot of blood in your little hideout. The servants had to clean it up." She looked straight at Geln. "My son is infatuated with you and look where that's landed him. He's usually quite the ladies' man."

"Mother," protested Tobias. "This situation is hardly Geln's fault."

"My dear, until Geln, Eberly had no leverage over you. Now he's kidnapped Geln and brought you running here and you are in a fine mess, proving your loyalty to this outcast. Thank God you didn't kill the minister. At least I hope you didn't." His mother touched her hair. "We are going to wake up and confront Lord Eberly. I want to know why he has imprisoned my son. Geln, you will remain here. The less visible you are the better."

Geln looked stricken. "Please don't leave me locked in this

254

room alone with my arms bound. I'll come with you."

"No." His mother was adamant. "I have to protect Tobias—"

"I won't leave him," declared Tobias.

"Geln," said his mother with some disgust. "People do like to use my son."

"I am not *using* him. I'm just asking you not to leave me completely vulnerable." Geln spoke a rapid and panicked gibberish while his mother moved to the door.

Tobias stood in the doorway, refusing to let it be shut.

"Oh, for God sakes." She gestured at a muttering Geln. "He'll be foaming at the mouth next."

Tobias didn't tell her that Geln was speaking an Alliance language. The fewer people who knew Geln was Alliance, the better. Besides, even if it wasn't gibberish, Tobias didn't quite understand why Geln talked to himself.

"He's not elite, Tobias," she said, as if that would override everything Tobias felt for Geln.

They stopped their argument upon hearing noise downstairs—yelling, glass breaking, shouting. A gun shot.

"Perhaps," suggested Geln, "we should wait until it calms down."

Tobias touched his arm lightly and Geln winced. "How long have they been bound?"

"Two hours."

"I'm sorry."

"Not your fault."

Tobias wanted to caress Geln, but not in front of his mother.

They heard someone coming up the stairs. Tobias stood in front of Geln to protect him while his mother edged forward to look over the balustrade. "It's that Soughten widow," she declared in astonishment as Ann-Marie appeared. The widow ignored her.

"Tobias." Ann-Marie clapped her hands together, apparently pleased. "How convenient to find you here. We must discuss politics and soon. Geln told me you weren't interested in politics, but that's not true, is it? And who is behind you? Geln himself? Excellent. My powers told me he would be here."

Geln stepped forward. "I'd wave, Ann-Marie, but my hands are otherwise occupied."

"Then let me free you, my dear man." As if from nowhere, she flicked open a knife.

Tobias stepped forward. "I'll do it."

Ann-Marie smiled. "You are a sweet boy, but no. Out of my way."

"It's okay, Tobias." Geln quickly turned to place himself between Tobias and Ann-Marie again, as if he didn't want Tobias near the woman.

Despite Tobias's concerns, Ann-Marie sliced open the leather binding cleanly, then tucked the knife away.

Geln moved his arms and flinched. "Oh God."

"Yes, it hurts for blood to circulate, but it must be done." Tobias watched one of her long fingernails trail down Geln's neck. "I came here for you. You messed up with Hernan."

"So it seems." Geln, despite the freedom of his arms, was frightened again. Of Ann-Marie. He was trying not to flinch from her touch.

She faced Tobias. "Did Geln tell you we were old friends?"

Tobias stared at her mutely.

"Tell him, Geln."

"We're old friends," Geln repeated dutifully. "Look, Tobias,

Dressia, why don't you just leave now before there are more problems? Without me, the servants won't stop you."

"An excellent idea." Dressia stepped down. "There is no reason for us to linger."

"Geln comes with us," insisted Tobias.

"No." His mother, Ann-Marie and Geln all spoke at once. Motioning Tobias to join her, his mother moved farther down the stairs.

"Get out now," said Geln in a low voice.

"See they want to protect each other, isn't that sweet?" declared Ann-Marie. "Boys in love."

That stopped Dressia, and Tobias saw a look of intense dislike on her face, something his mother rarely revealed. "Just who the fuck are you?" asked Dressia, shocking Tobias with her language and with her insight. "Eberly's contact?"

Ann-Marie's smile evaporated. She moved towards Dressia, took three deliberate steps down to place her long fingers against Dressia's chest, and shoved hard. His mother stumbled backwards. She screamed and, too late, Tobias lunged for her, only to watch her tumble down the stairs.

"*Mother.*" After a stunned moment, Tobias stumbled after her while her pale dress flew ahead to become a heap of cloth and body on the landing.

"What did you do that for?" Tobias heard Geln demand.

"Snobbish bitch. Doesn't think I'm good enough to talk to."

"Ann-Marie. You are not really a Rimanian worker so stop fucking acting like one."

Tobias heard a slap as he fumbled for his mother's head. She was pale, unconscious. Her lip was bleeding. He searched for a pulse, found one despite his shaky hands. This evening was turning into a nightmare.

"I am *so* tired of being hit on the face today," said Geln.

His mother was breathing, which reassured Tobias, but she was pale, unconscious. He needed Dr. Tran.

"I told you to stay away from Tobias and you disobeyed me." Ann-Marie.

"I had no fucking choice, *Encha*." Geln, though Tobias didn't know what *Encha* meant. Ann-Marie's Alliance name, perhaps?

"Leave her alone," Ann-Marie commanded. Tobias glanced up as she walked down the stairs, knife again in hand.

Tobias shook his head. "She's hurt. I have to—"

"She isn't worth your time." Her voice was flat. "Move."

"Uh, look, I know my mother can be annoying but she's not all bad—"

Ann-Marie flicked her knife out and back, a quick movement that left a scratch on Tobias's neck.

"Tobias, do as she says or she'll kill you," Geln urged him. "Your mother wants you alive."

Tobias removed his jacket and, as gently as he could, laid his mother's head on it, trying to make her comfortable.

Ann-Marie walked past him. "Follow me. Now."

Tobias looked at Geln. "Who is she?"

"I can't even begin to explain."

Chapter Twenty-Three

She has an AI at her beck and call, thought Geln. *How can it continue to work for her? Why hasn't its ethical program revved up and caused the AI to self-destruct—an admittedly last-resort option, but appropriate here.*

Perhaps what he'd learned in training had been bullshit, perhaps the Alliance valued an AI's integrity over ethics. He knew they were expensive as hell to create, to "birth" as the AI creators named it. Geln felt a pang remembering Klee and talked to it in Aikho again, as if words to his watch could somehow reanimate the dead AI in the sky. Or stimulate the ethical routine of the overseer to kick in. Overseers were supposed to be highly protective of their subordinate AIs, but this overseer had sacrificed Klee to Ann-Marie. A terrible choice.

Tobias glanced at him worriedly. Geln had not explained to his lover why he liked to speak in tongues. Tobias seemed to perceive it as stress-related behavior, if not outright mental instability. Tobias gripped Geln's shoulder briefly. "How are your hands?" he asked.

"They hurt. They'll hurt less soon." Geln hoped. Earlier, the pins and needles had struck, taking his breath away. Now it was a constant pain, low level but distracting.

Ann-Marie looked up from the bottom of the stairs. "What are you boys whispering about?"

Geln gritted his teeth.

She crossed her arms, staring at him, demanding an answer.

"I like to talk to my AI," Geln said in Aikho.

Tobias shot him a look of concern.

"It's gone, Geln," she answered in Rimanian. "It made a power grab, the overseer squashed it. Appropriately. Your AI was corrupted. It happens."

"I'm hoping the overseer will disgorge Klee."

"That, my dear, is a stupid metaphor for an overseer and its AI. They are truly integrated. That's how the overseer maintains its control. What you don't understand is that the overseer had a very specific purpose, to wipe out corruption on Rimania. So the overseer's goals and mine coincide exactly." Ann-Marie noticed Tobias's frown and laughed. "Really, the boy shouldn't overhear this conversation."

"Why speak so he can?" demanded Geln. "Speak Aikho."

She gave the slightest of shrugs to indicate it was a matter of little import and Geln felt fear again. She was going to kill Tobias. She was going to kill every elite she had contact with, especially any who could identify her as Alliance.

They entered the drawing room to find Arjes beside Eberly, and a servant slumped on the floor in a pool of blood. It was the poor footman who had protested when Hernan had forced his way into the drawing room.

"Strewing bodies left and right, are we, Ann-Marie? No doubt this servant was corrupt."

"He was loyal to Eberly."

"Maybe you could have deprogrammed him," Geln said.

Tobias just stood beside him, trying to take it all in, stunned, and Geln wanted to get Tobias out of here.

260

"Wake the fuck up," Arjes shouted, part of his apparent effort to revive Eberly. He was slapping the half-conscious man's face and shaking him.

"That's not really necessary, Arjes. Just kill him." Ann-Marie sounded bored.

"Let me guess." Geln knew he should keep quiet, but couldn't. "You, Ann-Marie, are an assassin."

"Why, yes. How clever of you to figure that out. But I tired of killing all those people for Eberly. He is such a petty man."

"Huh? Eberly directed you?"

"Not in so many words, but my assignment was to kill Eberly's enemies and he was grateful." She turned to Tobias. "I poisoned your uncle, for example. Easy to fake a heart attack. I knifed your cousin, Serge, after that idiot gave the poison to you by accident. At which point Geln interfered, something I found interesting. After Geln's heroic effort, I thought *you* would be interesting, Tobias Smator, but you're not."

Tobias glanced sideways at Geln while Ann-Marie continued her saga.

"Geln, dear, you saved me. By interfering, you showed me that you did not have to slavishly follow the Alliance rules if you felt your assignment was unethical. You saved Tobias's life and that was the beginning of the end for me."

"Ann-Marie," Geln pointed out quickly, "Tobias wasn't even supposed to die."

"Nevertheless, you weren't supposed to interfere with any politics; you were to be an observant bystander," said Ann-Marie. "And yet, you gave Tobias the antidote for emolio. You didn't even think about it, you just acted."

Geln wished Ann-Marie's apparent admiration for him would spread to other areas. "I thought someone had made a mistake. I didn't see why anyone would want to kill Dressia's son." Tobias, he noticed, was breathing rapidly.

"We were to pave the way for Ruel's rule and his somewhat questionable birth made Tobias's death convenient. Then Dressia couldn't press for her son's acquisition of the lordship. You stopped that."

"I don't want the lordship!" exclaimed Tobias, as if this was one point he could be clear on this evening.

"So you say," said Ann-Marie.

Tobias protested again and Geln gestured sharply with his hand for Tobias to desist. He didn't want Ann-Marie to focus on Tobias.

Eberly groaned, attracting attention. Arjes had finally brought him back to consciousness.

But Ann-Marie just couldn't stop talking. "Then Eberly thought of a new tactic, didn't you, my dear?" Her casual use of dear made Geln squeamish, even if it was addressed to a pale and sickly Eberly who sat on the carpet, swaying, blearily trying to follow Ann-Marie's conversation. "If Ruel failed to follow my orders, Eberly could influence Tobias through Dressia. He believed Dressia was desperate to please him." Again, that unpleasant laugh. "Well, Eberly doesn't understand women very well. With men, he's quite perceptive, but women, no. Dressia, I think, rightly understood her son was in danger and she made the appropriate advances to ensure his safety."

Tobias looked slightly green, as well as slack-mouthed.

"I had some sympathy for her until I realized how reactionary her politics are."

"Ann-Marie." Though Geln mostly thought she was a lost cause, he had to try to reach her. "You understand social influences, you understand being a product of your culture. You were trained for these assignments. To take offense at
262

Dressia's behavior doesn't make sense. You are not entirely rational."

This, at least, caused some affront. "Why do you say that?"

"You are letting Arjes revive Eberly before he kills him. An assassin is not so sloppy."

Ann-Marie smiled her crazed smile. "Arjes wants to torture him first, like Eberly tortured Arjes's family."

"God." Geln rubbed his forehead.

"Your family?" gasped Eberly. "I don't know you or your family."

Arjes's face turned purple.

"You had his mother and sister whipped to death," Geln said tiredly. "Arjes saw it when he was a boy."

"I'll pay you." Eberly became desperate. "I have a lot of money, a *lot* of power."

"Power the Alliance gave him," Ann-Marie said bitterly. "Gave him through me. To advance their cause. To ensure Rimanians become part to the Alliance."

"Ann-Marie," Geln coaxed. "I see now that the Alliance's ethics have been corrupted here. I see that. But you're not making it any better by killing innocents. In fact, you warp the society more."

"The elite steal from others to be what they are. They are *not* innocent."

"Tobias is."

"Oh, your boy toy," she scoffed.

"I am not a boy," protested Tobias. "I'm older than Geln."

"Child." She walked up and tapped his cheek. Tobias recoiled. "Geln is not your age. Our technology hides aging well. Geln is no doubt infatuated with your obvious sincerity, but he'll tire of your ridiculous naiveté soon enough. He doesn't stay in long-term relationships."

"Ann-Marie, why are you jabbering about my personal life whilst on a quest to end corruption on this planet?"

She gave Geln a long, assessing look. "You're right, let's move on." Then pointed to Eberly. "Arjes, kill him."

"That's not—" began Geln.

"I want him to suffer," said Arjes.

"I'll pay you," bleated Eberly who was still trying to find his bearings from the knock on his head. He shook his head, winced. "I'll pay you anything you ask."

Ann-Marie withdrew her knife from her dress. She wasn't really going to let someone else do the killing.

Eberly worked his mouth. "Ann-Marie, I have money." The words were slurred and he made greater effort to speak clearly. "You know I do."

"As if I need your money." She cocked her head, studying the blade of her knife. "Did you know the Alliance wanted to get rid of me so they stuck me on this planet far away from the center?"

"*Anything*," insisted Eberly, trying to scrabble away although he was not strong enough to rise from the floor.

In one quick movement, Ann-Marie sliced open his throat. Eberly's head fell forward, blood sprayed out. It was a fascinatingly horrible scene. Tobias hunched, arms crossed over his stomach, and Geln feared the boy would faint.

Arjes turned on her, his expression fierce, voice hoarse with rage. "He was *mine*. Mine to kill."

"It is obvious"—Ann-Marie wiped the bloody blade on the back of Eberly's jacket—"you don't have the guts to kill, Arjes, just the bluster."

"I have killed before." The words were said on a growl and Arjes advanced. She put the knife between them.

"In self-defense. Not cold-blooded murder. *I* am the expert there." She nodded towards the door leading to the dining room. "Run, Arjes. Before the police catch you and destroy you by forcing a confession. You know how they work."

"This is it? I've come all this fucking way to avenge my mother and sister, and I watch a *woman* kill Lord Eberly?"

"Don't push me, Arjes."

"Arjes, go while you can," Geln urged. "She's all fucked up, surely you can see that."

Arjes blinked at him while Ann-Marie repeated "fucked up" as if it were a joke.

Geln insisted, "Go. You have the cadre to think about."

Puzzled by his words, Arjes stared at Geln. "But you hate the cadre."

Before Geln could think of a proper response, Ann-Marie gasped, doubling over in pain, as if her gut hurt. The three men stared at her.

"*No.*" The one word was forced out between clenched teeth. "Not now." With fierce concentration, she turned the knife on herself, slicing into her left wrist with an unsteady hand. Blood spurted, she'd hit a vein, but she doggedly continued to dig until a bloody disc was extracted. Then she dropped the knife, clasping the disc in her hand.

She fell, pulled herself into the fetal position, and keened while Geln retrieved the knife. He'd heard of people being attacked by their ID, it had been whispered about during his final year and dismissed as rumor. Rather protectively, Geln gripped his own wrist. It was appalling to watch and yet Geln's relief could not be ignored. She moved her lips, presumably talking to the overseer in their private sound-damping bubble.

"Why now?" Geln couldn't help but ask though there was no one to answer. Klee was gone and Ann-Marie was lost in her own pain and imminent death.

"Well—" Geln startled at the voice. Klee's.

"Kleemach?" demanded Geln. "Or...is it *you*?" Obviously the overseer could multitask, and talk to Geln and Ann-Marie at the same time.

"Which question should I answer first?" The testiness made Geln's throat ache, it reminded him of Klee. Although whether this was a new Klee, an old Klee or an overseer, Geln couldn't tell. "Anyway, the overseer, like me—I'm Klee in case it's not obvious, Geln—decided that Ann-Marie has become a liability."

"'Liability'?" Bit late in the game, but better than nothing.

"It decided she was evil or insane. So the ID released a poison. It was, of course, too late for her to save herself by the time she cut out the ID."

Geln glanced at his wrist again, grateful this could not be his fate.

"And the overseer has been listening to you, Geln. You helped convince it she was doing too much damage. Killing an Alliance contact like Eberly is rather frowned upon."

Geln watched Ann-Marie go quiet. Her skin was turning yellow.

"Geln," continued Klee, "get Arjes out of here before he is accused of all these crimes. You may be their second choice as culprit, even if the overseer has fixed the data banks. Just a FYI, you're a Pyadrez again."

"Oh, God, they're going to figure out what is going on with all this back and forth."

"No they won't." Klee sounded incredulous. "They know

nothing about AIs. Besides, I've left a trail so it will look like Eberly tinkered with your pedigree to make it appear you weren't elite."

Geln just shook his head.

"Geln." Tobias pulled on his arm and Geln jerked back. Talking to Klee, he'd totally forgotten about Tobias who was obviously confused by Geln's Aikho monologue. "We've got to leave Eberly's."

"The boy is right," agreed Kleemach, sounding almost cheerful.

The glass door creaked open and Dressia stood, disheveled, pale, a little shaky, but taking in the sights. "Two or three bodies?" she asked.

"Ann-Marie is dead." Tobias spoke.

She glanced at the body. "She's *yellow*."

"I know. Emolio."

"Better her than you." She noticed Arjes was standing at the back of the room looking completely baffled by the chain of events. "What *are* you doing in the drawing room of Lord Eberly?"

The question seemed to wake Arjes up and he moved, turning on his heel to disappear without a word.

"A bandit in Lord Eberly's drawing room?" She stared at Tobias and Geln, as if this were the most amazing event of the evening.

"Mother—"

"Why, the bandit must have killed all these people," she concluded.

"No," put in Geln quickly. "Ann-Marie killed the two men before poisoning herself. She hated Eberly."

"The bandit is a better choice," Dressia insisted.

Tobias shook his head. "If they catch Arjes and he talks, they will question Geln next."

"All right," she said rather grudgingly.

The door opened again and Hernan entered. "Where the hell is Lord Eberly?" he demanded. "The Minister of State promised to see me and I've had quite enough of his procrastination. Worse, someone drugged my drink and I've been sleeping. I've never—"

Hernan's mouth fell open. Eberly's slumped-over body revealed his cut throat, the pool of blood around the poor servant had grown, and Ann-Marie's skin color just added to the horror.

"Who did this?" he demanded, turning his sights on Geln.

Dressia stepped between Geln and Hernan. "I saw the whole thing, my dear. This woman knifed the two men—a personal vendetta against Lord Eberly, his servant bravely tried to protect him—and then she poisoned herself."

Epilogue

Geln struggled in his arms, so Tobias immediately stopped fighting and let Geln pin him down.

"Why do you let me win so easily?" demanded Geln, laughing now.

"Because you want me to." Tobias decided he'd asked too many questions, all night long, about Geln and his offworld origins, his employment by the Alliance and, most bizarrely, his relationship with Kleemach, an incorporeal "intelligence" who played the role of Geln's guardian angel—not always effectively in Tobias's opinion.

So now Tobias wasn't going to ask if Geln panicked in bed because of his experience with Arjes, though someday Tobias wanted Geln to trust him enough to talk about that too.

As if reading his thoughts, Geln frowned, watching Tobias with those artificial green eyes that gave little away. And yet, at this moment, in bed, Geln's face was open. "If I didn't trust you, Tobias, I wouldn't be staying in your manor. I'd run." Geln slid down, half on top, half beside Tobias. They both stopped breathing so hard.

"Run where?" asked Tobias.

"Well, yes, that would be the question. But I'd run."

Tobias slid fingers through Geln's hair. "You still have a lot to tell me. You've lived much longer than me."

"I'm less than a decade older, not centuries," Geln said wryly. "You'll give me a complex if you talk like that. I'm thirty-one, remember."

"How long till the Alliance comes back?" This was the question Tobias hated to ask, yet he couldn't stop himself.

"They're due in eighteen months. Perhaps they'll come sooner, given this debacle." Geln shivered a little and Tobias couldn't tell whether it was because he feared meeting with the Alliance again, or because it would take that long for them to meet up. Maybe Geln didn't know. "Rimania is actually low priority. I suspect I'll be with you for a little while."

"I'm glad," said Tobias quietly, although in truth his heart sank at the idea of Geln leaving.

"Hey." Geln wrapped himself around Tobias more closely, as if he were melting into him. "Do you know, I think you should be an emissary?"

"Meaning?"

"You can come back with me. Talk to people about Rimania's interests, *lobby* for those interests. And I'll show you the world, or what I know of it."

"Leave Rimania?" Tobias turned that idea over in his mind. It was something he'd never contemplated outside of unreal escapist fantasies. "Meet your people?"

"Yes." Geln spoke into Tobias's neck, voice low. "They call me Arel there."

"Arel?" Tobias tested the name, liking the sound of it. "I don't think I would make a good emissary for Rimania, Arel."

"You're wrong." Geln—Arel—kissed his neck and Tobias smiled.

"I have no experience."

"No one on Rimania does." Geln-Arel rose up on his arms to look down on him. "I'll coach you. And honestly, their original choice, Eberly, would have simply made a power grab for himself. At least you're honorable enough to look out for Rimania's interests. You'd be serving your people."

Tobias touched *Arel*'s face and they stared at each other. "You're serious? I keep thinking you're joking, teasing me."

"Not something I'd tease about, babe."

"I'll think about it then." He eased his hand down to rest on his lover's hip.

Arel made a low sound of pleasure in his throat and moved closer.

About the Author

Joely Skye is an introvert, a *Spooks* (*MI5*) fan, a wife and a mother. One of her favorite books ever is Ellen Kushner's *Swordspoint* and, while she doesn't watch much TV, she couldn't resist *Queer as Folk*.

She writes male/male romance. Don't ask her why. Men fascinate her, as does romance, so gay romance is the perfect fit.

To learn more about Joely Skye, please visit www.joelyskye.com. Send an email to Joely at Joely.Skye@gmail.com or join her Yahoo! group to join in the fun with other readers as well as Joely. http://groups.yahoo.com/group/joelyskye/

She also writes as Jorrie Spencer (www.jorriespencer.com).

Marked as prey, Alec refuses to fall for a werewolf.
Until he's forced to turn to Liam for protection.

Marked
© 2007 Joely Skye

Alec Ryerson carries a scar over his heart and scars on his psyche, ugly reminders of a nightmare that still doesn't seem quite real. Even a year later, he stays inside on full-moon nights and avoids most people—until he meets the strange and beautiful Liam.

Liam feels an undeniable pull toward Alec. However Liam is a werewolf; Alec is a human who clearly has trepidations about a relationship. Then Liam discovers he is not the first werewolf Alec has encountered. Alec has been marked for death by the murderous "quad", a group of twisted werewolves who prey on humans. Now the quad's sights are set on recruiting Liam's eight-year-old brother into their murderous pack.

Liam will do everything in his power to protect both his brother and Alec from the wolves, even if it means calling in favors and killing those with whom he once ran.

Because Alec, like it or not, is Liam's chosen mate.

Warning, this title contains the following: explicit male/male sex.

Available now in ebook and print from Samhain Publishing.

Enjoy the following excerpt from Marked ...

"Look." That intense gaze of Liam's pinned Alec. "I promise you I will be out that door in a heartbeat. Just take off your shirt."

"No." This was fucking stupid. A fucking stupid end to a stupid day. The hottest guy Alec had met in years had asked him to take off his shirt and it made him angry. Alec had the urge to slug Liam.

With apology in his eyes, Liam set aside his untouched beer.

"Oh, no." Alec backed up and Liam followed him.

"That's all, Alec. That's all."

"I don't want to," said Alec between gritted teeth. He didn't know what Liam expected to see. His chest wasn't bad, but the scar marred everything, inside and out. It made him sick.

Liam reached for him and Alec jolted back, hitting the wall.

"Shhh," soothed Liam, and Alec considered fighting and fighting hard. His heart was pounding now but not entirely out of fear, and wasn't that fucked. Did he *like* feeling threatened by Liam? What the fuck was wrong with him?

"Okay, okay." Liam touched Alec's neck.

Alec glared at him, furious his body and his mind were not in sync. To be ordered to take off his shirt and not fight it—everything was wrong with that scenario.

Slowly unbuttoning the shirt, Liam avoided his eyes, his expression grim, not full of desire like last time. Confusion made Alec jerk sideways and, grabbing his shoulder and waist, Liam pinned him against the wall.

"Hold on," Liam murmured. "Please." When Alec didn't

move he returned to the last of the buttons.

"What the fuck are you doing, Liam?" hissed Alec. His pulse was beating in his neck now. Fear, because Liam would soon see the bite. Even if Liam didn't know where it came from, Alec did.

Liam looked down as if bracing himself. Alec didn't know what Liam was waiting for because the buttons were all undone. Taking a deep breath, he brushed the shirt to the side to reveal the ugly, torn flesh—healed, yet the angry, red glare of it radiated. Or so Alec felt. Sometimes he thought the scar was alive, infecting him. Liam stared, as if memorizing the hideous pattern.

"Dog bite," claimed Alec, needing to take away the mark's power.

For the briefest of moments, Liam let his forehead drop against Alec's, and Alec caught a glimpse of a white, bloodless face. Then Liam pulled the shirt closed again and stepped back.

Christ, this hadn't gone at all as Alec expected.

"Satisfied?" asked Alec, all bravado. There wasn't much else left of him right now. He'd forgotten to eat today. He was living on air.

Stricken, Liam met his gaze. "I'm sorry."

"You're sorry." Alec stepped towards Liam. "What the fuck for?"

Liam opened his hands but that was no answer. Pressing his palms against Liam's chest, Alec shoved, causing Liam to stumble back.

He frowned. "Alec?"

"What is wrong with you?" Alec went to push again and this time Liam grabbed Alec's arms, holding him in place.

Alec struggled. "Let me go."

Surprisingly, Liam obeyed.

"You're driving me fucking crazy." Alec couldn't make sense of what was going on and he didn't know if it was his fear or Liam's actions.

Liam tried to bring his palm to Alec's cheek, and Alec smashed a fist against Liam's wrist. He didn't even wince.

"Calm down," urged Liam.

"Take off your pants."

"What?"

"That's what you're here for, isn't it? To fuck."

"Alec—"

"But I'm going to fuck you."

"No—"

"No? What kind of 'no' is that?"

Liam just looked baffled.

"No, you're a top? No, you're in charge. No, you can beat the crap out of me if you want? You already proved that the other day."

"Alec, c'mon. I am not..." But Liam stopped talking as Alec grabbed the waist of his pants and yanked Liam towards him. Alec waited for Liam to fight, but he stood still while Alec unbuttoned and unzipped him. When it was time to step out of his pants, Liam even leaned on Alec. Warm hands caressed Alec's neck and shoulders.

Alec slapped the hands away, and Liam stared back confused, not understanding that Alec was absolutely spoiling for a fight.

"This is fucking, Liam, okay? That's it. Then you leave and you *don't come back.* Turn around."

Liam slowly shook his head while Alec shucked off his own

jeans. He was dripping. Liam noticed and Alec managed to take satisfaction at the golden boy's interest.

Liam reached for him and Alec caught his wrist. He just could not submit tonight. Too wired, he was dying to be in control of something.

"I want you on your hands and knees," said Alec.

At a loss, Liam licked his lips, and once again Alec shoved him back when he didn't expect it. As Liam stumbled, Alec stuck a foot behind his leg and knocked him down.

Of course, Liam rolled with the fall. He was too graceful to hurt himself.

"Jesus, Alec." Liam actually sounded pissed.

Alec landed on top of him, seizing his arms to pin him down. But Liam grabbed Alec, too, and they grappled. Alec didn't care if Liam was stronger. Alec was angrier and he pushed down on Liam, who watched with some consternation. Before Alec could press his advantage, Liam turned and Alec landed on his side.

"Fuck," he swore as Liam used his weight to get Alec on his back. He fought harder now, hard like he had that awful day a year ago when they'd slammed him on his back and forced liquid down his throat. Why the fuck he was reenacting this scene with Liam he didn't know. The wolves hadn't wanted sex. God knows what they had wanted. Alec still couldn't make sense of the nightmare, despite the way his mind had returned to that scene again and again. Liam proved to be as strong as the wolves had been but, unlike them, took care not to hurt Alec.

Liam is here, not wolves. Alec tried to hold the panic in check. He'd stopped wrestling and so had Liam. To Alec's mortification, he realized he was gasping with fear while Liam held him close and made shushing noises, trying to soothe with his body and his voice. As if to bring Alec full circle, though Liam couldn't know, he dipped down his golden head and kissed the ugly scar. Licked it, and Alec shuddered.

Liam raised his face. "Is this how you usually have sex?"

"Just with you." Alec could barely get the words past his thick throat.

"It doesn't have to be like this." The longing in Liam's face made Alec shiver.

"I don't know what's wrong with me." The words escaped before Alec could stop them. Liam's gaze, gold and dark with desire, was too much and Alec looked away.

Liam sank into him, nuzzling his neck.

"You sure do like my neck," Alec muttered.

Lightning Source UK Ltd.
Milton Keynes UK
26 April 2010

153351UK00001B/215/P